THE REWARDS OF TREACHERY

THE REWARDS OF TREACHERY

Rosemary Rowe

SEVERN
HOUSE

First world edition published in Great Britain and the USA in 2023
by Severn House, an imprint of Canongate Books Ltd,
14 High Street, Edinburgh EH1 1TE.

Trade paperback edition first published in Great Britain and the USA in 2023
by Severn House, an imprint of Canongate Books Ltd.

severnhouse.com

British Library Cataloguing-in-Publication Data
A CIP catalogue record for this title is available from the British Library.

ISBN-13: 978-1-4483-0833-0 (cased)
ISBN-13: 978-1-4483-1055-5 (trade paper)
ISBN-13: 978-1-4483-1040-1 (e-book)

All Severn House titles are printed on acid-free paper.

MIX
Paper from
responsible sources
FSC   FSC® C013056
www.fsc.org

Typeset by Palimpsest Book Production Ltd.,
Falkirk, Stirlingshire, Scotland.
Printed and bound in Great Britain by
TJ Books, Padstow, Cornwall.

To the two Sandras, Venton and Curnow, with many thanks for their friendship.

FOREWORD

I t is late summer, 198 AD and Britannia, the most remote
and northerly outpost of the Roman Empire, is settling
into an uneasy peace. Uneasy, because the last few years
have been dramatic ones. Since the assassination of Emperor
Pertinax (one time Governor of this province, and supposed
friend and protector of the fictional Marcus in this story) the
empire has endured tumultuous years.

First it had more or less been auctioned off by the same
Pretorian Guard which murdered Pertinax for not awarding
them the 'bonus' Commodus promised them. But the highest
bidder, Didius Julianus, did not last for long. He found there
really was no money to pay the promised bribe, the guard
deserted him, and three rival claimants to the Imperial throne
emerged.

It was Severus Septimius who finally prevailed, first by
doing the unthinkable and marching upon Rome, executing
Didius and seizing power, then – after a long and bitter civil
war – defeating Pescennius Niger, his most serious rival, who
had declared himself Emperor elsewhere and was issuing
coinage in his own name. (Indeed, he is sometimes listed
as an Emperor in the texts: he had been expected to be
Pertinax's lawful successor, and was the candidate most
favoured by the populace when Julianus fell.)

Meanwhile, the third claimant, Albinus Clodius, was prevailed upon to withdraw his claim (and thus not ally with
Niger) in return for the immediate title of Caesar of the West
and the promise that he would be named as Severus's heir to
the Imperial purple. This was never likely, since Severus
had a thrusting wife and children of his own, and was not
renowned for keeping promises. (Piscennius, offered exile,
thought it wiser to refuse and died in battle.)

Sure enough, once Severus's position was secure, Clodius
was duly denounced as an enemy of the state. Forced into

military confrontation of his own, he led his troops to Gaul, and for a time achieved a measure of success, but was finally captured, and executed too (beheaded and dismembered, the corpse trodden to pieces under Severus's horse, and thrown into the Rhine). His wife and family – though promised mercy if they surrendered – were subjected to the same barbaric death.

The problem for Britannia, and garrison towns like Glevum in particular, was that Albinus Clodius was at the time the Governor of this province and thus commander of the legions stationed there, and enjoyed a measure of popular support. But when the news reached Britain, these supporters either fled or changed allegiance as quickly as they could (outwardly at least), since it was the Emperor's fancy to execute sympathizers in the same way Clodius had died.

It was not the only gesture of revenge. The new Provincial Governor whom Severus installed was none other than Virius Lupus, whose troops had been decimated by Clodius's men during one battle in the succession war, and who therefore had a personal interest in supressing rebellious Britannia and keeping it subdued. (It appears that he was obliged to pay off the Scottish tribes, to 'buy peace' along the northern wall.) It is clear that the older struggle against the isolated pockets of rebellious Celts, south of that border, was intensified, presumably for fear that enemies of Severus might unite. For there were still some who continued to resist the rule of Rome, targeting military supplies on unfrequented roads and making the occasional raid on stragglers – who were generally beheaded and hung naked from the trees, as a warning to others, while the raiders disappeared, armed with the spoils of the ambush, to hang the heads as trophies in their sacred groves. (Indeed, Britannia proved so difficult to totally subdue that within six years it was divided into two, each with a separate Roman Governor.)

This is the background against which this tale is set, though, in contrast to the story, in fact there had been little evidence of native trouble near Glevum for some years, apart from the illicit trade in precious ores. All mining – gold and silver in particular – was governed by strict laws, subject to licence and mostly owned directly by the Roman state, who used slave labour under military supervision to extract the metal ore. (The few small mines permitted to be worked, under expensive licence, were limited both as to how much they could produce, and whom they could sell it to – while buyers also required a costly permit issued by the state.)

There were many deposits west of Glevum (Welsh gold is famous even now) and the native tribes were skilled in metalwork. The conquerors had co-opted the larger mines and seams, but there were still some small ones run by licensed families, and almost certainly others that were never formally declared. (Evidence of illicit silver mining and refining has been recently unearthed.) But all trade in metal was strictly state-controlled. Infringement could bring savage punishment, or even death. Gold, silver, bronze and brass were used for coins – which bore an image of the Emperor – and anything which might endanger that was treason, under law. Besides, illicit trade might fund the rebel cause. So anyone buying illegal gold or silver was at double jeopardy – from the state if he were discovered in the act, and from the Celts if he should cheat them or default.

Law of course was centred in the courts, presided over by local magistrates, but ultimately under the control of Rome and her officers. This was still a Roman province, criss-crossed by Roman roads, subject to Roman laws and occupied by Roman troops, albeit somewhat fewer than formerly.

It is not altogether clear what the strength of the garrison at Glevum was, at this period. (It has been argued that it had already been abandoned, but dating of repairs to fortress walls does not support this view, though records – rather sketchy at this point – do not show which legion, if any, was stationed in the town.) However, it is certain that shortly afterwards the fort was much reduced, much of the previous barracks area was used for other things, and fortress walls curtailed – suggesting that there may have been a military presence, but a far smaller one.

Most inhabitants, meanwhile, no doubt attempted to be invisible. Glevum was a thriving town and river port, full of a variety of trades. Latin was the language of the educated, people were adopting Roman ways, and citizenship, with the precious social and legal rights it conferred, was still the aspiration of almost anyone. Glevum, in fact, was so important – having been built as a 'colonia' for retiring veterans – that (among other privileges, including a degree of self-governance under an elected town council, the *curia* which could set taxes, as suggested in the tale) any freeman born within the walls was a citizen by right.

Most inhabitants, however, did not qualify. Many were freemen, born outside the walls, scratching a more or less precarious living from a trade. Hundreds more were slaves – mere chattels of their masters, to be bought and sold with no more rights than any other domestic animal. Some slaves led pitiable lives, but others were highly regarded by their owners and might be treated well. A slave in a kindly household – with shelter, food and raiment guaranteed – might have a more enviable lot than many a poor freeman struggling to eke out an existence in a squalid hut.

Power, where it existed, was vested exclusively in men. A woman of any age or rank was deemed a child in law, and although an individual woman might inherit an estate, she was always under the official tutelage of first her father and then her husband, if she had one, or some male relative. (If necessary, someone might be appointed by the state.) Wealthy females did little, even in the home – though they might to learn to spin. They were expected to bear children, preferably sons. There were slaves to do the work. Traders' wives often worked beside their husbands at their tasks, and in the poorest household everybody toiled. Bearing children was a risky business, too, and almost everyone – from all classes of society who could afford the fee and who did not have a trusted family female to assist – would call upon the services of a wisewoman (like the one mentioned in this book). Such women knew the properties of herbs and might be highly skilled, though some probably were not.

For details about the nature and formation of caves near Glevum, I am indebted to the Gloucestershire Speleological Society. I trust that I have managed to give a credible account, although there is no known cave in the actual location suggested in the text.

Information about the social life of the native Celtic tribes is sparse, since they kept no written records of their own. Such descriptions as we have are largely Roman ones, produced when the two races were at war, and thus not necessarily reliable. The little that we do know was almost certainly subject to local variation, and even the language differed slightly between tribes (perhaps as much as Portuguese and Spanish today) though they might be mutually intelligible. From these scattered sources, together with ancient traditions and archaeology, I have tried to create a credible picture of what might have been.

The rest of the Romano-British background of this book has been derived from a variety of (sometimes contradictory) pictorial and written sources, as well as artefacts. However, although I have done my best to create an accurate picture, this remains a work of fiction and there is no claim to total academic authenticity. Septimius Severus, and the events surrounding Albinus Clodius and Virius Lupus, are historically attested, as is the existence and basic geography of Glevum. The rest is the product of my imagination.

Relato refero. Ne Iupiter quidem omnibus placet.

I only tell you what I heard. Jupiter himself can't please everybody.

ONE

G reetings, this is Junio again. You may remember me. I am Libertus's adoptive son, and I have something to tell you. I'm not sure how to start, but Father always said if you want to tell a tale, start at the beginning. (Not that I have seen him for several years – not since he fled Glevum, following the death of his wife, under suspicion of having avenged himself on the one responsible.) And I suppose the beginning, from my point of view, would have been about a moon or so ago.

We live in troubled times, in any case, and that day had been especially troublesome. So troublesome that I'd shut the workshop early, leaving Tenuis, my apprentice-slave (a parting gift from my father), to sweep up and lock the doors. I was already not in the happiest of moods. I'd narrowly avoided a nasty argument with one of the chief magistrates of Glevum over a mosaic pavement for his house which I had finished earlier that day.

Very relieved to have finished it, as well. It wasn't a stock pattern – I've become quite skilled with those. But this client had wanted a particular design: a Cave Canem in his entrance porch, based on his own horrid, ugly pooch. The space was irregularly shaped, so it was no easy task – especially with no proper model that I could base it on. However, he was prepared to pay – and very handsomely – so in the end I had attempted to create my own design.

I confess the results were not exactly what I'd hoped. I'd miscalculated somewhere, and what I first produced was a hump-backed creature, more like an outsized toad. The owner gave it a single, contemptuous look and insisted that I take it up again and produce a better one, otherwise he refused to pay at all. Meanwhile, he showed it to some visiting fellow councillors – thus ensuring not only that my reputation slumped, but that his expensive residence became immediately known, all round Glevum, as 'the House of the Bulgy Dog'.

I could ill afford the bad publicity, far less to lose the handsome fee involved. Nor did I want to make a powerful enemy. So I'd spent several days removing it – a demanding task, when it was newly set – and still more days replacing it again. All unpaid, of course. The whole thing had cost me far more than it was worth.

Even then I was not very pleased with the result. The open mouth, which I'd meant to represent a snarl, looked much more like a yawn. But the client did accept it, and paid me what he owed.

That, at least, was a relief. But though I was glad to take home a bag of coins, it was less than half of what I might otherwise have earned. The whole thing was financially disastrous. Especially now there was to be an extra mouth to feed.

We already had three children (not counting one that died in infancy and another that had not survived the birth) and a fourth was on its way. Quite imminently now. So I was anxious to be home, although the sun was nowhere near about to set. There was some urgent building work I hadn't done – largely thanks to the extra hours spent on that entrance hall! It was late September, so daylight hours were fairly long. I might just finish it tonight, if it stayed dry until dusk.

I was riding Arlina (an ancient mule which was another of my father's parting gifts) and I tried to urge her to her fastest pace, so I could finish off my hut.

It was truly urgent, too. With my wife, Cilla, getting near her time, the extra room was a necessity – somewhere for the older three to sleep. They would need Brianus, our household slave, to be a guard at night – but as the master's children I could hardly put them in the dyehouse, or in the slave-hut with the two serving boys. There was not much space in there, in any case.

There's no room in our roundhouse either, in its present form. But I can't extend it while we live in it, and building a whole new one is an enormous task. So, with the older children growing fast, I'd settled on what I thought was a useful compromise. Not that my wife was very much impressed.

'Why bother with another Celtic sleeping hut? Your adoptive father might have been a Celt, but you're not and nor am I. Thanks to him you are a Roman citizen, so if you are going to build again, why not a Roman style of house? I don't mean a proper villa – nothing grand – just something small and solid, made of stone, that won't let in the rain. How often have I seen you climb up to mend the thatch on this, or have to spend the day repairing walls?'

'It would cost a huge amount,' I said, and it was true. Stone was not the problem – with the workshop I have good contacts in the trade, and the local stuff is fairly soft so I could turn that quickly into building blocks. But hiring labour, even borrowed slaves, is apt to cost more money than we could afford. Especially after losing earnings on that wretched dog! Though I did not say that, of course.

Perhaps I should have done. Cilla was not easily deterred.

'Expense, perhaps. But worth it, husband. And just think how pleasant it would be. We could have a little courtyard and a kitchen block, perhaps, and a nice atrium with separate rooms off it. You could do the floors yourself. That would impress your customers, as well. And don't say they wouldn't see it. You know how gossip spreads. With a house like that we could invite visitors to dine – a prospective councillor perhaps – and news would be round Glevum before you could say "Mars"!'

She was right, of course – as 'the bulgy dog' had proved. But we had no spare money now, and I wasn't to be swayed. 'A roundhouse hut is easy, we can manage that ourselves – especially now that I have Tenuis to help.' (That was specious, really. Tenuis was still too small to be a lot of use, and though he was willing, he had no experience. I did not have much, myself. Although my father had taught me what to do, I lacked his speed and skills – in this as so much else.) I glided over this. 'A stone house would be costly, and you can't build one yourself – especially not when you have a workshop to attend to – unless you are prepared for it to take you years. And our need is quite immediate.'

She humphed at that, and let the subject drop. But I knew I hadn't heard the last of it.

The trouble was that there was much sense in what she said. Few Roman citizens live in roundhouses. My father had, of course – and he'd helped me to build mine, which was why I was particularly fond of it. But a Roman house would give me greater social dignity, and would undoubtedly improve our children's chances too. Especially if I could show off the floors to a few important guests.

But that would have to wait. For now, I was just thankful to be coming home today with the full fee in my purse. It might not be the profit I'd been hoping for, but it was enough to afford some care for Cilla, if she required it now. At least the wisewoman to attend the birth, and perhaps even some nice, homely female slave to help with the newborn for a moon or two. We would have to accommodate her in the house, of course. Perhaps in the space where the children had been sleeping up till now.

Provided that I finished that new sleeping hut in time! I'd put the wicker framework up, and begun to thatch the roof, so all that remained was to finish doing that, then mix up the daub and fill the walls. It shouldn't take above another half a day at most – supposing that the rain held off, I thought, as I turned the final corner to where my roundhouse lay. I was calculating whether I had enough cut reeds to finish off the roof when I saw Brianus darting out from the enclosure gate and running towards me up the muddy lane.

'Master!' he panted as he came up and bowed. 'I saw you from the house. Thank Mars that you have come.'

I slid down from the mule and hitched her to the gate. I was damp and muddy, but I was at once concerned. 'Is your mistress . . . suffering distress?' (One doesn't mention the mechanics of childbirth, even to a slave.)

'Impatient and uncomfortable, that is all. Though I think her time is near.' He peered anxiously in the direction I had come. 'Tenuis is not with you?'

'He stayed back in the shop. There was time for him to follow me, but he preferred – he said – to bed down there beside the fire. Did not relish walking home alone, in case he got caught in the forest after dark.' Tenuis has grown a lot in size and confidence in the years since Father left, but he's still a nervous soul. And at present there is plenty to be nervous of. The local garrison has been depleted recently (for disturbing reasons). And fewer troop patrols on unfrequented roads means more chance of thieves and bandits – to say nothing of the wolves and bears that roam the woods at night.

Brianus made a disapproving face. 'A pity. I might have sent him for the wisewoman. I think it would be prudent to have her very soon.'

'Well, I'm here now,' I said, abandoning my building plans at once. 'I'll go for her myself.'

I was quite glad to be of help, since I happened to be available (unlike many Roman fathers who leave all that to slaves, even avoiding the house if possible). Not that I would be of any use whatever at the birth – Cilla knew what she was doing by this time anyway, and the wisewoman from the woods would take charge when she came. That, and her fee, had already been agreed, following the death of the infant last time round.

What I could do was supervise our three other little ones. Take them into the forest to gather nuts and herbs, perhaps. And kindling, if the ground was not too wet. (Strangely, it is often drier in the woods, where the trees are thick and the leaves have yet to fall. I know at least one thicket where the weather does not reach and there are several shallow caves and clefts cut in the limestone hills, where our forefathers dug out rocks to burn for lime – or even crush for seams of lead and silver, rumour says. Places one can hide until the rain has stopped. The worse of it, at least.) The children might even relish doing that.

Then, if the birth was mercifully quick, they could help me build the hut – mix the mud and straw and throw it at the walls. They would enjoy the mess, though I would not. Though by then it might be a dreadful rush to get it done. I might have to drape some capes around it, like a sort of tent, for now.

I wished, not for the first time, that Father was still here – and my adoptive mother too. Gwellia could take the children and let them help her bake, till the pains began in earnest. Then Father would tell stories until they fell asleep.

That is what had happened at all successful births – but my parents and their cosy roundhouse were both gone. Last time round it had been difficult enough – though the stillbirth was all over before it had begun – but this time it was clearly up to me. At least, I thought, I had a sort of plan.

'I'll fetch the wisewoman,' I said. 'And I'll take the children too, and find things for them to do while the private female business is going on. I'll try and wear them out. If the birth is quick and simple, I'll come back and do the hut. But, if necessary, they can sleep in Tenuis's bedding space tonight, and I'll stay there with them. You can sleep inside, and attend your mistress through the night. You'd best get back to her. Soothe her brow while I am gone and stand by to fetch and carry when the wisewoman arrives.'

(That was another change from Gwellia's time. She always came in when things got critical. There'd been no need, in those days, to call on wisewomen – or anybody else.)

But Brianus did not hurry to obey. He looked so doubtful that it prompted me to add, 'It's only for a day or two at most, until the hut is done. Your mistress will be glad to have the children somewhere else, tonight. There's little enough privacy in a roundhouse, at the best of times. But don't fear to sleep inside. She may require your help.'

He bowed. 'Obviously, master, I'd be honoured to oblige. And no doubt your other plans are good. But you are wanted. There have been messengers . . .' He jerked his head towards the dyehouse, just inside the gate.

The dyehouse is a simple structure, round and thatched with reeds, with a fire in the middle where my wife boils up the ingredients for dyes, and colours yarn with them. (Some people do not bother with a chimney space, leaving the smoke to filter through the roof, but Father always said there was too much risk of conflagration from the sparks, and insisted on a central hole. And he should know: his workshop building nearly burned down once.) Like any roundhouse, it had no window-space, but the door was open, and I could see into the gloom. I was expecting nothing but a cauldron hanging on the hearth, but as I looked more closely I realized there was someone sitting in the shadows next to it.

A youngish fellow, squatting on the floor, greedily spooning something from a bowl. He wore a short tunic, so a slave, perhaps? But as he moved his arm again, it caught a beam of light, and I realized what uniform it was. A scarlet tunic with a cloak to match. The livery of the previous owner of this piece of land: Marcus Septimus Aurelius, ex-patron of my father, and one of the wealthiest men in all Britannia.

One of the most influential, too. Again! He had slipped from favour for a time, because of his connections to the first Imperial house. But after the dreadful upheaval of the last two years – when Clodius Albinus, the last ill-fated Governor of Britannia, had actually led his troops against the current Emperor – Septimius Severus was now firmly on the throne, and the succession settled.

(I have some private sympathy with Clodius. He was promised, in return for his support when Severus was fighting another pretender to the throne, that he would be next in line, and was actually given the title 'Caesar of the West'. But only Clodius could believe that promise, Father used to say, because Severus has a healthy, living son. And sure enough, last year the son was named as heir – and Clodius was declared an enemy of state. That left him little choice except to rebel. He put up a good fight too, but was defeated in the end – decapitated and his dead body spread out on the ground so Severus could trample on it with his horse. The resultant pieces were not even given decent burial, but thrown into the Rhone, along with the bodies of his murdered family.)

So now we had a new Provincial Governor, Virius Lupus. A quite deliberate choice. He had been humiliatingly defeated by Clodius once, in Gaul, as part of the revolt – so he had an especial interest in seeking out 'traitorous' supporters of his predecessor. Especially in garrison towns, like Glevum, where loyal legions had followed Clodius to Gaul (he was their overall commander, after all) and been part of Lupus's defeat – with enthusiastic sympathizers in the populace.

It had changed Glevum. The disgraced detachment had been partially replaced, but the fort was under-strength, although very active on Lupus's behalf. People had been executed or had simply disappeared – including two of our

local councillors – among rumours that they'd been secretly
denounced.

But it had all been good for Marcus, in the end. Those who
were merely related to previous Emperors were, by comparison, no threat. Indeed, Pertinax (a friend of Marcus's who had
once been Emperor) was now restored to the Imperial pantheon,
and his supporters were in favour once again.

Meanwhile, normal citizens like me kept their opinions on
Clodius to themselves, and concentrated on being anonymous
and invisible.

'Master?' Brianus broke into my thoughts. 'His Excellence
has sent a messenger.'

'Surely Marcus isn't wanting me again?' I puffed my cheeks
out in a sigh. I did not want this now.

Even since my father fled the area, Marcus (who lives in a
villa nearby) has turned his attention on to me. This can be
welcome – as when it results in civic contracts for new mosaic
floors – but less so when he calls upon me to resolve trivial
problems at his country house. And things had been going
missing over the last moon. He'd asked for my advice about
it twice before.

I believe he thinks it a kind of compliment – a tribute to
that old relationship – though it isn't even that. He only asks
in a symbolic way. None of the serious public matters which
Father used to deal with so effectively. For which, I suppose,
I should thank all the gods. I have enough to do. Marcus
would not think of paying anyone – the invitation is supposed
to be a privilege.

I said, 'He wants to see me?'

My slave-boy nodded. 'Urgently, it seems.'

'What is it now? Another joint of pork has disappeared?'
If I were Marcus, I thought bitterly, I should interview the
cook! But I dared not voice that, even to my slave. I sighed
again. 'With this birth impending, do you suppose I could
refuse to go? I don't imagine I can be the slightest . . .' I
tailed off as a thought occurred to me. 'Wait a moment! Surely
he did not tell that messenger to wait for me? He could not
know I would be home so soon.' I do not usually get home
till after dusk.

Brianus shook a warning head at me. 'He will know very shortly, master, when his slave returns to him. It is unfortunate. If you'd been a little later, the courier would have gone, and no one would have looked for you until tomorrow, as you say. But as it is . . . it's my fault, I suppose . . . I offered him refreshment.'

He was so apologetic that I was moved to say, 'As anybody would. It's what your mistress would have ordered you to do, if she had not been occupied with other things.'

Brianus looked grateful, but he still felt the obligation to explain. 'He had run here all the way, and he was out of breath. Just some homemade bread and cheese and water from the well. Dull pickings – but without bothering the mistress, it was all I could provide. I did not really expect him to accept – the villa feeds its servants very well – but he did so eagerly. You would think he hadn't eaten for the day. Ah – and now he's seen you.'

This was obviously true. The boy had dropped the crust of bread with which he had been scraping out the remnants of the cheese, and was scrambling to his feet. He brushed the breadcrumbs from his tunic, clearly embarrassed to be caught in the enjoyment of his snack. His face, which I could see as he moved out into the light, had turned as scarlet as his uniform – all the more vivid against his bright ginger hair. He caught my glance and paused to give a sweeping bow, then started towards me down the enclosure path.

'Oh, by all the gods!' I muttered. 'Now I suppose I can't refuse to go. Though it could not be less convenient.' (I don't know how often I heard my father saying that!) 'And probably just for another piece of missing meat! Marcus is the richest man for miles. He would hardly notice it.'

'The matter does appear to be more serious this time,' my slave replied, dropping his voice discreetly, though I had not lowered mine.

I stared at him. 'You have heard the message?' But, of course, he would have done – thinking to relay it to me later on.

'There's a piece of missing jewellery. Some problem with a clasp. A solid silver one, inlaid with gold and jewels and big enough to close a cloak. It had quite a value I believe.'

Certainly more serious than disappearing food. My status was improving! But now of all moments? Aloud I simply said, 'Belonging to Marcus, I assume?'

Brianus raised his hands and shoulders in a shrug. 'That, master, I can't tell you. I did not ask, and the fellow did not say. But here he comes, himself. Better, perhaps, to question him direct?'

TWO

'Citizen Junio, greetings!' Marcus's messenger had fastened the enclosure gate behind him, and turned towards me as he spoke, scarlet all over and bowing abjectly.

I frowned. There was something familiar about that voice. Then, as he straightened up again, I saw the freckles and recognized the face. 'Letigines?'

'Citizen Junio, you remember me?'

Slaves do not expect to be recalled by name, but in this case it wasn't very difficult. 'Letigines' means Freckles – and he was covered with them from head to toe.

'Of course,' I said. 'We've met before – in rather unhappy circumstances, I believe.' He had been witness to some of the events which forced my father to leave town, though the boy had obviously risen in importance since. Back then, he was a mere humble household page – occasionally entrusted to deliver messages. Now he was a liveried courier, a much higher-status post. The voice had broken in the meantime, too. I said as much to him.

He flashed me a sheepish grin, but supressed it instantly, in favour of the serious face appropriate to his role. 'I bring a message from His Excellence—'

'So I understand,' I interrupted. 'Some trouble with a clasp? Tell me about it.'

He looked nonplussed. Messages are generally carried word for word, and he was not expecting to extemporize.

I offered him a prompt. 'Something of value, belonging to your master, I presume?'

He shook his freckled head. 'The lady Julia.'

I gave an inward groan. This put more pressure on me to attend the villa – Marcus would do anything to please his wife. To refuse his summons was always dangerous, but disobliging Julia made it doubly so. I turned to exchange a glance with

Brianus, who had been standing close behind. But his attention was now engaged elsewhere.

Unseen by me, my eldest son had pottered from the house and was tugging at the slave's tunic hem. (Carus was almost six and knew enough never to interrupt me if I was talking to a messenger or potential customer.) Brianus had bent down to listen to the boy, so I turned back to Freckle-face again.

'The lady Julia?' I repeated. 'Part of the pattern of petty theft, perhaps?' Maybe I should have paid more attention to that disappearing pork. 'Or,' I added daringly, 'is it possible it has simply been mislaid?' Julia was charming, but she could be scatterbrained.

Letigines did not smile. 'This jewel did not go missing while it was in the house.'

Stolen at the baths or while visiting, perhaps? This was more alarming than I had supposed. People don't steal from Marcus and his family as a rule – they have more concern for their future health. Supposing that they have a future! 'No doubt it is a valuable thing?'

'The mistress does have finer brooch pins, citizen. But this was her favourite. My master gave it to her years ago. He had it made for her when they were wed – inlaid with gold and set with precious jewels. Then perhaps a moon ago she broke the clasp off it – trying to pin a cloak that was too thick. She did not wish to have His Excellence involved – she felt he might be vexed that she'd been careless with his gift – so she sent to have it mended, secretly.'

'Dear Mercury! Where did she send it to?' I was imagining all kinds of fantasies – from travelling fraudsters to the shady workshops behind Glevum marketplace.

The reply surprised me. 'To Gaius Vitellius.'

I whistled in surprise. This was a wholly different matter then! Gaius was one of the best silver craftsmen in the whole colonia – not that I had ever called upon his services. But I knew his reputation, which was for excellence. And for colossal prices. 'Vitellius? You are quite sure of that?'

'Absolutely certain,' Freckle-face replied. 'I took it there myself. He has worked for the master many times before, so the mistress naturally sent him the repair. But what came back was just a copy, made of some base metal and simply dipped to silver it. I might not have noticed, but she spotted it as soon as she undid the leather bag. A different weight, she said. And she thinks the stones are glass. So, of course, she had to tell my master after all.'

'Surely, then, they must confront Vitellius direct!' I was beginning to wonder why Marcus felt he needed me. 'There will be witnesses, no doubt. If there was a proper contract, there would have to be.' If Marcus simply wanted my advice, I could offer that from here.

But Freckles shook his head. 'But there wasn't. The customer was officially my mistress, after all, so a formal contract was not possible. We were not expecting one – this was a mere repair.'

I should have thought of that. A woman cannot make a binding contract under law – and Letigines was right, even at Vitellius's prices, the sum concerned for simply fixing back a clasp was probably not large enough to warrant one. 'But, even so, if you have any sense, you don't hand over precious things without a witness there.'

The courier winced. 'Unfortunately, citizen, that is exactly what I did. In fact, I waited purposely for everyone to go before I gave it to the jeweller. It was supposed to be a secret – which he swore that he would keep. It all seemed perfectly in order at the time. He gave me a receipt, including a written statement of how much it would cost. Only a piece of bark-paper, of course, but there was nothing at all unusual in that. I've had such things from him before. The last occasion was a moon or two ago, when the master sent me with a ruby ring that had to be resized.'

'Do you still have this document – the one about the clasp?'

He shook his ginger head. 'When I retrieved the item, I gave it back, of course. That is the system. You hand it back and pay the stated sum, and are given the mended article in exchange. I even checked the contents of the bag before I left. It looked all right to me.' His voice trembled and the words became a wail. 'There should have been no problem. There has never been any trouble up till now. That's why, on this

occasion, suspicion falls on me. Citizen Junio, if you can find
out the tru—'

We were interrupted by an anguished cry. 'Brianus! That
water!' It was Cilla's voice. She sounded in distress.

Brianus stepped forward, deferentially. 'Excuse me, master,
I didn't wish to interrupt. But the mistress sent the boy to ask
for water – she feels she wants a drink – but I gave the last
of what was in the pail to the courier, so I'll have to fetch
some more. But I don't wish to leave her unattended as she
is. What shall I tell her?'

'That I will take the children to the spring and fill the pail,
and then fetch the wisewoman to her – as soon as I have
finished with this messenger. Which will not take me long!'

Brianus bowed in swift acknowledgement and hastened
off, accompanied by the child. That cry of anguish had strength-
ened my resolve. Whatever trouble this might land me in, I
knew what I must do.

I turned to back to Freckles. 'My wife is in childbed. This
is not the time. Tell Marcus I regret it very much, but I cannot
come just now.' (Not that he was likely to sympathize, I
thought. Roman fathers tend to make a point of not being in
the house while their wives are giving birth – it is thought to
be ill-omened, requiring ritual cleansing afterwards. I would
take care to do so later on myself – by washing in the running
waters of the spring.) I smiled at Freckle-face. 'In the
meantime, if he is asking my advice, I should send to Gaius
Vitellius, just to make sure there hasn't been some terrible
mistake. If this does not solve the matter he can let me know,
and I will come – of course – as soon as possible.'

It was a dismissal, but he did not bow away. 'Citizen Junio,
he has already sent to Gaius Vitellius. This morning at first
light. By me, as it happens – he did not suspect me then. I
arrived the moment they took the shutters down. Gaius
Vitellius was not there himself – it seems he's gone to Corinium
for supplies – but the slave who served me yesterday swears
that his master had no other clasp of that description in the
shop, nor have they ever had one.'

'And you believed him?'

'He invited me to look, and believe me that I did – on every shelf and work-table and in every drawer – but there was nothing remotely similar. And then he showed me something written on a slate, which I could not really read, showing that it had been paid for and returned. "*Caveat emptor*" – that is what he said. "Let the purchaser beware."'

'And you're sure the bag he'd given back to you was the same one that you brought?'

'I'm certain about that – there is a mark on it. And to my eyes the clasp itself seemed just the same. I did not think about the weight. But having agreed to take it, there is apparently no recourse in law. My master is absolutely furious, of course.' He sounded desperate. 'But the lady Julia suggested I might come to you. I think she hopes you might save me further punishment.'

I was in the act of turning back to Brianus – who was hurrying from the roundhouse, carrying the pail, with my children at his heels. But he saw me still talking and paused beside the door – waiting politely till I'd finished. Which I thought I had. But Freckle-face had made me hesitate.

'Further punishment?' I'd been a slave myself and knew what that could mean. 'Your master has already had you whipped?'

'Not yet.' The voice was quavering again. 'Just a few angry blows he gave me with his switch. But he has had them stop my meals – until this thing is found.' (So he hadn't eaten since shortly before dawn. No wonder the poor boy had been so glad to have the cheese!) 'The mistress has spared me a formal beating up till now. But as the one who carried the item to and fro, of course, unless it's found . . .' He tailed off, hopelessly. 'But I did not take it, citizen. I swear it on my life! They've seized all my few possessions and searched my sleeping-space. But of course they did not find it, because it was not there.' He flung himself on to his knees, and would have grasped my tunic if I'd not stepped briskly back. 'The master was for flogging me at once, but the mistress said I was to run and fetch you back as soon as possible. I think she feels responsible – both for sending me, and for breaking it

to start with – and so making the master furious. Master Junio,
I beg you . . .'

I felt for him, of course. When Libertus was my master he
never struck me once, but I have seen a formal whipping. It
happened in the house where I was born a slave. All the
household servants were compelled to watch, and I've not
forgotten it. I was not intended to. Marcus, I knew, was
not unjust and cruel, but a formal flogging is something I'd
try to protect anybody from.

I sighed. 'Then tell the lady Julia I will surely come, and
do what I can to help – though Mars alone knows what good
I'm going to be – but not at this moment. My wife is close to
giving birth, and I am needed here, as you can clearly see.' I
turned to Brianus. 'You go and tend your mistress – it sounds
as if already she has need of you. Tell her that the wisewoman
will soon be on her way. I'll take the children with me to the
spring, then fetch her straightaway – just as soon as I have
turned Arlina out to graze.' I turned back to Freckle-face. 'I'll
have to leave the villa till tomorrow, I'm afraid. Assure them
that I'll come then, if the child is safely born.'

The messenger, however, did not move a limb. He simply
knelt there staring at me in dismay.

I gave him what I hoped was a disarming smile. 'Marcus
can't have been expecting me tonight, in any case. It's only
chance that I happened to be here.'

Brianus looked extremely dubious, too, as he handed me
the pail. 'Are you quite certain, master, that you ought not to
go?' he murmured. 'His Excellence will . . .'

He clearly wished to urge what I already knew – that keeping
Marcus waiting overnight, when he was already angry and
sure to learn that I was indeed at home, was likely to be injuri-
ous to my health and happiness. But it is not a slave's place
to question what his master does. I scowled at him, to remind
him of the fact.

'Very good, master,' he went on, clearly deciding he'd
already said too much. 'But with your permission, might I
have a private word?' He gestured me a little further up the
path, out of earshot of the courier, who had risen to his feet
by now, but was still hovering.

I was impatient. 'Well?'

Brianus dropped his voice still lower, so we could not be heard – even by the children who were nearby clamouring to go. 'What should I say to the other messenger?'

THREE

I stared at him, startled.

'I think I mentioned, master, that there had been more than one.'

He had done, when I came to think of it. Messengers. Plural. I sighed. Another interruption to the urgent tasks I had to do. But this might be business – which I could ill afford to lose.

I looked around. There was no one else in sight. 'So, where's the other one? And who is he? Not another of Marcus's messengers?' (Given this sudden mistrust of Freckle-face, that was not impossible.)

Brianus shook his head. 'Some sort of Celtic freeman, by the look of him.' He moved closer, making sure we were not overheard. 'And one who very clearly did not want to be observed – at least by anyone connected with His Excellency. When Marcus's messenger arrived, he darted off without a word. I don't know where he's gone. Or even who he is. He gave me some outlandish name I did not recognize. Though he clearly knew who you were. And your trade. He spoke about the workshop – but said that for private reasons he preferred to see you here.'

I gave him a sharp look. 'Rather suspicious, wouldn't you have thought?' If this Celt was frightened of authority, I wasn't sure that I wanted to talk to him at all.

Of course, there are many Celts who are very Romanized and live happy, peaceful lives – but there are still rebels, hiding in the caves, actively opposing Roman rule. These men were extremely dangerous to know – especially since I look half-Celt myself. (My mother was probably a Silurian slave, though I shall never know for sure, because her owner – almost certainly my sire – sold me on as soon as I could walk.) So I was particularly anxious not to be suspected of rebel sympathies. The Emperor, having defeated his rivals to the throne, was turning his attention to stamping out all other threats to his authority.

And these rebels certainly were that. They knew the hills and forests perfectly, appearing from nowhere to ambush any 'occupying troops' – or anyone with overt ties to Rome – foolish enough to march in small parties through unfrequented woods. The victims were likely to be expertly deprived, not only of weapons, armour, horses and supplies, but also of their heads, which were hung as trophies in grisly 'sacred groves'. Their hapless corpses were then strung up on trees – naked – beside the roadside, as a dreadful warning to everybody else, though one terrified survivor might be permitted to escape – bruised and bleeding and without his clothes – to stammer his story at the nearest market town. It served to magnify the legend – and the fear.

The tension had been worse, if anything, in recent times. The local legions had supported Clodius, of course, and several companies had been withdrawn to help his fight in Gaul. (The local commander had actually been killed, before he could be captured, with many of his men.) After their defeat – and subsequent disgrace – not all of them had been replaced. That left fewer men to man the garrison. So, though there had been no raids now for a little while – the rebels having simply disappeared into the mist – another might be expected any time.

So what was I to do, if this message was from them? Virius Lupus, after his humiliating – if temporary – defeat by Clodius and his men, was anxious to impress the Emperor, and anyone in Britannia found dealing with the rebels could be in danger of his life. But one dared not cross them either – they were not kind to enemies.

'A wanted man, you think?' I said to Brianus.

He considered for a moment. 'You might think so, master, from the way he fled. But there can't be anything too secret about his being here. He must have asked about to find you. And in some detail too. He called me by my name. Someone must have told him what it was. More likely that – with you living in a roundhouse – he took you for a Celt yourself, and simply preferred to come and meet you here.'

I allowed myself to be convinced. 'Come to offer a commission, possibly?' Some local chieftains have built Roman homes, trying to seem as civilized as possible (Cilla would doubtless have approved) and distancing themselves neatly from awkward dissidents. And what could be more Roman than a mosaic floor?

This had to be a possibility.

I said, more cheerfully, 'Hoping for a discount from a fellow countryman, perhaps? Then I'm afraid he's been deceived. Though you can't judge by appearances. Some Celts are rich these days. Did he wear a torc, or lots of golden rings?'

Brianus looked doubtful. 'Not that I could see. He looked travel-stained and dusty, as if he'd walked for miles, though if he had baggage he's left it somewhere else. In fact, at first I thought he was a slave, since he was unattended – but he insisted he was not. Said he had been sent here by an elder of his tribe. And he had a message for you. That's all that he would say. Refused to talk to anyone but you.'

'Ah!' I understood. Or I thought I did.

There had been recent proclamations in Glevum market-square – first offering an amnesty, which no rebel was fool enough to claim, and then rewards for information about the dissidents. Local citizens, preferring on the whole to keep their heads, prudently elected to be ignorant. But anyone knowing the rebels' whereabouts – or even remotely suspected of doing so – could expect to be brought in for unpleasant 'questioning'.

No wonder this tribesman had avoided seeking me in town, and then rushed into the woods when Letigines arrived wearing that distinctive scarlet uniform. Marcus was the highest authority for miles.

I swallowed hard. If I was right, I really did not want to be involved. As a Roman citizen, I was less likely to suffer physic-ally for 'having information about an enemy of the state' – but there might be fiscal penalties. On the other hand, it was not wise to make enemies among the tribes. 'You didn't offer *him* refreshment?'

'I didn't get a chance. The courier arrived and – since he was from Marcus, I went to greet him down the lane. When I turned round, the Celt had disappeared. I didn't see him go, and I haven't seen him since. He may have given up. What should I tell him, if he turns up again? We don't know what he wants.'

'Well, it can't be important, can it?' I said impatiently. 'Or he would have told you what it was. I can't see him this evening, obviously enough. But it might be business. Don't simply send him off. Tell him to come by in the morning – supposing that he ever does in fact come back.'

'He has already done so,' a voice said at my ear, and I whirled around to find the man in question standing behind me on the track. Clearly a Celt, as Brianus had said. Not only did he wear a long plaid tunic and a hooded cloak in native style, but underneath he sported a pair of those outlandish 'trews', which – though far less civilized than proper Roman dress – are still favoured by Celtic tribesmen from the country farms. (Father once told me that every family wove a slightly different pattern of colours in the plaid – though they all look very much the same to me.) Even the lower legs were wrapped in strips of the same cloth, and in place of sandals – or even Roman shoes – he wore a pair of uncouth 'country boots', pieces of raw cowhide tied around the feet and left to cure until they shrank to shape. To my relief he carried no weapon of any kind, beyond a walking staff – at least that I could see.

All the same, he was an intimidating sight – a strapping lad, a hand's breadth taller than I was myself. And he'd unsettled me, though I did my best to hide the fact. He'd appeared as if by magic, and without a sound – though he had probably been lurking in the woods throughout.

'You wanted something, stranger?' I enquired.

He seemed amused by that, I saw it in his eyes, but when he spoke he was gravely courteous. 'A private word, citizen, if that is possible?' The voice was deep and cultured and the Latin excellent. Not a trace of the heavy accent many tribesmen have.

He pushed back his hood and I could see him clearly now. His hair was cut close around the face and lime-bleached in native style – though it might have been naturally as red as Freckle-face's, judging by the eyebrows, unusual bushy beard and typically Celtic long moustache. But there was something familiarly Roman about his eyes and nose – product of master and a slave, perhaps (as indeed I was myself)? But that was not a question one could politely ask. Nor was this moment for asking anything.

'You can leave us to it, Brianus,' I said, as coolly as I could. 'But I will not be long. Fetch me a dry cloak from the dyehouse – and put the children in their capes and stoutest sandals too. Then bring them back here with a basket each so they can come with me.'

My servant bowed acknowledgement and shepherded my little flock away.

I turned towards the newcomer. He flashed a charming smile. 'I am sorry, citizen, if I startled you!' He kept his voice deliberately low. 'I did not wish to draw attention to myself. Though I fear I may not altogether have succeeded there.' He jerked his head towards the corner of the lane.

Freckle-face, who was still loitering indecisively, bent down to adjust his sandal-straps, trying to pretend that he had not stopped to stare.

'I think he's merely hoping to delay the beating he expects when he gets home,' I said, inwardly praying to all the gods that this was true.

It made the stranger smile. 'Then let us hope it does.'

I looked at him sternly. 'And you are?'

He gave me a strange look. 'They call me Anlyan.' That meant nothing to me, but he offered nothing more.

I was impatient to be rid of him. 'You have a message for me, man? Deliver it, if so. I am in a hurry – I have many things to do. I have even been obliged to refuse to answer the summons of an important magistrate. So, what is your business, Anlyan?'

He glanced towards Letigines again and seemed to change his mind. 'Nothing that can't wait a little, citizen. It's quite a complex tale. And there are documents which you may wish to see. But no answer is required, so there is no special haste. You have other pressing matters to attend to, as you say. Though, if you wish, I could assist you there.' He gave that smile again.

I glowered at him, more impatient still. 'Assist me, how?'

'I was close by and could not help but overhear. Marcus

Septimus requests your presence at his house – but you feel that you must fetch the water which your wife requires, and also go and ask the wisewoman to come. But I could do that for you. I could even take the children with me when I go, and keep them in the forest afterwards, as you sensibly proposed, to pick some herbs or find some kindling wood. I have experience with youngsters. So do not fear for them.'

Such a thing had not occurred to me. One often leaves one's offspring with an unfamiliar slave, who might well be a Celt. But a freeman, with connections to the local tribes? That was different. However, he was already reaching to his belt.

'I have a letter that would recommend me, here.' He proffered me a scroll. It had not been carried in a scroll case, as a Roman might, but in a sort of linen bag, so it was slightly damp and dusty, but it was nonetheless a scroll.

That surprised me. Writing formal messages was not the common Celtic way. What's more, this was not mere linen or a piece of rolled-up bark. It was proper parchment – which involved expense. And the message was a lengthy one. A palimpsest by the outward look of it. (Since parchment is costly, it is quite usual for people to reuse a letter in this way, by writing a new message crosswise – and on both sides too, which was evidently what had happened here.) It seemed to be in Latin, rather than in runes, which I had briefly feared.

The scroll was tied with ribbons, four of them in all, and each knot was fastened with a seal. An unfamiliar one. That was disturbing. Most of the local tribal chiefs had ones I'd recognize.

I picked at the knots, but age and dust had rigidified the wax and I could not open them. 'I'll have to fetch a knife.' I was exasperated, and could not disguise the fact.

'Then take it upon trust. It commends me as hard-working and of good character,' Anlyan said.

I shook my head. 'From someone I don't know?'

He was about to answer, but Brianus had come back with the children by this time, and caught the last few words. 'Apparently the writer is not entirely unknown. A tribal elder who had dealings with the workshop in your father's time, it seems. And that seal should mean that writing's not been tampered with. Though I did not recognize the imprint of the ring.'

'You've seen it?'

'He offered it to me when he first arrived, but of course I cannot read. And this was no time to show the mistress anything.'

Not that Cilla could have deciphered it easily herself. (Though, despite her humble origins, she has taught herself to read a little by studying the inscriptions on the tombs outside Glevum's walls.) But Brianus was right. If Anlyan was so anxious to have the message read, presumably it could be counted on.

I looked at this curious visitor again. I had no recollection of meeting him before. But there was something familiar about him, all the same. Red hair was typical of the Salurii, a local tribe my father had had cordial dealings with. And it was true that I'd met one or two of them – a family with no (known) connections with the rebels in the woods. Perhaps I could have confidence in this stranger after all.

I would gladly send him to fetch the wisewoman. She is brilliant at her trade, and Cilla dotes on her, but she is formidable – to me at any rate. (She's old and only small and slight – eccentric looking, with wild grey curls and piercing eyes, and often dressed in several layers of tunic at one time – but intolerant of fathers, whom she once described as 'necessary nuisances'.) So I'd be more than happy for the Celt to go. Especially as matters were urgent and I was wasting time. 'Since Libertus knew the writer, I could accept your help, I suppose,' I said, relinquishing the scroll.

'Could you, master?' Brianus was visibly relieved. 'It would comfort the mistress very much, I think. She's worrying about you failing to appear when His Excellence has summoned you. And this way I could stay with her throughout. Besides, that messenger will have to go back to the villa very soon – or he will get a whipping.' He nodded at Letigines, who was still dawdling in sight. 'He has already been too long. So he is almost certain to be flogged – though, if he brought you with him, that would alter things, of course. And I'm sure if you requested it, he would not find it necessary to report what else he'd seen.'

I kicked the gate impatiently, and wished that I had not (I was wearing sandals). But it was now clear that I would have to go to the villa after all. Otherwise, Marcus was going to hear, quite soon, not only that I had been at home to greet his messenger, been offered an opportunity to come and had rejected it, but also that I'd been consorting with an elusive Celt.

'Oh, very well then,' I said, crossly. 'But let us, by all the gods, be quick.' I raised my voice, and cupped my hands around my mouth to call. 'Letigines!' The boy, who had moved not half a dozen paces all this time, made to come back to me but I waved him on. 'I have changed my mind. You set off, and I'll catch up with you.'

I was unhitching Arlina as I spoke, to general relief. Brianus hurried back to Cilla's side, and Anlyan shepherded the little ones away, stopping them to wave as they turned up the hill.

I urged the mule into her reluctant trot and we soon caught up with Freckles – who had been walking slowly to make sure that we did. He jabbered his relief at me the whole way down the lane.

But I was hardly listening. Something uneasy about the scene that I'd just left was niggling at the corner of my brain. It was not until we reached the villa gates that I realized what it was.

Anlyan would clearly get directions from my slave as to how to reach the wisewoman, when he came back with the pail. But how had he known which way to go to find the spring?

FOUR

B ut there were other things to think of by this time. We had reached the villa and the slave on duty was already opening the gates at our approach. 'Welcome, citizen!' he said. 'And courier, it is well that you are back. I'm to tell you that the master is awaiting you in the atrium. You're ordered to report at once, if not before!'

Letigines turned as pale as his freckles would allow. He was already in trouble and such a summons clearly boded more. I did not really wish to make it worse by irritating Marcus further – as I was likely to if I intruded, uninvited, into this interview. But, with the state of Cilla's health, I did not have time today to be kept dangling for hours.

I thought quickly. His Excellence was obviously not expecting me. And it was not my place to be there while he chastised his slaves. Like any wealthy man, Marcus generally left his lower-ranking visitors to wait some little time – the lower, the longer. And as his visitors go, I was among the lowest. But he had sent for me and, besides, I might be able to speak for Freckles, too.

So – despite the attempted protests of the slave at the front door – I insisted on being shown in straight away, walking so close behind Letigines that I could not have been prevented except by force.

'Simply announce me. I'll take responsibility,' I ordered loftily, but as we entered the atrium I realized my mistake.

Marcus was already entertaining company. Patrician company. Thaddeus Quintus Flavius, a rich but querulous and ageing local magistrate, was there, sitting on a folding stool consuming honeyed dates and wine. He raised his head – which was completely bald – to give me a disdainful look as I came in. I knew exactly why. Not only was I clearly a man of lowly rank; he had been one of the councillors invited in to jeer at my first attempt at the House of the Bulgy Dog!

If I could have slunk away, I would have done. The councillor's spotless toga, with conspicuous purple stripe, was in striking contrast to my shabby working clothes. I wished devoutly that I'd stopped to change – as a Roman citizen I had a toga too (although a humbler, dingier one) and social convention said I should have put it on, in any case, to visit somebody of Marcus's high rank. Even my cloak (which I'd declined to shed on entering, being 'in a hurry' as I'd told the slave) was only an old one, stained with years of wear.

Meanwhile our host, as usual, looked immaculate, in a pale-green synthesis – that useful combination of tunic and toga, which Marcus generally prefers to wear at home – together with a golden torc around his neck and a vast gold-seal ring on his hand. For all his otherwise informal dress, Marcus was emphasizing who had status here. Even his folding stool was deliberately higher than his guest's.

As a humble tradesman, I was distinctly out of place. But there was no escaping now.

'Letigines, master, as you requested!' The slave who had escorted us into the atrium pushed Freckles forwards as he spoke, then shot a look at me. 'And the citizen Junio. Apologies, master, but he was adamant that he must come as well.' He bowed low and made a swift escape, before he could incur a reprimand. I only wished that I could do the same.

I bowed, too, as low as possible – expecting fury at my impudence. 'Your indulgence, Excellence, this is entirely my . . .' But the outraged anger which had crossed Marcus's face had instantly vanished as he realized who I was.

'Junio!' He rose to meet me and his voice was cordial. 'Forgive my slave. I fear he sounded rude.' His Excellence was apologizing for his staff! To me! No wonder Thaddeus was looking mystified.

'Your page had every reason, Excellence!' I said. 'I would not normally have dreamed of pushing myself in—'

Marcus cut me off. 'In general, of course, I'm not to be disturbed, especially when I'm entertaining visitors, and my slave would not have admitted you, whatever you might say. But since I sent Letigines to summon you, and then required that he should be sent in here to me at once, my house-slave clearly did not know what he should do with you. But he made the right decision. I have urgent need of you.' He held out both his hands. 'Citizen, it was good of you to come. And so quickly, too. You know Councillor Thaddeus, I think? He's spending a few days here at my villa while he has a floor installed.'

He gestured to the older councillor, who was staring at me like the fabled basilisk. With his pale skin, cold eyes and general hairlessness, he looked like a marble statue of the First Emperor (a similarity I suspect he cultivated quite deliberately). And he was visibly annoyed at being required to share this private audience with someone of low rank.

'Know Councillor Thaddeus?' I murmured as I bent to kiss Marcus's proffered ring. (Unlike my father, I did not actually kneel. His Excellence was not officially my patron, after all.) 'The donor of the fountain outside Minerva's shrine? Of course I do, if only by repute.'

This was not wholly the compliment it seemed. Thaddeus was certainly well known around the town, but chiefly for his young, expensive wife (who'd brought a handsome dowry and whom he famously indulged) and for perpetually fretting about his health. Even the fountain had been at his wife's behest, so rumour said – as a gesture to the populace, intended to ensure his re-election to an honourable (and often lucrative) post.

His birth and wealth alone would probably have guaranteed that anyway, though his record on the *curia* was not a sparkling one. My father, who had briefly been a councillor himself, used to say that Thaddeus was chiefly notable for 'voting rarely, saying little and doing even less. Though he does have a talent for somehow emerging on the winning side of every argument – without appearing to take part in it.'

He was also, famously, a stickler for proper dignity. And it was clear that I'd offended against this code today. He had been obliged to stand when I arrived – since Marcus did, as Marcus was both his host and a man of higher rank. But I, emphatically, was not. And now he had been formally introduced to me, meaning that he might be expected to converse! These were not courtesies he wanted to accord and I feared he would resent it, when Marcus wasn't here. Councillors have ways of making their displeasure felt.

I was anxious not to make a powerful enemy, so gave him my warmest smile as I bowed to him. The deepest I could manage – I could not have improved upon it for the Emperor himself. 'Your servant, councillor.' I straightened up. 'And yours too, Excellence.'

Hastily, I did the bow again, lest Marcus should suppose I was now insulting him. These political civilities are an eel-trap of complexity. To say nothing of wasting precious time. So, to avoid entangling myself in them any further, I decided that my best course was to be businesslike. 'I trust my appearance has not interrupted you in important private business. I answered your summons as fast as possible, but I fear I must be swift. My wife is in childbirth . . .'

Marcus waved the words aside, expansively. 'Not at all. I am glad to have you here. We were discussing the very matter on which I sent for you. Letigines, bring the citizen a stool. Take his cloak. And have them send another plate and goblet. Now!'

The final word was sharp enough to startle everyone. Freckles turned scarlet and hurried to obey. I dared not demur again about the cloak and he scuttled off with it, clearly still terrified of punishment.

I attempted to put in a supportive word for him. 'It is only chance that made it possible for me to come at all. I came home early and found your courier there. I fear I have delayed his getting back to you.' Letigines, propelled by fear, was back again by now, obediently carrying another folding stool, which he set down for me, at the same time flashing me a grateful glance.

I wanted to decline the seat, but Marcus interposed. 'Citizen, your chair,' he said, and then sat down himself. Thaddeus did the same. So there really was no option but for me to sit down too. In my dusty work tunic with my knees bare like a slave's, I felt that I was guilty of a dreadful lapse. I mumbled my apologies again.

'I was in haste to get here and am needed elsewhere now. So, please, very little wine,' I added, as a blond-haired page appeared with a fresh jug and goblet on a tray. 'And, I regret, I must forgo the dates. Delicious, but today I really cannot stay for long.'

Marcus said nothing, simply watched as the pageboy filled my glass (to overflowing, naturally). I tried again. 'You have some problem with a missing *fibula,* I understand?'

His Excellence frowned and shook a warning head. 'Slaves, you may leave us. We have private matters to discuss. Be about your business, Niveus. Letigines, you will remain outside the door. I shall want to speak to you again.'

I was both rebuked, and very much surprised. It was not like Marcus to be careful what he said before the slaves. Generally, he behaves as if they have no eyes or ears. (I've heard my father very often warn him about that.) Today he seemed to have taken that advice to heart, waiting until all the staff had left before he spoke again.

He saw my expression of incredulity. 'I can't be sure of their discretion,' he explained. 'You know my doubts about Letigines. And that page, Niveus, is relatively new, and so nervous that he might be pressured into saying anything. I made a mistake in buying him, I think.'

Thaddeus raised an eyebrow. 'I might take him from you. He seems nicely trained. Might have the makings of a messenger, one day. Expensive?'

'Not at all. He was a bargain, at the time, since his former owner had all his assets confiscated by the state. Niveus was his sole surviving slave, in fact – the others were all killed defending him.'

'And he was not?' Thaddeus withdrew as if he had been stung. 'Then I can see why you are doubtful about his loyalty. And why you called him "Snow". He melts away. I thought it was a reference to his hair.'

I laughed politely at this little pleasantry, but Thaddeus did not smile. 'So, forget my interest in him, Excellence. There was something that you wished to tell us, privately?'

'Something I'd like Junio to see. A cloak-clasp has gone missing, as you know.' Marcus ran a distracted hand through his now-greying curls. 'Solid silver, of the highest grade, set with gold and precious stones – quite a valuable thing. I gave it to Julia as a wedding gift, so it has some sentimental value too. In fact, that is what caused the problem, I'm afraid. She broke the clasp off it and sent it for repair – without my knowledge – but what was returned was a worthless replica. As you can no doubt see yourself.'

As he spoke, he reached for a drawstring leather bag which had been on a little table at his side. He loosened the tie-strip, shook out the item it contained and handed it to me.

I gasped. I had expected some crude copy, but this was a handsome thing: a cloak-clasp in the Celtic manner, fashioned of two dragons, intertwined, their heads together to form the centrepiece. The intricate scales which ran from neck to tail were picked out with graduated insets of glittering blue, while the eyes appeared to be glowing rubies. The rim around it was inlaid with what look liked rings of gold.

Only when I held it closer could I see that there were imperfections here and there, where the gilt and silvering was lifting off, and that – when one considered it – the weight was slightly wrong. What at first sight appeared to be bright jewels were little chips of glass – fragments of a broken vase, perhaps. But for all that, it was a pretty thing.

I was still staring at it, dumbfounded, when Marcus spoke again. 'I was saying to Thaddeus that the fault was mine, perhaps. If I gave Julia less allowance, she would not have had money to pay for mending it.'

'Excellence, you cannot blame yourself. Like my own wife, Cornelia, yours brought a substantial dowry when she wed, so you could do no other than be generous.' Thaddeus was obsequious but he contrived to smirk. 'You and I may have the use and profit while they remain our wives – but arguably the money is still theirs, in law.'

Marcus brushed this off with an impatient hand. 'Either way, a valued piece of jewellery is missing now. The sapphires alone were worth a pretty sum; I had them imported specially from Rome. Since I can't believe that Vitellius would try to cheat my wife, I am inclined to think that courier had a hand in it – but he swears there's merely been some terrible mistake.' He looked at me. 'That's why I wanted your opinion, citizen.'

I handed back the object in my hand. 'I think that's possible,' I ventured, carefully. 'This is, in its way, a splendid thing itself. It must have taken hours of skilful work to make – not something rushed out in a day or two. There would scarcely be time, while yours was in the shop. Did Vitellius make the original himself?'

Marcus was impatient. 'So I understand – though following some pattern that he'd obtained from Rome, he told me at the time.'

'So could he have made some sort of mould?' I said. 'I believe that's viable – though I don't really understand how silverwork is done.'

'If you are implying that he made other versions, for differing customers, I suppose that's possible, though he swore to me that Julia's would be unique. Swore a formal contract to that effect, in fact, so I would have a case against him if it were proved otherwise.'

I shook my head. 'He may have been telling you the truth. I think the answer might be a simpler one. This may be the pattern that he was working from.'

Thaddeus snorted. 'That's unlikely, surely? And why would he have kept it, if that were the case? It's not made of precious metals, or real gems.'

I bowed in his direction. 'Forgive me, councillor. As a craftsman, I know the value of a pattern-piece like this. Working without one is far more difficult.' I was thinking of that wretched pavement, as I spoke. 'Besides,' I added, 'Coloured glass like this is hard to make – and costly in itself – though possibly a broken vase has been reused. The workmanship is good, and the design is excellent. He must have paid quite handsomely for this – even if it's only made of base materials.'

Marcus paused in the act of putting it away in its leather bag, to look doubtfully at it and then at me. 'You think so?'

'I do. Such a pattern would be most desirable to other people making jewellery. Vitellius would not destroy it, I am sure. I suspect he generally keeps it under lock and key – perhaps in a strongbox somewhere, to keep his word to you – but got it out to model the repair.'

'In which case this may be a simple error, after all – especially if he was working late to get it done?' Marcus sounded hopeful, suddenly. 'It would be easy to mistake by candlelight. This does look impressive, at first glance.'

I saw a chance to speak up for Letigines. 'Certainly, if I had been a slave – with little experience of fine jewels – I would have been deceived. It's even possible Vitellius's servant did not know, if he's not entirely in his master's confidence. Which seems to be the case. Perhaps, Excellence, if you call at the premises, yourself . . .'

Thaddeus could not resist an opportunity to sneer. 'Strangely, citizen, we might have thought of that without your help. But, alas, it is not possible. As I was just explaining to His Excellence before you burst into the room so unexpectedly.'

I frowned. 'Tomorrow's not ill-starred. The shops will not be shut. There are no more holy-days or festivals this moon, and there's only a couple of half-*nefas* days to come.'

'Then why,' Thaddeus demanded, in a triumphant tone, 'did I find that workshop shut and bolted when I called there today?' He sat back, glowering.

I was still trying to make sense of this. 'But I understood from Letigines that a slave was left in charge. He was gone as well?'

A faint inclination of the head was all the answer I received.

It was Marcus who answered. 'No one there at all, apparently. Just a crude notice chalked up on the door saying that the premises was closed.'

'Until further notice,' Thaddeus said. 'And this is not merely a report. My litter happened to be passing close nearby, so I called there myself.'

'But found that it was shut?'

'Indeed.' He permitted his thin lips to curl into a smile. 'And if that's the way Vitellius treats his wealthy clients, it's the last time that he'll have my custom, I can promise you. I know he has been having money worries recently – difficulty meeting the new increase in tax – but this oversight is unforgivable. I had made it clear that I would come today to pick up a pair of silver toe-rings for Cornelia. She particularly wanted them, as we were coming here – she'd lost one, and we'd asked him to make a replica. He promised that he would – but obviously he found better things to do.'

I raised an eyebrow. 'Like going to Corinium, to pick up supplies?'

Thaddeus glanced at me in some surprise, then waved his thin, ringed hand dismissively. 'I don't know where you heard that, but it appears it's true. He was seen leaving by the silversmith's next door – so they told me when I stopped to question them.'

I nodded. Of course, the neighbours would be silversmiths as well. As with many other trades, all the silver workshops are together in one street, so prospective customers know where to go and can compare the price and quality. 'And they were not surprised to see him go?'

'Not at all. Apparently, he does it several times a year. He goes by arrangement to meet some contact there who brings him gems and copies of the latest styles from Rome – presumably that pattern-piece was one of them. And he mentioned to the neighbours only on the Nones that he proposed to go again.'

I was still frowning. 'So what happened to the slave? I understood that he'd been left in charge.'

Marcus was nibbling at a date and sipping wine. 'Evidently not. Gone with his master, wouldn't you have thought? I would not care to travel to Corinium alone, without an attendant – especially if I were likely to bring back precious goods.'

'But Letigines told me . . .' I began, then trailed off.

Thaddeus pounced at once. 'If your freckled friend says otherwise, I fear it was a lie – one of several, if I am any judge, though doubtless the truth can be beaten out of him.'

'And there is no doubt of what the neighbours saw?'

'None at all. Vitellius said that he would go and they saw him doing it. He was right outside the shop, filling the panniers on a donkey in the rain – just as the noonday trumpet sounded from the basilica. Which means they could even be certain of the time. He can't have been gone for very long when I arrived – which heightens the offence.'

'So about what hour would you estimate this was?' I demanded. I did not have time for social games today.

Thaddeus clearly did not care for this direct approach. His reply was snappish. 'I don't know, exactly. I was in a double litter with my wife. We had been visiting another councillor last night and were on our way here to see His Excellence. I suppose it was perhaps an hour or two past noon. Hard to judge with the sky so overcast.'

'Today?' I persisted.

'Well, of course today.' The councillor was brisk. 'What do you suppose that I've been telling you?'

I sighed. 'Then I fear,' I said, 'that alters everything. I begin to think that Vitellius has gone for good. Along with the jewellery belonging to your wives.'

'Dear Jupiter!' Marcus sounded shocked. 'I thought you were convinced it was a mere mistake! What makes you change your mind?'

'The fact that the slave has disappeared, and when! Letigines goes this morning and is sent away again. But he tells the slave about the forgery and the next we hear, he's gone. That looks suspicious, Excellence, I think you will agree.'

Thaddeus shook his carefully powdered head again. 'You are leaping to conclusions, citizen.' Whatever I said, he seemed determined to urge the opposite. 'As far as the missing fibula's concerned, I'm still inclined to think that freckled courier had a hand in it. We only have his word that the original was not actually returned. He could quite easily have stolen it, and hidden it somewhere along the route.'

Marcus ignored the unlikeliness of this. 'So how would he get the pattern-piece, instead – if that is what it is?'

Thaddeus gave a shrug. 'In collusion with that missing slave perhaps?'

'And the disappearance of the jeweller?' I said. 'You don't think that might be significant?'

'I was irritated, certainly, to find that he'd let me down.' He seemed to have turned quite pink with indignation, now. 'But there's no reason to suppose that he won't be coming back. We know where he is gone. There is no mystery.'

'Except,' I said, 'why Vitellius would deliberately choose

to set off quite so late – when it had been raining very hard for hours, and the roads would be especially slow and difficult. Not to mention why his slave should tell Letigines this morning, shortly after dawn, that his master had gone to Corinium yesterday.'

FIVE

'Yesterday?' Thaddeus was disdainful. 'Where did you hear that? From that freckled courier, no doubt? Then that simply proves what I've been saying all along. That boy can't be trusted. That must be a lie. The neighbours were very clear about what they had seen.'

'I suppose it's possible that the page was misinformed.' Marcus, at least, was softening towards Letigines. 'If Vitellius's servant told him otherwise . . .'

Thaddeus gave a scornful snort. 'We only have your courier's word for it that there was a slave at all.'

'Vitellius always had assistance,' Marcus said. 'He used to have a skilled apprentice, but I hear he died – fell into the fire or something similar – and I supposed he'd taken someone new. He would need a helper, wouldn't he?'

'Vitellius would hardly have bought another slave, if he could have a youngster in the shop who would pay him an apprentice fee for doing the same work,' Thaddeus declared. 'Especially if he was struggling to pay the taxman, as I heard recently. And there would be no lack of applicants – any aspiring freeman, who could raise the cash, would wish such a future for his son. But the accident to the former slave was not very long ago – there's scarcely been time for people to apply. I think the whole idea is an invention, first to last.'

Marcus said what I dared not voice myself. 'If there was no slave, Thaddeus, Letigines could hardly have been in league with him. To say nothing of how he could have got the piece that he brought home, unless it was from Vitellius himself.'

I was emboldened now. 'But if there was a slave – as I believe – no doubt the neighbours could corroborate the fact. They could hardly have missed him, if they work next door.'

Thaddeus looked thunderous, but made no reply.

Marcus, though, was energized. 'And if they agree there was a slave, I think Junio is correct, and this disappearance is a suspicious one – especially given the discrepancy about when it occurred. I suppose it is just conceivable that Vitellius somehow changed his mind – forgot some item and came back for it, perhaps, and the silversmiths saw him leave the second time . . .' It sounded feeble, even to himself, and he abandoned it. 'Though that would not explain why the slave has gone as well.' He looked at me expectantly.

'I could make a guess,' I said.

'Gone to warn his master that the attempt to pass off the imitation clasp had failed?' Marcus was delighted at his own cleverness. 'If Vitellius really has current money troubles, as Thaddeus declares, he may have hoped to swap the two versions for a while. To use the original as security on an advance, maybe? It would be accepted with alacrity if the sum involved was not too large. Though, frankly, I'm amazed. Vitellius has a reputation for total honesty, and with his prices, I find it hard to understand how he would need a loan.'

'The latest rise in property tax is quite a swingeing one,' Thaddeus said, with feeling. 'No doubt the Emperor needs to pay for recent wars.'

'And, with due respect, you're not a tradesman, Excellence.' I found myself agreeing with Thaddeus, for once. 'There is a common problem, I'm afraid. It has almost happened in my workshop, once or twice. You make a costly object, from materials which you have to buy yourself, but when you pass it to your customer it may be some considerable time before you're paid. Especially, forgive me, if the customer is rich, in which case money is not always a priority.'

That was daring. Neither of these men had ever had to earn a quadrans in his life. And Thaddeus himself was famous for not settling bills on time. It was rumoured he hadn't finished paying for the famous fountain yet.

He looked outraged, and I was expecting a rebuke. But Marcus went on, as though I was simply supporting what he'd said. 'You're quite right, citizen, again. And it would make sense of what I said before. Vitellius makes a temporary swap. When his debtors pay him, in a day or so, he can "discover" the supposed "mistake", and change the items back – without damage to his reputation for financial probity. I can see that rumours of trouble could only make things worse – if he fails to pay one person or doesn't meet his tax, all his creditors would come knocking on his door, fearing that he might default on them as well.'

Thaddeus looked thoughtful. 'I did hear a story, a moon or two ago, that he'd been buying gold and silver from the Celts out to the west – he has some sort of family connection through his late wife, I think, though he was born within the walls, so he's a citizen himself. I don't know how true it is, of course. I only heard it in the barber's shop, when they were scraping off my beard.'

I gasped. This was something that I certainly had never heard before. If Vitellius was flirting with the Silurians he was juggling with fire. The tribes know where the seams of metals are – have done for generations and do fine work with it – but if they were selling to Vitellius, it must be clandestine. The Romans have taken over the existing local mines, and declared a monopoly on all precious ores. And, though expensive licences can sometimes be obtained, it was certain that the Silurians had not been granted one – for fear they'd use the proceeds to help the rebels in the woods.

'If this is true, Vitellius was taking dreadful risks,' I said. 'The courts would exact a swingeing fine if he was caught, and the gods alone know what the tribes would do to him if he somehow failed to pay.'

Marcus looked doubtful. 'I find it hard to credit, anyway. He has always been a man of probity. But I suppose – with property taxes due to rise again, as Thaddeus pointed out – he might have seized a bargain, if it was offered him.' He glanced at me. 'You look troubled, Junio?'

In fact, it was this talk of Celts which caused my frown. It had occurred to me to wonder, suddenly, whether my own mysterious visitor might be some part of this. I did not mention him, of course – I did not want to jeopardize his safety, or my own – but I would be sure to ask him when I got home again. As I was keen to do. I was anxious to get this meeting over and return to Cilla as soon as possible. 'This disappearance worries me,' I said.

'Dear Mars, all this is supposition, nothing more!' Thaddeus stood up, suddenly – which showed how roused he was. (It was socially improper, of course, since Marcus had not risen.) The old man turned crimson with embarrassment and sank back like a punctured water-bag. 'You really think he's gone? Taking the toe-rings with him? And won't be coming back?'

'We have to contemplate that possibility.' I almost felt sorry for the councillor. 'You say you found the workshop shut this afternoon. There was a slave in charge this morning, earlier – wherever Vitellius himself was at the time. So, if there has been a closure, it was a very sudden one. It may be permanent. The question is: how much he has taken from the shop? I imagine his neighbours could tell us something about that.'

Marcus said, grimly, 'Let me follow this. If Vitellius has fled, he may have taken the remainder of the stock – and everything that he had been given for repair? And, obviously, at dawn he had not really left the town at all. The slave was simply lying, to give him time to flee.' He cocked a brow at me. 'Something of that kind? That is what you are thinking, Junio?'

'There was certainly something being stuffed into those saddlebags, if the neighbours are to be believed. The question is, has he taken everything?'

Thaddeus was stung into defensiveness. 'If he'd taken all his chests and furniture, I think the neighbours might have mentioned that. Which they did not, of course. They simply said that Vitellius had gone, as he told them that he would, and they'd seen him loading up the panniers, today. At the time it all seemed unremarkable. Except of course, that he had not let me know!'

Marcus was looking at me, ashen-faced. 'But you do not believe that, do you, Junio? You think he's run away? And probably for good?'

'Well, perhaps tomorrow this could be resolved. Vitellius has a flat above the workshop, doesn't he?' (I'd almost said 'used to have', but corrected that.) 'If he's run away, that will be empty, too. In the morning, it might be possible to look. Until then it is impossible to judge.'

'Well, we'll go to Glevum in the morning and find out,' Marcus said, firmly. 'And perhaps we could send to Corinium as well, and discover where he generally stays – presuming that he does sometimes stay there overnight. We might even find him there.'

'Do we know whether the ass was his property or not?' I asked. 'If he merely hired it, that would help a bit – at least we'd know when he was due to bring it back, and whether the hire was scheduled for today or yesterday.'

Marcus seized on this with some alacrity. 'I don't remember hearing that he owned an animal, and he would not need one in a general way. We'll send to all the hiring-stables and enquire. So perhaps we'll make some progress – though, as you say, we can't know anything for certain yet.'

'Except that Letigines had no part in it,' I said.

Marcus looked at me sharply. 'What makes you sure of that?'

'How could he profit, Excellence? His belongings have been searched – in his absence, as I understand, so he had no time to hide anything – and there was nothing found. And I'm quite sure that you searched him when he came home again. He has no money, so could not have paid to have a copy made, or to buy the pattern, come to that – and it would have been reported to Julia if he had. Besides, who would buy anything of real value from a slave, without enquiring how he came by it? All he stood to gain was a flogging,' I replied.

Thaddeus stubbornly refused to be convinced. 'Unless Vitellius bribed him to play his part in it, as he could easily have done. The boy claims that he looked into the bag, and did not recognize it was a forgery. Yet anyone must realize that, by comparison, it's crude.' That was a childish dagger-thrust at me, but I did not respond, and after a moment he began again. 'Suppose the boy took money and has hidden it somewhere? He knows the road to Glevum; he rides it all the time. He must know a dozen places it would be secure – always supposing he did not lodge it with a friend.' He looked meaningfully at me.

It was outrageous, but I did not rise to it. I did, however, permit myself a jibe. 'All this is merest supposition, as you say yourself. I am quite sure the boy is innocent. After all, he has always been quite honest up to now – enough to be entrusted with a valuable clasp! There is absolutely nothing to suggest that he was bribed,' I appealed to Marcus.

'And no proof that he was not,' he replied, to my dismay. 'But I concede you have a point – and Julia pleads for him. I'll have his meals restored, and order that the flogging be revoked – for now, in any case. But meantime I will keep him under lock and key. Until something is proven, either way.'

It wasn't much, but it was all the concession I was going to gain. 'Excellence, you are renowned for being just.' I bowed my head, relieved to have done something, at least, to help the boy. 'So, if there is no further assistance I can give, with your permission I will hurry home. My wife . . .' I was getting up to leave.

'Indeed!' Marcus acknowledged this with a condescending smile. 'We have kept you far too long – and it will soon be dusk. Besides, it is almost time for us to dine. I'll lend you a slave to light you down the lane. Finish up your wine, and I will have them fetch your cloak.' 'He flicked his fingers, and the steward hurried in – to be sent away again to fetch my cape, and help me into it.

Marcus watched with an indulgent air. 'So, we will see you tomorrow, at first light, citizen. Thaddeus has a personal litter, so I will bring the gig and driver and you can ride with me.'

I looked at him, appalled. 'Tomorrow, Excellence? You're hoping I will come?'

He held his hand out so that I could kiss the signet ring. 'Of course. We could not do without you, citizen. You are your father's worthy son.' He bent forward, dropped his voice and grasped my fingers, suddenly. 'You have not heard from him, I suppose?'

'No word since the day he fled to exile,' I replied. It was the truth – though the day in question was not the one His Excellence supposed.

Thaddeus had been growing increasingly incensed, as though hunting for a thief was beneath his dignity. But since

Marcus had involved him, he could not refuse any more than I could. He turned his bitterness on me. 'Wise of your father to stay away. He is still a wanted man.'

'Wise not to try to contact you.' Marcus chose to ignore the latter half of this. 'In the current climate, even messages are traced. Though beyond the northern wall, he should be safe. I hope so, for his sake. And for yours, of course.'

I did not answer, merely bowed across the ring – not least because I had my own suspicions about where my father was.

Marcus pressed my fingers and released my hand. 'Go well, citizen, and I hope the child and mother both are safe – and, naturally, that it is another son. I know too well the problems of too many girls.'

I thanked him and bowed myself away – taking care to give due deference to Thaddeus as well. I only wished my promised escort could have been Letigines: I harboured deep suspicions about that jeweller's slave, and had been hoping that the boy might give me a private description of the man. But that was clearly now impossible.

So when the pageboy Niveus met me at the gate, with both Arlina and the lighted torch, I assured him I could manage on my own. To prove it, I swung up on the mule and held the flame aloft. 'Tell His Excellence that I excused you, Niveus,' I said. 'It is raining and the torch won't last for long. You would have to walk back in the dark.'

He was easily persuaded, with the gatekeeper to witness what I'd said, and a moment later I was lurching down the lane. It was an awkward struggle to keep the torch alight – especially in the mounting wind and wet. In the end I just abandoned it and let Arlina take me – slow but sure – to the enclosure gate. By the time we got there I was drenched through to the skin.

I was pleased to see Brianus watching for me at the round-house door. When he saw me, he came hurrying out, carrying a taper which he shielded from the storm. 'Master! I am glad to see you. You have been gone so long. I hope there was no trouble. Were you able to assist?'

I slid down from Arlina and handed him the reins. 'Perhaps

a little, though it's not over yet. It seems that Gaius Vitellius and his slave have disappeared. Marcus has demanded that I go to town with him, tomorrow, and help to look for them – but if Cilla needs me here . . . How is she? I have been concerned.'

Brianus's face was smiling in the flickering light. 'Resting, master. Listen, can you hear?' Behind him, as he reached out to take the mule, I heard a welcome sound – a thin, high, unmistakeable newborn baby's cry.

'The child,' I said. 'Already born?'

'A boy. And healthy, too.'

I heaved a heartfelt sigh. 'And Cilla?'

'She will pull through, with rest – though she has lost a lot of blood. Or so the wisewoman reports. I am to tell you that you may go in and see her briefly – and your son – but you must sleep elsewhere, tonight. Though I can only offer you Tenuis's sleeping space, I fear.'

'But what of the other little ones? Are they not in the slave room there with you? Better that I sleep in that half-completed hut. Or in the dyehouse. At least it would be dry.'

'No need, master, thanks to Anlyan's help. He went and sent the wisewoman to us, then took the children gathering kindling in the woods. But obviously he could not keep them there for long. They were getting fractious – hungry, tired and wet – so he brought them home again, gave them a little bread and cheese, and kept them occupied by helping him complete the sleeping hut.'

He held the taper so that I could see.

'A splendid job.' Better than I could have done myself, I thought. 'As a Celt, I suppose, he's done it many times.'

'I thought that you'd be pleased. By the time that it was finished the birth was very close, so we put the children in there on some reeds. He's keeping watch on them. Or rather, when I looked, he was fast asleep himself.'

'And well deserved,' I murmured.

So Brianus took Arlina to her field, while I crept into the roundhouse to see my newest son, and my exhausted wife. Very briefly, because I was soon chased out by the wisewoman again. 'Come back in the morning, when she has some rest.

And do not touch that pot. I'm brewing up a strengthening medicine for her.'

I grabbed an apple. That would have to do. I was beginning to wish that I'd had a sugared date. Or maybe two. But all was well, I thought. I glanced into the new hut as I passed and glimpsed the sleeping forms.

'Anlyan must have been sent to us by the gods, I think,' I said to Brianus, as we settled down ourselves and snuffed the taper out.

If only I had known.

SIX

I woke, in broad daylight, to find Brianus shaking me. 'Master! I hate to disturb you. But a page is at the gate. Marcus will be here for you within an hour – before the sun is over the tall oak, he says.'

I groaned unwillingly, and scrambled to my feet. 'You'd better fetch my linen tunic then, to put on top of this, and then help me wash and put my toga on. If I'm to ride with Marcus and Thaddeus today, I'd better look my rank. Though Jove knows it will be difficult, walking around town in that formal dress all day.' I was splashing cold water on my face and neck, and reached out blindly for the drying-rag.

Brianus deftly handed it to me. 'I have your Roman clothing ready, master,' he replied. 'I realized that you would be needing it. And I've put some chicken's eggs into a pan for you. I'm afraid there is no bread or oatcake for you to break your fast – obviously there was no baking done last night. I'll see there's some tonight – even if I have to mix the dough myself.'

'I'm sure the mistress can instruct you from her bed,' I said. Brianus does not usually cook – Cilla prefers to do that task herself – and his few attempts have not generally been a great success. 'Perhaps Anlyan can help you, if he's still here by then. He seems a man of talents. Where is he, anyway? I'd like to talk to him.' Quite apart from asking why he wanted me, I was thinking of Vitellius and the rumoured purchase of precious metals from the Celts.

Brianus shook his head. 'Taken Carus to the forest for mushrooms, I'm afraid. Apparently they saw some yesterday, near where the wisewoman has her little hut, but they didn't pick them then, because their baskets were already full. He thought we might cook them for the children now, since there's no bread left at all. There was one oatcake, but the wisewoman wants to steep that in warm milk and honey for your wife. And we have eaten all the cheese, though I will set more milk to sour.'

'I'll bring some food from town when I come home,' I said, resigned. 'Egg and mushrooms will have to do for now. What a strange breakfast!'

But even that was not to be. Before the mushroom foragers returned, the gig was at the door. I was wrapped into my toga by a hasty Brianus and was on my way to Glevum with His Excellence, and Niveus the page crammed in at our feet, before my egg was half-digested.

On the road we soon passed Thaddeus and his litter-boys. They were trotting townward as quickly as they could, but it was clear that we would be there well ahead of them. It is a jolting journey, especially at speed, and there was little chance to talk, so I was surprised when the driver drew up short before we reached the gates.

'Here we are. The hiring-stables.' Marcus turned to me. 'You go and talk to them. I will see you at Vitellius's workshop later on.'

I was not delighted, with my toga on – making a long walk a longer one – but it had been my suggestion, and I obediently dismounted and went through the wicket gate to the establishment. The stable yard was muddy (not ideal, with trailing hems) but my toga soon had the owner fawning at my feet. He was sorry, but he had not hired Vitellius an ass. But he knew who might have done – the other hiring-stable, at the Eastern gate, was known to provide Vitellius with transport now and then.

I thanked the man, gave him a quadrans from my purse, then walked on into town. Thaddeus's litter overtook me at the entrance arch, but he had the curtains shut and did not even pause. I walked on glumly till I reached the Street of the Gold and Silversmiths.

Not having had occasion to use his services, I was not altogether sure which was Vitellius's shop. Most of the workshops here were rented ones, downstairs spaces in one of the residential blocks – each with a counter opening on to the street, and goods for sale piled up beside the door. (Presumably these each had a living area behind, which might – with luck

– give out on to the court, or the bottom of one of the public staircases.) But I guessed that Vitellius's shop would be at the farther end, where a few of the more prosperous tradesmen owned their own small premises outright.

I began to walk towards the area. Being in my toga and on foot alone, I was accosted instantly by hopeful traders, clutching at my arms, all trying to drag me off to view their wares. 'Best silver, citizen. Special price for you.'

I wondered about asking directions as I shook them off, but I soon saw there was no need. It was quite obvious which workshop I was looking for. There was quite a little gaggle in the road outside, in the middle of which I could make out Marcus, Thaddeus and their slaves. News of their presence had obviously spread and people were beginning to congregate to look.

I had to elbow my way into the group. In the centre, being questioned by His Excellence, stood an ageing man, with a huge nose and straggling grey hair, dressed in a tradesman's tunic, and a younger version – evidently his son. They were gesticulating wildly – and looking terrified. Clearly these were the neighbours that I had heard about.

Marcus looked up and saw me. 'Ah, citizen!' he cried. 'We are glad to see you. We're not making progress here. Have you discovered anything?'

'Only that Vitellius hires an ass, and where he gets it from,' I said. I turned to the older silversmith. 'I believe you people saw it yesterday?'

The man looked round in desperation. 'Citizen, there is nothing further I can say. What are all these people? What have we done wrong?'

'Nothing, townsman,' I said, since no one else replied. Everybody turned to look at me.

I waited for Marcus to resume, but he said nothing. Nor did Thaddeus. Suddenly I seemed to find myself in charge.

'I'd like to hear the story from your lips, that's all,' I murmured. I took the father gently by the arm. 'But not out here, perhaps. Is there somewhere more private we could talk. Your workshop, possibly?' I gestured to what clearly was his door, behind the piles of silverware for sale. From somewhere inside, a rhythmic thumping clang was issuing. 'If you could ask them to stop hammering meanwhile?'

The old man nodded and led the way inside. We found ourselves within an outer showroom area, where the open counter gave out on to the street, and yet more piles of goods were on display. Beyond, behind a half partition, was the workshop proper, where the noise was coming from.

There was a huge chimney-niche built into the back wall, and a skinny youth, who might have been a slave, was squeezing a pig's bladder between two bits of wood as a sort of bellows to further fan the fire, which was already uncomfortably hot. Something was bubbling in a cauldron over it, while – nearer to us – an ageing woman and two small boys were squatting on the floor, each busy hammering a pattern on a pot.

'Leave us!' said the owner, and without a word they all four dropped their tasks and disappeared, scrambling up a ladder to what was clearly a sleeping-room above. Even then, it was hot and overcrowded in the shop, though the younger man quickly produced a pair of folding stools and set them for Marcus and Thaddeus right behind the counter, where there was a least a draught. Their attendant pages took up station behind them, at the doorway to the street.

I was left to stand against the half-height inner wall, on which all manner of silver vessels were displayed, and I was soon perspiring in the roaring heat. But the owners seemed oblivious to the temperature, and went through to the workshop to give us space and talk to us from there, still visible across the barrier of their glittering display.

The younger of the silversmiths glared angrily at me. 'I don't know what you want of us. We've told you what we saw. At noontide yesterday, I heard the trumpet blow, and looked out in the street. And I saw Vitellius filling up his panniers. That's all there is to say. I knew that he was going, so I was not surprised – though it was rather late to leave. I didn't go out to speak to him. It was raining at the time.'

And then, of course, it struck me, as it should have done before. 'Raining? But of course it was! So Vitellius presumably was dressed for it? In a cloak and hood, perhaps?'

'Well, naturally! What else would one expect?'

'Then, if he had his hood up, you did not see his face?'

The man looked startled. 'Well, since you mention it, I suppose that's true. But I'm sure it was Vitellius. It was certainly his cloak. It is a russet birrus britannicus, which his late wife wove for him. He was very fond of it, so much so that he's twice had it patched. I'd know it anywhere.'

'But was it Vitellius who was wearing it? Or did you simply see what you expected to? As anybody would?'

Thaddeus was staring at me, like a startled duck. 'You mean it might not really have been him after all? That's what you're suggesting? But that's preposterous. Who else could it have been?'

'Almost anybody!' Marcus sounded grim.

'Anyone who had access to the cloak,' I said. 'That missing slave, for one. I have been rather suspicious of that fellow from the start.' I turned to the silversmiths. 'How long has he been working with Vitellius, do you know?'

The two men exchanged a helpless glance. At last the younger spoke. 'I am not exactly certain. A half a moon or so. Since that young apprentice died so tragically.'

I looked towards his father. But the old man only shrugged. 'I'm sorry, citizen. I can't tell you more than that. Vitellius told me that he'd acquired a slave, but I've only actually seen the fellow now and then, putting something on the midden heap. And then only from a distance. Certainly, I never spoke to him.'

'But you could describe him, somewhat, all the same? As a silversmith you'll have an eye for detail, I'm sure.'

If that was flattery it appeared to work. The old man fairly preened. 'Well, I suppose he was of more than average height. Lean and scrawny, with thin straggling brown hair and somewhat bulging eyes.' He stopped, considering. 'Rather sullen, from what I could detect. Not a handsome fellow, even for a slave – though I might have thought differently if I'd ever seen him smile.'

For someone who could not describe the man, this was remarkable. Though all I said was, 'But Gaius Vitellius was content with him? It seems he trusted him enough to leave him with the shop?'

'I was surprised to hear that,' the younger man put in. He had lost his grumpy manner, suddenly – perhaps because he was anxious to atone for having leapt to unwarranted conclusions earlier. 'As Father says, I'd only seen him throwing rubbish out. I did not realize he'd progressed sufficiently to deal with customers. Vitellius was complaining, not many days ago, that he had a lot to learn.'

I was becoming increasingly alarmed. 'Yet he was left in charge?'

I looked at my two companions – both patricians, even more out of place in this cramped, overheated workshop than I was myself. Marcus was discreetly dabbing at his brow, and Thaddeus was sweating in a most un-Roman way – and from his anxious manner, possibly not entirely from the heat. (Wealthy Romans are a superstitious crowd and – much as they love skilful metalwork – are often slightly wary of those who fashion it, believing there is something almost supernatural in the art.) I decided that the time for talk was done.

'Excellence and councillor,' I said, 'I fear we're wasting time, and keeping these good workmen from their trade. The more I hear about this slave, the more concerned I am. If there is a mystery, I think he holds the key.'

Marcus looked doubtful. 'I was beginning to think the opposite. It appears that what he told my courier might be true. His master had already genuinely left – and it may be that he shut the shop to set off after him.'

'Meanwhile, also, borrowing his cloak?' I said, and instantly wished that I had not.

It was a daring challenge, which I might regret, but all that Marcus muttered was, 'He might have had permission . . .' He knew that was unlikely, and he corrected it. 'Or thought it so important to find Vitellius, and tell him that Julia's fibula had been missed, that he took it anyway to shield himself from rain?'

The silversmiths were goggling at this: one could only imagine how Marcus would react, if one of his servants dared to wear his clothes. I turned to them again. 'There's one way to be certain, isn't there? I assume that Vitellius has rooms upstairs, like you. Is there any way of reaching them, other than through the workshop? I'd like to take a look into his shop, but I understand the front door has been locked?'

'That slave might have been stealing things, you think?' The younger man looked knowingly at me. I did not answer, and after a moment he went on. 'Well there is a tiny courtyard at the back, and our wall abuts it. If you stood on that, you might just reach the window opening, I suppose. Though it would be a stretch.'

'Or run a ladder up there from his yard,' his father said. 'You could borrow that one!' He jerked his head towards the set of rungs still propped against the entrance to the family's sleeping-room. 'My slave will help you!' He called up through the open aperture. 'Macilentus, come down here at once. Go and tie the dog up, so it does not bite our guest, then come back here and take the ladder out. Meanwhile, the rest of you come down as well, before we move the steps, or you'll get trapped upstairs. You have planishing to finish, anyway. This way, citizen.' He gestured me through to join him in the workshop as he spoke.

There was a clattering from upstairs and the skinny slave climbed down. He lifted a heavy wooden latch, opened a door in the wall beside the chimney-niche, and disappeared outside, shutting it after him. I heard snarls and barking, and the slave came back, looking flushed and dishevelled but otherwise intact.

By this time the two boys had skittered down the ladder, too. It was becoming very crowded in the overheated room. 'Hurry down, wife, we are waiting for the steps!' The old man stepped forward, pushed the outer door ajar, and ushered me outside into an evil-smelling sort of yard beyond.

It was too narrow to be called a court. Simply a space surrounded by high walls on all three sides, and made even narrower by a series of stone bins: storage compartments set into the wall, along most of the boundary with the next-door property – waist-high boxes that sloped up towards the back, with heavy wooden lids. One of these was propped open with a wedge, and evidently held domestic goods: amphorae, presumably of oil and wine and flour, piles of turnips, fuel, and jumbled cooking pans. The other two were closed and sealed, their covers bolted down. Beyond them a large dog – even more ugly than my picture on the floor – was tethered to a post, growling in a low but threatening way. It strained towards me, baring all its teeth.

'Don't worry about Rex Canis, citizen,' the old man said. 'He can't reach you from there. That's why we generally have him running loose. Something of the kind is a necessity. There is a small fortune locked into those bins, and we cannot keep a vigil all the time. The place is as secure as we can make it, naturally.' He gestured to the high walls around, in which, I noticed there was no rear gate at all. 'A good guard dog is the only real defence. He'll attack any stranger. But he cannot harm you now. Where would you like my slave to put the steps? I will go and get him. Would you like to choose a spot?' He gestured vaguely down the yard.

I nodded, and he disappeared inside. Keeping one wary eye on Rex, I edged my way along the storage bins. An area of blackened stone and ash beyond gave evidence of yet another, even bigger, fire.

I was just wondering if this open-air hearth was reserved for summer days, and screwing up my nose against the stench of a midden-pile from the alleyway behind, when Macilentus joined me, carrying the ladder in his scrawny arms. (His very name means 'skinny' and it was well deserved.) Mercifully his presence seemed to calm the dog, who retreated snarling, and curled up by the wall.

The slave-boy flashed a smile, showing blackened broken teeth. 'Forgive me, citizen. I had to help the mistress down before I came.' He gestured to the wall. 'Where would you like the ladder?'

I stared at him, aghast. I had no intention of climbing up myself – in a toga it would have been impossible. Then, of course, I realized he was not suggesting that. I tried to sound efficient. 'Wherever you can get it closest to the wall – up at this end, perhaps. Then if you jump down, I'll pass it through to you, and you can see if it will reach to Vitellius's window-space. He does not seem to have left the shutter closed.'

Macilentus might be skinny, but he was lithe and strong.

He swarmed up the ladder like a legionary storming a defence. At the top he grasped the wall, and vaulted to the ground on the other side, landing as softly as a butterfly.

As soon as he had disappeared the dog began his snarling again, making me anxious as I clumsily tried to raise the ladder from my end. The slave took it from me and wrested it across as though juggling with ten-foot poles with projecting footholds was an easy, daily task. Which perhaps it was, for him.

In a moment he had it set up against Vitellius's inner wall. It was evident at once that it was not going to reach – it was designed to be vertical, up into a hatch, and here it had to slope – but a tall man, like Macilentus, might manage to look in, if he could balance on the topmost rung.

I should not have doubted. As soon as he had wedged the base against a stone, he was up the ladder like an acrobat and standing on tiptoe in a way which made me wince. Even then he had to grasp the window-space and hoist himself a little to get a proper view. It was so precarious that I closed my eyes, expecting any moment that there would be a frightful crash, and the slave-boy would be injured in the fall. It would be my liability: he was on loan to me.

So I was heartily relieved to hear his voice again. 'Citizen.' It sounded very close. I opened one eye, but there was no sign of him, then I looked up and saw his head appear above the wall. He was coming back. I prepared to take the ladder, but he shook his head.

'You had better get the master!' He was deathly pale. 'He will have snips that will cut through the lock. I am not quite certain, but – if I did see what I think I saw – someone should go in and have a look. I guess that both those patricians will be magistrates. Take one of them with you. You might need witnesses. Vitellius was a citizen, I think.'

'Was?' I said. But his ashen face had disappeared again. A moment later, I thought I heard him being violently sick.

With growing trepidation I hurried back inside, and reported all of this. Without a word the elder silversmith picked up a pair of snips – so long and heavy they were thicker than my arm – and led the way out to the road. Marcus – who of course had been listening to my tale – made to follow, but Thaddeus held back.

I paused, unwilling to walk in front of him.

'His Excellence should deal with this,' he muttered. 'It obviously requires someone of higher rank than mine. With your permission, citizens, I will leave you now. I have some rather urgent business in the town. I'll get my bearers to carry me to the forum now and take me back to your villa later, Excellence – if that's acceptable – to join my wife and look forward to another evening in your company.' He launched into paeons of effusive praise, but Marcus silenced him by extending an imperious hand for him to kiss the ring. Thaddeus did so with a flourish, and stood back to let us past, only adding as we reached the door, 'But you'll let me know if the toe-rings can be found?'

Impatiently, Marcus said, 'Of course!' Then, raising his eyebrows expressively at me, and accompanied by his pageboy, went out into the street. Then I was able, at last, to do the same.

The previous curious onlookers had by now dispersed, but the presence of a purple striper quickly attracted more as – together – we approached Vitellius's door. The silversmith was already busy with his heavy snips and soon cut through the hasp.

With the lock removed, he worked the bolt and opened the front door. 'There you are, distinguished citizens,' he said. He stood back, deferentially, obviously hoping he would be dismissed.

'You have been more than helpful,' I declared. 'But now I'm sure that you have work to do.'

The old man looked gratefully at me. 'I would be glad to get back to supervise,' he said. 'My wife is skilled but my two grandsons are not.' He turned to Marcus. He knew where power lay. 'With your permission, Excellence. Naturally I will stay if I'm required. Otherwise, forgive me, I may already be losing customers.'

Marcus could take a hint when it was justified. He pressed a silver coin into the old man's hand.

The silversmith brightened as he slipped it into a purse beneath his sleeve. 'Glad to be of service. I'll leave my slave and ladder, in case they are of use.'

'Tell him to wait in the garden, until we call for him,' I said.

Marcus looked astonished.

'We don't know what we might be dealing with. Give him a lighted candle,' I told the silversmith. 'Pass it across the wall. And if it has not burned halfway before we call him in, tell him to climb back to you, and bring some lusty help. Armed with knives or clubs, if possible.'

The old man murmured that he would, and bowed himself away.

'You think there might be someone hiding in there now?' Marcus had visibly blanched at the idea, but was too much a Roman to admit to fear. 'We shall soon discover. Niveus, you stay out here and guard the door – and if I shout, be ready to fetch aid.' He looked round at the gawping spectators. 'The rest of you, disperse. By my orders, before I call the watch.' Then as the little gaggle moved reluctantly away, he turned to me. 'Junio, lead the way.'

And there was nothing for it but to go into the shop.

SEVEN

t was very dark inside. And very smelly, too. The stench, which I had taken to be from the midden-pile, was overwhelming here. I was reluctant to move, fearful of what I might stumble into.

I took a step forward, encountered something with my foot – mercifully metallic – and, as my eyes got accustomed to the gloom, I realized there were shadowy objects everywhere. The shutters to the street-counter aperture were shut, but faint light seeped down from the hatchway to the upstairs room. With care it was possible to edge my way along the window-wall and take down a portion of the shuttering.

The boards were heavy and I was hampered by my formal Roman clothes, so it took a moment to let the daylight in and stack the shutter up against the wall. But as I did so, I heard Marcus's startled gasp. I whirled around – and saw what he had seen.

Gaius Vitellius had not gone to Corinium. Not all of him, at least. His severed head was sitting on a piece of bloodstained cloth in the middle of the floor. It had attracted flies. I had only seen the man from a distance once or twice, but there was no mistaking that high brow and flattened, broken nose. The bulging eyes were open as though staring in horror at the chaos elsewhere in the room. The swollen flies were swarming over them, as well. I was forced to look away.

I told myself to concentrate on something else. Father always said that, if there was a crime, it was important to take in details of the scene. I tried to do that now.

The building was a mirror of the one next door (probably built by the same man, in fact) but otherwise the two could not have looked more different. Here every shelf and surface appeared to have been stripped, and finely decorated silver bowls and trays lay scattered everywhere. Some of them were dented, or splashed with what I realized must be blood

– though it was dried by now. But there was no sign of the rest of Vitellius – or of anybody else.

'It looks as if whoever is responsible has gone.' I had been holding my breath till now, I realized. Not only from the smell.

Marcus had picked up a heavy tray, which might have served as a weapon or shield. He didn't put it down. 'Best to be certain,' he replied, nodding towards the workshop area.

I ventured round the half-dividing wall. There were more streaks of spilt blood across the floor here, too, apart from a section where the floorboards had been lifted up and not replaced. Beneath it, clearly, there had been a secret cavity where Vitellius kept his box of cash. The box was still in it, open – forced, by the appearance of the splintered sides – but completely empty.

I looked at Marcus, who had followed me, still clutching at the tray. 'That answers several questions, Excellence,' I said. 'Vitellius has been robbed. The thief has clearly gone. And Letigines was obviously told an outright lie. The jeweller is dead, and has been for several days.'

'By the hands of that mysterious servant, do you think?' Marcus was trying to be calm, but he sounded shaken. He did not often witness scenes like this. He put the tray down, and edged around to look at what I'd found.

'I'm almost certain of it,' I replied. I had been crouching to peer into the hole, but there was nothing else in there. I got back to my feet. 'And he has made no effort to conceal the deed. No pretence that it could be an accident – he almost seems to be advertising what he's done.'

'Then we must have him found and punished. As severely as the law permits. Vitellius was a tradesman, but he was a citizen – born within the walls! And murdered by his slave. Who then must have impersonated him!' (This had clearly just occurred to him.) 'That alone is a capital offence.'

'They'll have to catch him first,' I said. 'That might be difficult. We don't know his name, or where he's gone. It won't be to Corinium, wherever it might be. My instinct would be to try the other way – the wildlands to the west. But they'll be hard to search. And I think the hiring-stables can say farewell to their ass.'

'You think he timed this purposely for when Vitellius was due to be away? And was therefore unlikely to be missed for several days?' Marcus seemed pleased with this deduction, though it seemed obvious to me.

I didn't say so. 'It's warm in here, of course,' I murmured, gesturing to the hearth, where a pile of charred remains and a few last embers still gave a feeble glow. Around it lay a scatter of abandoned tools. 'There must have been a roaring fire, much like the one next door, probably as recently as yesterday. But that's not wood or charcoal ash on the top. Looks like a bundle of something pushed into the fire . . .' Suddenly alarmed at what it might contain, I picked up a pair of tongs and poked at it, but it crumbled into blackened fragments instantly. I let out a thankful sigh. 'Not human anyway – looks like a roll of cloth. Burnt to a cinder, so the fire was very hot. And that would hasten things, of course, but – judging by the smell – Vitellius might already have been dead the first time that Letigines was here and was given the false clasp.'

'But that can't be so. The boy would have noticed. You could not mistake a thing like that.' He gestured to the head. 'Though I suppose it could have been put there afterwards. What gives you that idea?'

'The smell, for one thing. And the flies. And the fact that Vitellius was unlikely to have left the slave in charge. He did not trust him much, from what we hear.'

Marcus was frowning. 'With good reason, if you are correct. But it's extremely strange. You would have thought that if this killer took the money from the chest, he would have stolen these as well.' He gestured to the tray and the other goods which were strewn everywhere. 'These are valuable things.'

'I've been thinking about that. He only had one donkey. The rest may simply have been too heavy to carry easily. Which reminds me, we ought to look upstairs. He's moved the ladder, by the look of it – or thrown it on the fire – but I know where there is one . . .' As I spoke I went to the yard door, and after a short struggle with the latch, contrived to open it. 'Macilentus,' I called, relieved to have let in some fresher air. 'Come here, and bring that ladder too.'

Macilentus was standing in a yard much like the one next door. He was still looking dazed and leaning against the alley wall. He held a lighted candle which he was watching fixedly, as though it were not a timer, but a protective charm. When he saw me, he looked relieved, blew out the flame and hurried in – carrying the ladder, which he quickly set in place. It was not secured at the top, of course, but if he held it, I could get up safely – though it was not a prospect which delighted me. And I would have to take my toga off. But it was obvious that it would fall to me to go.

I turned to find him gazing enquiringly at me. 'You see what's happened here?' I gestured to the empty coffer in the cavity, then through the gap to the horror that was lying on the showroom floor beyond. Macilentus stepped forward, took one look around the barrier and staggered back, appalled. For a moment I thought that he was going to retch again.

I tried to give him something else to think about. 'Wedge that door open, and let out the smell a bit.' Then, as he hurried to obey, I added, 'In a moment I am going to look upstairs. But first I want to work out when this happened if I can. It's difficult to judge. Nothing occurs to you, which might be relevant? You did not see any strangers in the last few days? Or hear unusual noises from in here?'

'Unlikely to do that, citizen; there's too much hammering.' He was so shaken that he clearly found it hard to speak, but I waited and at last he blurted out: 'And strangers would not be unusual. People came for miles for Vitellius's wares – though some of his customers were Glevum customers. Like that ancient councillor who came with you today. He's been here once or twice. And your household, Excellence, of course,' he added, with a nervous glance at Marcus.

'Normally Vitellius would come and call on me, if he had something special to propose,' Marcus said, defensively. 'But if I want anything at other times, I send a slave, of course.'

'Of course.' The slave-boy had turned pink with terror but he persevered. 'In fact, forgive me, I've seen one recently. I noticed the distinctive livery. On two occasions, on successive days.'

'We know about those visits – they are what brought us here,' I said, reassuringly. 'But well done for having noticed them. But nothing remarkable, apart from that?'

Macilentus shook a doubtful head. 'Citizen, all that I can tell you is that the only stranger I have seen for weeks was a farm-boy that I encountered in the alleyway, looking to remove the midden-heap to put on to his fields – and even he was put off by the barking of the dogs. Apart from that I've seen nobody unusual at all. Though I would not have been looking all the time.' He hesitated. 'But if you are asking about things which might be significant – I expect you have observed it for yourself . . .'

'Go on,' I said, as he paused uncertainly.

'Well, I have never been inside this shop before – of course – but I know Vitellius specialized in casting pretty things. And making silver wire to twist into designs . . .'

'What sort of things?' I prompted to encourage him. He seemed much less troubled, talking about the trade he was familiar with.

'He used to buy hammered objects from my master at one time, and attach raised patterns on to them. Little cups and dishes and all sorts of things. He often had a whole display of them, outside. And silver eyes for statues – he had a contract with a local sculptor for providing those. But he was chiefly famous for making personal ornaments. Amulets with jewels, and lovely fibulae . . .'

'Like my wife's cloak-clasp,' Marcus interposed. 'What of it, anyway?'

'Only, Excellence, that I see nothing of that kind in here now at all.'

'Just what I was saying, to His Excellence!' I exclaimed. 'Anything easily portable has gone. Cloak-clasps and toe-rings among other things. Of considerable value, I expect?'

'Extremely costly,' Macilentus said. 'He asked high prices, but his goods were exquisite. Beautiful strigils, all inlaid with gold. And all the lovely jewellery . . .'

'And now it's vanished.' Marcus looked around as though the missing items might suddenly appear. His gaze alighted on a storage chest. 'Though there are boxes here. He's brought things out for me to choose from, several times, in one like that. Slave, have a look in it.'

Macilentus went obediently across and tried the lid. It was stiff, but it was unsecured. He flung it open. There was nothing in there but a pair of shallow wooden trays. He handed them to Marcus who looked at them with dismay.

'Dear Jove!' he muttered. 'The last time I saw these, they were full of lovely things. Silver ankle chains and necklets, all beautifully wrought. Rings and brooches set with precious gems. And twisted bracelets, with cunning dragon clasps. Exquisite objects. I wish I'd bought a few.' He gave a heavy sigh. 'But there will be no chance of that again – unless we catch that slave. You think he could fit all that into a pair of panniers?'

'I expect he had a bag or two with him, as well,' I said. 'He must hope to sell it.' I looked at Macilentus. 'Wouldn't you agree? You're looking doubtful.'

'Citizen, forgive me.' He was unwilling to contradict. 'It might be difficult. People don't happily buy fine items from a slave.'

I had said the same thing yesterday myself, but I found that I was arguing. 'Though it's not impossible, at the right time and place? Vetillius's previous apprentice used to man this shop, you said. And we think this man has fled – somewhere far from Glevum, where he would not be known. Wearing that expensive cloak, he'll look respectable.'

Macilentus nodded, rather doubtfully. 'If he was willing to take less than things were worth, someone might snap up a bargain, I suppose. Or he might find a trader in another town, who'd be prepared to buy in bulk.'

'But that would draw attention to him, wouldn't it? Without a licence, trading in silver is against the law.' Marcus was in his magisterial role.

'Not necessarily, Excellence,' replied the slave. 'Not if it's something you already own. We've had customers send slave-boys in to us, offering silverware for us to melt down and reuse. Or just to sell again. Especially if their masters were in need of cash. This man might claim that he was doing something of the kind. There is nothing illegal about that.'

'I've never heard of it.' Marcus was scornful. He had never been short of money in his life.

'It isn't something that we advertise. Clearly the citizens concerned don't want the town to know, for fear of bringing all their creditors to their door at once. But it does happen every now and then.'

'And you buy it?'

'Sometimes, citizen. Depending on the client. And the quality. And on the mix, of course. You can't use pure silver for things in daily use – it discolours and it bends too easily. But if we're making plates, for instance, and it was suitable, we might make an offer. Of course, with—' He was interrupted by a loud noise at the outer door.

Marcus whirled round and seized the heavy tray again, and – though this was unlikely to be the killer coming back – my own heart skipped a beat. But a moment later the door opened and Niveus ventured in, accompanied by a striking-looking man with olive skin and tawny hair, who was dressed in a tradesman's tunic, but held himself with a freeman's dignity.

'Master, your indulgence.' The pageboy sketched a bow. 'This person begs admittance. He claims acquain—' He broke off as he caught that still-unpleasant whiff, then registered the sight of the dreadful fly-blown head. He clapped a hand across his mouth and rushed outside.

The newcomer was staring at it too. He gulped and paled, but then controlled himself. 'Well, that answers my first question, citizens,' he said, in faultless Latin, making a deep bow to Marcus and a briefer one to me. The voice was educated and polite, though clearly neither from Britannia nor Rome. 'Freedman Draco at your service, gentlemen.'

EIGHT

Marcus put the tray down, with more displeasure than relief. 'I don't recall the name – or face. Unless, Junio . . .?'

But I was staring at the newcomer. 'I have seen you somewhere, I am almost sure . . .'

A deprecating smile. 'That will have been through His Excellence, citizen. I very briefly was a slave of his. He bought me as a potential bodyguard, when he was expecting a visitor from Rome, though I never gave him personal service. I did attend your father once when he was ill. One of the other councillors bought me after that, and – thanks to your father's intervention – quickly set me free.'

All of a sudden, recognition dawned. 'Of course,' I said. 'But I did not recognize the name . . .' It was a stupid thing to say, as I realized at once. Most men choose to lose their slave names once they're free.

As he had done, it seemed. 'They call me Draco – because of my tattoo.' He pushed his cloak back so that I could see the impressively detailed dragon that ran up his outer arm.

It was distinctive enough that even Marcus recognized him now, but failure to recall his former slave had irritated him. His tone was cold and formal. 'Of course, the Dacian. So what brings you here?'

'Excellence.' Draco managed to be courteous. 'You may recall I am a silversmith myself. I have a little workshop further down the street. I believe that you yourself arranged the lease.'

Marcus said, 'Hmmph!' and looked annoyed again.

I said, appeasingly, 'No doubt you heard this shop had closed and we had broken in? I know how rumour spreads.'

'More than that, citizen. I was told that Vitellius had disappeared, and run away – suspected of having taken all the stock, including items sent in for repair.' He nodded at the head. 'Though that's clearly quite untrue.'

'But you – alone – were inquisitive enough to come and have a look?' Marcus sounded grim.

'Excellence, I have an interest in the place. Vitellius and I were planning to combine. He lost a skilled apprentice fairly recently, and his replacement has no aptitude at all. I, on the other hand, have skills – but not much strength, due to an ancient battle injury.' He held up the dragon arm again, showing a long scar along the inner side, running from wrist to armpit. 'Struck with my own falx! So pouring molten metal is difficult for me.'

'Can you not find an apprentice of your own?' I asked, surprised. Dacians are famous for their silverwork. 'Men would be clamouring to place their sons with you.'

'I might have done, but I can't afford the keep – not until I've built a greater trade. It's hard enough to find the money for the rent. I already have an aged maidservant to feed. She cooks and cleans – but she's no help with heavy things. Vitellius and I had complementary skills. Together we might have built a partnership – I would have rented space with him and lived upstairs, and that would have helped him pay the higher taxes on this place.'

'So he was struggling financially?' Marcus sounded sharp. 'I'd heard rumours, but I found it hard to credit them.'

'Not financially, as far as I'm aware.' Draco seemed genuinely surprised. 'The money would have been an added benefit, that's all. But physically, perhaps. He too was finding it hard to work alone – which was effectively what he was doing now. That slave of his was useless.'

'You don't know his name?' It was not much, but any information might be a help in tracking down the man.

But Draco was smiling ruefully. 'He nicknamed him Inutilis, because he was so bad – though obviously he can't have been called that when he arrived.'

'And certainly won't be what he's calling himself now.' I glanced at Macilentus. 'You don't know the proper name, by any chance? Perhaps as fellow slaves you sometimes exchanged a word or two?' Wasting time by chatting was firmly frowned upon, but I'd been a slave myself once, and I know how they seize these little opportunities.

The slave-boy shook his head. 'He seemed to be avoiding me, if anything. And I never heard Vitellius call him anything but that.'

'Inutilis. Yet he selected him?' Marcus surprised me with his acuity. 'At the slave-market he must have had a choice.'

'Not in this case, Excellence,' the Dacian replied. 'He told me so himself when we were discussing terms. He took the fellow in part-payment of a debt. From somebody important, as I understand, so he could not well refuse. He would not tell me who, though he did confide that he regretted it. If we had formed a partnership, he meant to use the occasion to absolve the debt – calling it a gesture to the donor, naturally, but actually so he could politely send him back.' He glanced towards that dreadful head again. 'Better if he had done so, by the look of it. As his prospective partner, Excellence, may I be so bold . . .?'

He hardly waited for Marcus to agree but went across and did what I should done myself, before. He raised the borders of the cloth around the head and covered it. The room felt less alarming, instantly. 'Poor Vitellius,' he murmured, standing up again. 'Not only killed but robbed of all his finest things.'

'And possibly his stores of raw materials?' I said. 'We have not looked outside. He will have had ingots, won't he – and gold and jewels as well.'

'The thief might not have taken those,' the Dacian said, to my surprise. 'Unworked metal can be very difficult to sell. Without a licence, anyway. People tend to be suspicious – most gold and silver is state property, reserved for making coins.'

'But there's a rumour of a secret Celtic trade,' I said. 'Or so we've been informed.' It was a gamble. Marcus was the town's most senior magistrate. If Draco did know anything, he might not wish to mention it in this company.

He was startled, but dismissive rather than alarmed. 'The tribes have skilled workmen of their own. They would hardly require Vitellius's services. And even if they did, you'd have to have good contacts to sell anything to them.'

'Or buy from them?' I murmured.

He frowned at me. 'What are you hinting at?'

'You don't think Vitellius might have done so, now and then? Bought ores from them, and failed to pay, perhaps? This looks rather like Celtic handwork to me.'

'I hadn't thought of that.' The Dacian's face cleared. 'But I'm absolutely certain he would not have done. There was no need for it. He had a proper licence – and one pays enough for that. As I have cause to know. I cannot afford a full one. I am only authorized to remelt and repair.'

'Macilentus was explaining about that.' I glanced towards the slave, who was standing listening, still looking shocked and pale. I had almost forgotten he was there. 'But one can make a living?'

'Scratch one, citizen. But I did make one or two things, with the metal I acquired. Simple things, but as good as I could fashion them. Vitellius saw them on display and he was quite impressed. He bought them there and then embellished them and made a pleasing profit out of them. He came to see me, after that, suggesting we combine. His licence would provide sufficient silver for us both.'

I was remembering something else that Macilentus said – that his master had sold items to Vitellius in the past. So was there resentment, now his wares had been replaced? I glanced at the lad but he was staring into space, as if still seeing what he'd glimpsed upstairs. Not the moment to discuss it now. I said, 'So the jewellery and smaller things would be easier to sell?'

Draco nodded. 'Even then it would be best to keep away from the formal marketplace, where there might be aediles, asking awkward questions.' He saw my enquiring look. 'Vitellius marks his pieces with a special sign, so they could be recognized, by anyone with knowledge of the trade. On smaller things, the marks are smaller too – one might not see them, if one did not know that they were there. But that slave would be aware, and know the dangers of items being traced. So set up a stall by any roadway – there are always people passing by, who know a bargain if they're offered one, and won't enquire too much. Though he'd have to move on afterwards as fast as possible.'

'Making him almost impossible to trace.' Marcus sounded quite dispirited. 'But easier than selling ingot silver, I can see. Though there may be may be unset jewels or ivory, as well. We ought to look outside . . .' He stopped in mid-sentence. 'What is it, Junio?'

I'd given a sharp gasp, struck by a sudden thought. 'What happened to the dog? I understood that having one was a necessity? I've seen – and heard – the one next door. Surely Vitellius must have had one, too?'

Draco looked puzzled. 'Well, of course he did. No silver workshop would be safe without a guard. I assumed the thief had taken it – or murdered it as well.'

I turned to Macilentus. 'Was there any trace of it outside?'

He shook his head. 'Your pardon, citizen, but there would not have been. That dog's been dead for days. I saw its body on the midden-pile. There was no injury. It was getting very old, but I thought it had eaten something – possibly a rat: there was one half-chewed beside it, and they can carry death.'

I looked at Marcus. 'Poisoned by the slave? That seems most probable. Leaving a hungry dog to bark would draw attention to the place.' I turned back to Macilentus. 'How long ago was this?'

'I can't recall exactly. A day or two at least. Vitellius was looking for another one, I know – he spoke to my master about where Rex came from, and was going to see the breeder when he returned, he said. In the meantime, Rex was fierce enough to frighten anyone and would certainly alert us if someone climbed the wall.'

So, the neighbours were still friendly – in appearance anyway. But what I said was, 'If the dog was deliberately poisoned while Vitellius was alive, then this whole affair was planned quite carefully. The missing cloak-clasp did not cause the slave to flee, as we first thought – it was simply one of the things he chose to steal. No doubt he found the pattern-piece – Vitellius must have worked with it to fashion the repair – and seized the opportunity to make a quick exchange. Which reminds me, we have not found the rest of him. I suppose I ought to go upstairs. Though in this toga . . .'

Macilentus had turned a deathly pale. 'Better to take it off in any case, from what I saw – though of course I only got the briefest glimpse. I will hold the ladder, citizen – and assist you with your robe.' If he had dared, he would have begged me openly not to send him up – but I understood the message.

'Very well.' Not that I really wished to go myself – I'd been delaying it – but I felt I really had to see with my own eyes what lay upstairs. It was Draco who surprised me.

'I will come with you, citizen,' he said, as Macilentus unwound the heavy folds from me. 'It may be useful to have witnesses. Besides, if the rest of Vitellius is there, the guild should be informed. Someone will have to arrange a funeral. As his prospective partner, I should be happy to request their services. And if I go first, I can secure the ladder at the top for you.'

I nodded. 'Lead the way, then.' And without another word he swarmed lightly up the steps, without even waiting for the slave to steady them. I paused until he had tied them into place before I reluctantly followed him upstairs.

NINE

I will not dwell on what we found up there. Some things should stay in nightmares and this was one of them. Suffice to say that Vitellius must have suffered as he died – or just before he did.

His bruised and battered torso was propped up naked on the bed. The body had not only lost its head. The killer had also hacked off both the arms and legs, and then roughly reassembled the remains – the mutilated hands and feet still bound. The corpse had turned a horrid colour, too, a gruesome parody of what had been a man. The place looked like a scene from the arena – you might have thought there'd been a dozen deaths, from the amount of blood. Except here, there was no one to clean it all away. The smell was terrible and yet more flies were swarming everywhere.

And not only on the corpse. They were buzzing all around us, where every chest and shelf had been emptied out on to the floor, and spattered by the gore. Even the household gods had been thrown down from their niche – somebody clearly did not fear a curse – and they were bloody and the flies were crawling on them, too.

If Macilentus had glimpsed this through the window-space, no wonder he had been so shaken he could hardly speak. I was about to call to him – something reassuring, I was not sure what – when I realized he had climbed behind us now and was standing on the ladder, with his head up through the space. 'Citizen, is it . . . rebel handiwork?' He was white around the lips. 'With the head, and everything?'

'It rather looks it,' I replied. 'This is the kind of thing they can inflict. Though Jove alone knows how Vitellius could have offended them.' I turned to Draco, who had gone across to stand beside the bed. 'Unless, of course, he did have trade with them – and defaulted on payment, or something of the kind.'

Draco looked disbelievingly at me. 'You can't believe that, surely, citizen? Vitellius was well respected in the town. He had a licence to buy good silver from the state. He had lots of wealthy clients. And a reputation for quality. I don't believe that he would risk all that – and possibly his life – by going outside the law, for metal whose quality could not be assured. Or dealing with the rebels in any way at all. I think you can forget that possibility.'

Put that way, it was unlikely, I could see. 'Though possibly Inutilis thought otherwise?'

'You think he is responsible for this?' Draco's obvious surprise reminded me that he could not know what the neighbouring silversmiths had seen.

'It looks clear that he had a hand in it, at least.' I gave him a brief outline.

Draco looked genuinely shocked. 'I realized that he wasn't here, but I assumed he'd simply run away – rather than die defending Vitellius. That would fit with what I knew of him. He was ineffective, but I did not think him capable of this. I still find it hard to do. Bad enough to kill your master – perhaps because he caught the fellow in the act of theft – but why inflict all that?' He gestured at the corpse.

'Perhaps precisely to suggest it was the Celts, and so deflect suspicion from himself? It made even this slave here think of them at once. It occurs to me that this might be a desperate ploy to send the authorities on a different trail, when they might otherwise be seeking him.'

'But it will hardly stop them, will it? For a slave to desert his master is a capital offence – there would have to be a search for him in any case. And it would be more than reck-less to have done as you suggest. The rebels would exact a terrible revenge for implicating them and stirring the garrison into another full-scale search for their retreats.'

'Like us, they would have to find him first.'

'I have no doubt *they* could, even if the authorities could not. They have eyes and ears in every little town. And many rebel sympathizers in the countryside – the only place a runaway slave could try to hide. So, if Inutilis was really trying to put suspicion on the Celts, he must either be an even greater fool than I supposed – or have borne some dreadful grudge against the rebel cause.'

I joined him at the bedside. 'Unless he had links to them, somehow? Could it have been him who tried to trade with them? Without Vitellius knowing?' I was suddenly struck by the possibilities. 'Could he have found a route for their metallic ores – unassayed silver in particular – to find their way into the marketplace, by swapping them for legal Roman versions of the same? To be made into items bearing his master's sign?'

'Of uncertain quality? I would not even think about it, citizen.' Draco seemed unwilling to discuss this any more. He turned away and began to fold and sort the various blood-stained garments and blankets on the floor. A swarm of flies arose and buzzed around his head. He batted them away.

'But it might be undetected if it were melted down at once,' I persisted, waving away the flies myself, and talking to his back. 'I presume that would be part of his duties as a slave? Melting down the ore – or softening it at least – so it could be moulded or pulled out to that wire that you were speaking of? Even if he was not trusted with much else.'

'Who knows? And it hardly matters, does it? Inutilis will be wanted by the law in any case. First as a runaway, and even worse, for failing to defend his master. The punishment for that is terrible enough, but if it's proved he killed his owner, he might be crucified. Just as well Vitellius had no other slaves, or they might have suffered too.'

There was a gasp of horror from Macilentus, who had climbed right up by now and was hovering by the ladder, listening to all this.

Draco seemed alert to his distress. 'But we can't just stand here inventing possibilities. For one thing we are causing a delay, and for another it's not respectful to that unhappy corpse. Help me to find something suitable and we'll cover him at least.' The slave-boy made a movement to join us in the search, but Draco turned to me. 'Meanwhile, citizen, perhaps you'd authorize that slave to call the guild? They can begin arrangements for a funeral.'

He had deferred to me because officially the slave was lent

to me – but, since he had previously offered to alert the guild himself, I felt there was something else behind the courtesy. However, I was happy to agree. I said to Macilentus, 'You know where to find them?'

An eager nod. 'My master is a member. I've been there before.'

'Then go and tell them to send their undertaker here. As soon as possible. Tell them that Vitellius is dead – but nothing else, as yet. Though you'd better call in first and tell your master where you're going. And inform His Excellence.'

Macilentus gave another nod and disappeared. Gratefully, I thought. Downstairs, I heard murmuring, then Marcus calling, 'I've endorsed your orders, what have you found up there?' as the front door squeaked open and then closed again.

'Vitellius's body, Excellence. We will be with you in a moment and explain.' I turned back to Draco, who had picked up a cloth – the least bloodstained of the blankets from the floor – and was covering up the mangled corpse. It deterred the flies, which rose up in a cloud and the Dacian flapped them towards the window-space.

I went to help him, but he placed a finger on his lips, warning that he did not want Marcus to hear us from downstairs. He gestured me nearer. 'Now, I'll answer your question, citizen,' he said, in a low voice. 'Too dangerous to do so when the boy was here.'

I frowned at him in surprise.

'Vitellius was a tradesman, but he was a citizen. This murder cannot be ignored. The army will be notified, and will be looking out, both for Inutilis and for the Celts as well. Obviously, from the method of this death, we were supposed to think of them – whether they were actually involved or not – and that will soon be common knowledge round the town. But your theory about secret trading is another thing. On reflection, I can see it's possible. But if you're right, we must be circumspect. One false word and we are in danger too.'

That made me swallow, but I said, 'But surely Marcus, as chief magistrate, will have to be informed?'

'If you happen to be right, you don't want the neighbours – or His Excellence – telling people what your suspicions are.

As they almost surely would. If that story got about, you might be silenced, too. With equal violence.'

'But surely the authorities must . . .' I began again.

'Possibly later, if there is any proof – which at this moment you don't have at all. And perhaps not even then. The murder of Vitellius – and the way that it was done – is sufficient on its own to turn the whole force of the law on to looking for the rebels without involving you. If they are traced they can only be executed once.' He looked at the shrouded body, pityingly. 'And the same goes for the slave, who was clearly guilty of treachery, at least – whatever happened here. Poor old Vitellius, I liked him very much. To think he harboured such a serpent in his house!'

'But you think I might be right? Inutilis could have managed to exchange some of their illegal silver for what his master had?'

'I think it very risky, but it must be possible – if he was prepared to face the awful penalties if he was even suspected of defrauding anyone. By either side – but especially by those beyond the law. Though presumably he would be highly paid.'

'But suppose he did? And Vitellius found out? It would give a motive for this killing, wouldn't it?' I said, pleased with my deduction.

'For a killing, possibly. But a killing such as this?' He shook his tawny head. 'You saw the fingers had been broken, I am sure. This looks more like vengeance – or a punishment.'

'Or an attempt to extort information?' I put in. 'About what, I don't quite know. A slave would already know most everything that went on in the house.' I had a sudden thought. 'You don't suppose that by fleeing yesterday, he defaulted on some contract with the Celts – and that the rebels did this as a consequence? They may have thought that he was just a go-between, and that they'd really been dealing with Vitellius secretly. The slave might just have left his master gagged and bound.'

'I don't believe so – given the condition of the corpse. I have experience of corpses on the battlefield. Even with the fire to speed the putrefaction, as it obviously would, I'm sure this can't have happened yesterday.'

I had said much the same myself. The implication struck me, suddenly. 'You mean that Vitellius's body was up here, hacked apart – all the while that Inutilis was serving customers below us, in the shop?' The thought was so frightful I felt unwell myself.

'So it would appear. He must have coolly brought the head downstairs before he left! The body was dismembered shortly after death, or there would not be so much blood. Supposing the victim was not actually alive.'

It was such a dreadful picture that I had to shut it out and follow a different line of thought. 'Perhaps it was the rotting that persuaded him to flee – he realized that the smell would soon be noticed, and that he could not disguise it any more. That makes a kind of sense. But it still does not explain why Vitellius was killed in such a gruesome way.'

'Or why there is so much spattered blood downstairs, if the head was up here for so long,' Draco said, surprising me.

I should have thought of that myself. And it must be true. It could hardly have been there when Letigines arrived!

But before I could pursue this tantalizing idea, Draco went on. 'But, citizen Junio, we are wasting time. We must go back downstairs. His Excellence is waiting. He will be losing patience with us by this time.'

He was quite right, of course. Irritating Marcus was never very wise – even for a favoured citizen like me.

I said, 'And the undertakers won't be very long, since they'll be told that Marcus summoned them. They won't want to keep him waiting, either. But perhaps before they get here, we can go and search the stores. If we find evidence of Celtic ores out there, it would prove my theory, wouldn't it?'

'Support it, anyway. Though for Jove's sake, don't tell His Excellence what you hope to find. Simply say we're checking if there's been theft from there. Now you go down, and I will follow you.'

I set off down the ladder. I saw Draco reverentially picking up the household gods and wiping them in his tunic hem before replacing them gently in their niche. Then I was below the level of the floor and had to concentrate on my descent.

Marcus was waiting in the outer shop. He was impatient. 'What took you such a time?' His expression altered. 'Nothing pleasant, judging from your sleeve.'

I glanced down to see what he was looking at and realized that my best tunic had been stained. 'He's been dismembered. We've covered him,' I said. 'The thief has been there too, and ransacked everything. Even the household shrine.' I explained about the gods.

Marcus looked appalled. 'That slave will wish that he had not been born, when we catch up . . .' He broke off as two things happened both at once. Draco came skittering down the ladder too, and there was an imperious knocking at the outer door.

It opened suddenly and Niveus reappeared, still looking slightly green. He sketched a hasty bow. 'Your pardon, Excellence. The councillor Rufus Fulvius Quintillius is here and craves admittance.' He was talking to Marcus, but his eyes kept flicking towards the bloodstained parcel on the floor.

Marcus looked at me. 'Tell him to wait a moment, till we have finished here.'

But Rufus had pushed the slave aside and was already in the room.

TEN

I knew this Rufus slightly, from his official role. As one of the local aediles, he had responsibility for the marketplace. He had a reputation for being pompous, stern but fair – but mostly pompous. I did not care for him. He was diligent enough, but self-important to the point of arrogance: a youngish man, with a sallow face, a receding chin and an air of having the right to power – as perhaps he did. The broad purple stripe around his toga edge marked him as a member of a high-born family.

Draco clearly recognized him too, and was bowing very low – as a tradesman, he'd no doubt had dealings with him before. (There was a rumour that it was actually Rufus who'd bought the Dacian from His Excellence and set him free, in payment of some debt of honour that he owed. But I never believed that. Acts of kindness would not be typical.)

Certainly the aedile did not show the slightest sign of recognition of him now. Or of me, either. Tradesmen were beneath his dignity. He acknowledged us both with the faintest nod, then turned to Marcus. 'Excellence. I am here as market officer. I was informed that there was trouble and that the shop had closed, leaving some customers as creditors.'

'Trouble?' Marcus said bleakly. 'You might say that. Vitellius is dead and it seems his slave has run away with half his stock.'

Rufus managed to look shocked, and even more self-important, both at once. 'Then I must instigate a formal search for him. And if stolen silver goods are likely to reach the marketplace, I should send a warning message to the surrounding towns . . .' He paused, giving a fastidious sniff, and looked around. His eyes alighted on the bloodied object on the floor. 'What . . .?'

'Vitellius. Or his head. The rest of him's upstairs. Also in pieces, as I understand.' Marcus's tone was grimmer than the news.

'Murder?' Rufus made a gesture of disgust, lifting the hem of his toga from the floor. 'I was told Vitellius had closed the shop and fled in order to escape his creditors. But murder? We must notify the priests.' ('We', suddenly, I noticed. Rufus was anxious to share responsibility.) 'And this premises will need a proper cleansing ritual. Burning herbs will not suffice.'

It was an obvious suggestion and I should have thought of that, when I sent Macilentus out. A *quadrans* would have bought some rosemary, and a little more a sprig of hyssop, which was famous for its power.

But Marcus said coldly, 'That will be for the undertaker to arrange. The guild has been informed. They have a burial society, I understand.'

'Then the funeral women must be warned what they are going to find – no simple washing will purify a body that's . . .' He tailed off, aware of Marcus's forbidding stare, and began to fuss instead. 'If I had realized that this was a place of death, I should have worn an amulet, at least. Now I shall have to go and purify myself at the temple – as will all of you, no doubt. Should we not nail a piece of cypress to the door, as a sign to passers-by that this place is now unclean?'

'The guild will arrange that, too, I have no doubt.' Marcus was still frostier than snow. 'As a precaution in the meantime, I have set my page on guard – with instructions to let no one in.' He nodded at the boy, who escaped outside again.

'Ah!' For a moment Rufus looked abashed. 'Excellence, I fear I over-ruled him there, in my capacity as aedile. I felt it was my official duty to attend since Thaddeus, my fellow councillor, told me that valuable items which belonged to customers had somehow gone astray. He did mention that he'd come here with you but I supposed you'd left together too. I did not realize that you had stayed and taken charge.' He looked around. 'Hard to believe a slave would dare do this. Has the wretch escaped with much? Some quite costly things are left, I see.'

'Things that were too big to carry on a single ass, we think. He seems to have packed it up and gone quite openly.' I explained about the cloak. 'But we don't know if he's stolen from the outside stores, as well. He might well have done. It seems he took the precaution of first poisoning the dog who used to guard the court.'

Rufus puffed his chest, importantly. 'Then we must go and make a search. As aedile, of course, I shall accompany you.' He gestured to the open door into the yard.

I glanced at Draco. This was not at all what I had planned. But there was no escaping it.

The Dacian bowed low. 'With your permission, aedile, we may require some tools. The storage containers may possibly be locked.' He gestured to the scattered implements beside the hearth. 'At least the snips, perhaps?'

Rufus gave him permission with a nod so Draco picked up a heavy pair – rather like the ones that were used to let us in. Marcus, however, clearly felt the need to reassert control.

'I will wait here until the undertakers come,' he said, 'After that, aedile, I will leave this in your hands. Then – when I have purified myself, as you so helpfully suggest – I will go and inform the garrison. It will be too late to alert them now to keep a watch out for this fugitive. But I've met the new commander of the garrison. He's keen to make his mark. I'll get him to send a message with the imperial post to notify the towns nearby, and spread the word to other units to watch all the roads.'

'A runaway slave who is a murderer and thief certainly calls for the utmost efforts of the law.' Rufus was anxious to have a part in this. 'But he'll want to interview the rebels most of all. A severed head and mutilated corpse? Exactly what they do to victims. He'll want to talk to them.'

'If he can track them down,' Marcus said wryly. 'But no doubt he will try. That would impress the Provincial Governor.'

'Exactly. And if the story spreads, as it is almost sure to do, it might cause public panic, unless the crime is put to rest. Somebody must be caught and questioned – at the very least – to show that the authorities are still in charge, and criminal activity will be rigorously pursued.' (When he said 'questioned' he meant the torturers, of course.)

Marcus nodded. 'Beasts in the arena, I shouldn't be surprised. Virius Lupus would expect no less – especially since Vitellius was a Roman citizen. Though I suspect the rebels might prove difficult to catch. But we'll find this slave, at least, and have him punished for his crimes. We'll need a full description, though, if we're to set a useful watch. Draco, you have met him, I believe?'

'I've seen him, anyway,' the Dacian said. 'Though I never spoke to him. Not quite as tall as I am, rather stooped and sallow, with pale protruding eyes. Thin hair cut short, the colour of dead grass, and long thin legs and arms. That's all I can report, except he had a shifty manner – would not meet your eyes, as if there was something that he wished to hide. When I saw him, he had a brownish-yellow servant's tunic on – though of course that could easily be changed.'

'And we know he had his master's russet cloak, as well.' Marcus was approving – unsurprisingly. The description was precise. 'I'll get the neighbours to describe him again too, before I leave, in case they can give me extra details – which I rather doubt. You are a good witness, Dacian. But if we could find his previous owner, we might discover more – scars, or moles, or even just a name. An important person owned him, I believe you said?'

Draco said, 'Somebody too important and wealthy to refuse. I know no more than that.'

'Rufus, you might look into that when you have finished here. Ask around the forum – all the councillors you can. If a member of the curia gave this slave to Vitellius – in part payment of a debt as we believe – it should not be impossible to find out who it was.'

Rufus acknowledged this commission with a little bow. He had turned quite pink with pleasure (or with self-importance, it was hard to guess). He was about to speak when there was a rapping on the door, and the page appeared again. 'The undertaker that you sent for, master, and his funeral women too. And the head of the gold and silverworkers' guild has come as well.'

He had, and it was he who entered first. A large, red-faced fellow, with shoulders like an ox, and dressed all in black – like Mors incarnate – in a full-length Grecian gown and hooded cloak. 'Your Excellence!' He gave a sweeping bow. 'This is very grave. I felt it was incumbent on me to attend myself.' The carefully mournful expression and doleful voice could not conceal his glee at dealing with a man of Marcus's high rank. 'We are flattered that you have taken an interest in this death – but I assure you that Vitellius has paid all his dues, and the guild will attend to everything. May I present the undertaker whom we use?'

The undertaker – who was as pale as the other man was pink – bowed, smiled wanly and looked obsequious. 'If you could instruct my people where to go?' He gestured at three women who were loitering by the door, each carrying a basket of cloths, oils and herbs. 'I presume that the deceased is upstairs – and, from the smell, that he's been dead some little time?'

Marcus said. 'Most of him is up there. The head is in the cloth.' He gestured to the parcel on the floor. Then, as the visitors exchanged shocked, startled looks, he added, 'You will oblige me, though, by not discussing this with anyone. I fear there have already been gawpers looking in, and no doubt the story will soon be everywhere, but there is always gossip and it may not be believed. I would be glad if you could keep the details to yourselves – and do not speculate about what happened here, at least until the funeral is over. Enough for customers to know Vitellius has been killed and robbed. I don't want panic spreading through the town.'

He waited for the newcomers to blurt their promises.

He smiled. 'So, if you are ready, I will leave you to your tasks. In the meantime, Rufus, you may go and search outside.'

Rufus – who had not been deferred to or addressed throughout all this – looked flushed and mutinous'. But it was all the invitation I required, and I led the way at once, back through the inner room and out into the court, moving the wedge and closing the door behind us as I went.

I had been looking forward to getting out into the fresher air again, but even here the smell was evident – to my surprise

– perhaps because of the high walls all around. Or perhaps it was simply that midden-heap again.

The yard was narrower than the one next door, but rather tidier. Clearly it had been swept not very long ago – and from the presence of a broom and bucket standing by the wall, and the tracks of brushmarks on the paving-stones, I guessed that someone had roughly scrubbed it fairly recently. The last task of that useless, missing slave perhaps? Even the ashes in the outside hearth were neatly piled.

It seemed too, as we began the search, that it would not take us long. When I say 'us', I speak of me and Draco, naturally – Rufus had no intention of doing anything. He saw his role as merely to direct, while we two struggled with the heavy lids. (I was still in my tunic, at this time, of course – my toga was still folded up indoors, so the aedile probably did not recall my rank, if indeed he'd ever noticed it. But I was interested in the outcome, so I did not demur.)

It did not seem that there was much to find. The first stone bin, when we had wrested up the lid, was (rather like the neighbours') full of pans and amphorae and sacks – none of which yielded anything more interesting than a few turnips, hazelnuts and leeks. The next, to my dismay, contained not even that. It was completely empty. Even when Draco climbed right in and searched the floor, he found nothing but a single amethyst, still uncut and nestled in its piece of stone, which had somehow found its way into a corner and been missed.

This find was given to Rufus, who'd put out his hand for it, and we turned our attention to the remaining bin. This time there was a lock, one of those ingenious little barrels made of bronze, with a spring and chain securing the hasp. There was no key of course, and it was hard to cut because the device was so close against the bin, but Draco was clearly practised with his snips. After a little the chain gave way, and he threw down the implement and put his shoulder underneath the lid to help me open it.

There was an immediate, strong and quite distinctive smell. Even before I saw it, I knew what we should find. The body of a man. Someone not quite as tall as Draco, at a guess –

though it was hard to tell, because he was in several pieces now. The legs were long and thin, and lying on the top. So were the arms, which had been hacked off too. The pieces had been pushed in quite haphazardly – as if to fit into the space – not reassembled, like the corpse indoors. The severed head had clearly gone in last. It had sallow cheeks and the pale, protruding eyes were open and staring up in an unnerving way. The thin hair – where it could be seen among the blood – was short and the colour of dead grass. There was no ochre tunic (or russet cloak) – the battered torso was bare of any clothes – but otherwise the Dacian's description was exact.

I turned to Draco. 'Inutilis, I presume?'

He nodded grimly. 'I'm afraid so. So, he hadn't run away. It appears that I misjudged him, citizen.'

'But he didn't save his master, did he? Or die in the attempt. He was still alive when Letigines was here, and keen to tell him lies.'

'You are supposing that was actually him, citizen. But I am not so sure. That might have been the killer – he must still have been nearby. Someone arranged the corpses in this way, and it must have happened after Marcus's slave had left. Inutilis may have been a prisoner by that time. He died more recently than his master, if I am any judge. Of course, he has been out here, in the cold, rather than in the workshop with the fire, and dismembered bodies are harder to assess – but this one is fresher, I am fairly sure of that. The stiffness of death has hardly started to wear off. I could believe that he was murdered yesterday.'

'By the same person?'

'It rather looks like that. Even the fingers have been broken in exactly the same way.'

There was a strangled noise behind us. I turned around to see Rufus leaning on the wall. His eyes were closed and he was retching in a most un-Roman fashion. I ignored him – as I guessed he would prefer – and turned back to Draco.

'So perhaps he didn't kill his master? Then who did? And why? Do you think it was the Celtic rebels, after all?' I sighed. 'We're back where we started.'

'Further back, perhaps. This raises still more questions, doesn't it? Who killed Inutilis? And why not both at once?'

'And, if it wasn't either Vitellius or his slave, who was it loading treasure on that ass?' I said. 'And who . . .?'

I was interrupted by a cough behind me. I spun round to see Rufus, pale but evidently more collected now, standing at my shoulder. 'Townsmen, thank you for your help. This second find is most unfortunate, of course, but I think that you can leave this matter now with your superiors. You may be on your way.' He had clearly realized that I had noticed his distress, and his next words confirmed it. 'And – you heard what His Excellence said – please do not speculate about this any more, or discuss what you have seen here with anyone.'

I was ready to demur – there were lots of questions that I wanted answers to – but the Dacian forestalled me. 'Aedile,' he said, 'you can count on our discretion. We swear by all the gods. We will not discuss this with anyone at all – except, naturally, His Excellence himself – other than at his express request.'

That was clever. Marcus had asked me to investigate, so whatever questions I might choose to ask could be said to be already at his 'express request'. But Rufus could hardly argue with the promised oath.

He seemed to feel it, because he frowned at me. 'You swear it?'

'Willingly.'

'Then you may be on your way. I will deal with remaining matters here. Except, perhaps, that if you are going back to your trades, you could call in at the slaves' guild on your way and ask them to pick up this unfortunate. I presume that Vitellius will have paid his dues in full. If not, don't discuss it further with the guild. Come back to me and I will see what's to be done.'

I sketched a bow. 'With pleasure, aedile.' It occurred to me that if anyone might identify the slave, and even know who the previous owner was, it could well be the guild (to whom regular subscriptions must be paid). Not that it was going to help us find the killer, now, or retrieve the stolen goods, but I was curious.

Rufus gave me the briefest of brief dismissive nods. 'And shut that lid again before you go; I don't wish to look at that.' We complied and he waved us towards the workshop door.

Draco bowed and went obediently inside, but I did not follow him. I paused just long enough to murmur, with a smile, 'Of course I am very happy to assist. Don't hesitate to ask, if there are any other errands you require. If you'd just permit me time to put my toga on . . .'

It wasn't wise. I could be making a powerful enemy. But I did have the satisfaction, as I turned back to go inside, of seeing the look of startled horror on his face as he realized he'd been dealing with a Roman citizen.

ELEVEN

The funeral women had been working hard. We had been outside for hardly any time, and already the inner workshop had been tidied up. The scattered silverware and tools were sorted into piles, the boards which hid the safe cavity had been replaced and the floor was newly swept. The air was better too – the sick-sweet odour masked, in part, by a pungent smell of burning herbs. Downstairs was empty, but professional keening noises and clatters from above told me someone was busy up there, attempting to prepare the corpse for its journey to the pyre.

Draco left, to go and purify himself. I found my toga, neatly folded on a shelf, and – rather inexpertly – contrived to wrap it on. (It isn't easy to fold a toga properly oneself – usually I have Brianus or Tenuis to help – but I managed to get it to stay on, and to walk in it, with care.)

I rather hoped that Rufus would come in and see me in my Roman finery, but when I dared to peep around the door he was leaning on the fence again. So I left him to it and went through to the outer shop – the intervening shelves were now full of piles of rescued goods, so I could not really see it until I walked round the barrier.

Out here, too, it was already looking very different. The shutters to the counter were completely taken down and leaned against the wall, and light from the aperture was streaming in. The front door had been left ajar, presumably to air the room, though I could see a piece of cypress nailed on to it, as a sign that death had made this place ill-starred, and thus to deter the curious from peering in. It seemed to be effective – there was no one doing so.

If they had been looking there was not much to see. The parcelled head had vanished – presumably upstairs. The undertaker and the chairman of the guild had disappeared as well.

But even as I stood there, two of the undertaker's women

bustled in. They had managed to procure both water and a priest – probably from Thaddeus's fountain and the Minerva shrine, respectively, since both were close nearby. (As protector of craftsmen Minerva was much revered, and her little local temple was quite a wealthy one, although the priest – who must have been part-time – was very old.)

Once across the threshold, the women got to work at once. They started scrubbing at the blood-spattered floor, walking backwards, while the old man tottered behind them with a bowl, scattering the contents and muttering a prayer. It took him a moment to look up and notice me, but when he did, he gestured me across. 'Citizen, you will need purifying too, before you leave. I've already done it for your tradesman friend. We met him on the street.'

That would be Draco, I thought as I went across and knelt obediently. He marked my forehead with a stripe of what proved to be a mix of water, salt and perfumed oil, then poured a little of the liquid over both my hands, murmuring an incantation all the while. (The women deftly swept away the overflow.) 'Go in peace, citizen,' intoned the ancient voice. 'I declare you cleansed. Though a little sacrifice – a pigeon or a dove – made at the temple, would assure the purification is complete.'

'Thank you,' I said. I was not sure if I should tip him, but – after the fiasco of the Lumpy Dog – I did not have funds to spare, so I sidled past and out into the welcome open air.

Glevum streets are not noted for their pleasant smells. But the usual odours – midden-heaps, donkey-droppings and unwashed humanity – seemed wonderfully wholesome by comparison to what I'd left within. Even the clamour and the clutter, and the tradesmen plucking at one's sleeve, were almost pleasing now – part of decent, everyday normality.

I shook off the would-be salesmen (and those simply curious for news – gossip in Glevum travels very fast) by declaring that I had an urgent mission from the aedile and had been forbidden to tell them anything. This had the advantage of being broadly true, and Rufus's reputation was enough to discourage even the most determined questioners. So I was able – quite quickly – to hurry through the town and reach the marshy area just inside the eastern walls where I knew the slave guild had their premises.

The land here is boggy and regularly floods, and those who can afford it choose to live elsewhere. It has none of the broad pavements of the central town, just narrow shadowed streets and narrower alleyways, where my toga caused considerable attention as I passed. But among the warren of neglected buildings and decrepit sheds, I found the hanging painted sign that indicated – even to those who couldn't read – that this was where the slaves' guild could be found.

Inside it was more respectable – a neat entrance and a proper little anteroom where visitors could wait, though unfurnished except for a little table and a stool. It was manned by an aged individual, in a tunic of appropriately sombre hue, who was standing with his back to me, engaged in making chalk marks on a board hung on a wall. It appeared to be marked into a sort of grid, and he was writing something in small letters into spaces on the chart. Clearly he had been an educated slave, since he could read and write.

He turned his head when I came in, saw the toga and dropped the chalk at once.

'Citizen! Forgive me.' His long face lit in a lugubrious smile. 'I was marking where the ashes from our pyre tonight are going to go.'

The guild had a private columbarium, I knew – a simple wall with holes in it, providing a resting place for urns. I said, politely, 'Then I am sorry to have interrupted your important task. Clearly the guild will need a record of whose ashes are placed where.'

The flattery was rewarded with a bow. 'Exactly, citizen. And which niches are still vacant. That is becoming a concern. We may have to think of having another set of "dove holes" made. But we would need a generous donor to help us pay for it.' He paused to give me time to volunteer.

I didn't.

'But, forgive me, citizen. That's none of your concern.' He tugged at his tunic as he walked across to me, and I realized that his left arm finished at the wrist (an injury that no doubt explained why his former master was induced to let him go and why he was working here). 'How can we be of help? One of your slaves has had an accident, perhaps? And you have paid his dues? Or did he pay his own?'

I winced. That happened sometimes, but it was unusual – generally it meant the master was too mean to pay for them. (A veiled allusion to my failure to donate?) I gave a cheerful smile. 'Not my own slave, in fact. But certainly a dead one, and in need of your immediate services. I am not quite certain who his legal owner was. He was on loan I think, to Vitellius the silversmith, but he may have been a gift. I was hoping you could tell me. He will be in your records, I assume.'

The guildsman looked at me uncertainly. 'And your interest in him, citizen?'

Of course, it must sound as if I'd accidentally killed the slave myself, and was attempting to have the corpse removed without paying the (legally required) compensation to the owner. I hastened to defend myself. 'I happened to be there when he was found. Rufus the aedile was with me at the time – and he suggested that I come to you.'

'Ah! I see! In that case – naturally – citizen, I will look through the records and see what I can do.' (The mention of the aedile swayed him in a way that I – as a mere tradesman citizen – did not.) He sat down at the table, and pulled from under it a wooden box containing several rolled-up linen 'scrolls' – long strips of cloth which had been written on. (Much cheaper than parchment or even bark-paper – though on cloth the ink does tend to run, as had clearly happened here. Black marks were showing through. Proper squid ink, though, by the look of it: financial records clearly needed something more durable than soot.)

The guildsman looked expectantly at me. 'The name of the deceased?'

It was my turn to look uncertain. 'I don't know that either, I'm afraid. Vitellius called him Inutilis, but that can't have been his name. I was hoping you could tell me what that was, presuming that Vitellius paid his dues.'

The guildsman selected the largest of the scrolls and, holding one end steady with his stump, deftly unrolled the

rest across the table top with his other elbow, using a finger
to check each column entry as it went. 'Vitellius. Here he is.'
He consulted the squiggles which accompanied the name. 'He
did indeed make payments, but no recent ones. This account
is closed. We arranged a funeral for an apprentice-slave not
very long ago.' He closed the scroll with one smooth movement
of his hand.

I sighed. 'I hope this doesn't mean the dues have not been
paid.' If they had somehow been allowed to lapse, Inutilis
would not qualify for free burial by the guild and someone
else would have to pay for it. To make it clear that it would
not be me – and no doubt adding to my reputation for being
miserly – I added, 'Let's pray his former owner kept his
subscription up, or I will have to refer this to the aedile.
Even if the dead slave paid the dues himself, without his
name there'll be no way to prove the fact.' I gave a hopeful
smile. 'You don't know of any councillor continuing to pay
the fees for a male house-slave that he's lent elsewhere?'

'A general slave?' He shook his head. 'Not that I'm aware
of, citizen. The only case I know of is a courier on loan – and
I'm under strict instructions not to mention that.'

'Which you've just done,' I said.

The mournful face turned scarlet. 'I mean, I am not to
mention who the owner is.'

'A man of some importance, though?' I urged, and when
he failed to answer I went on, 'Since he had a private courier
to lend? And very likely on the council, too, since he's important enough that his wishes must be implicitly obeyed.'

'Well, I suppose there is no harm in confirming that,' he
said. 'But I can say no more. Obviously, a man in public
life does not wish to have it generally known that he was
unable to repay a debt – or not with coin, in any case. So his
name is not to be disclosed. He made a point of stipulating
that. Even if anything happened to the slave, he was not to
be involved.'

'Yet he agreed to go on paying the subscription dues?'

'As I said, the loan was in payment of a debt. I imagine the
creditor had demanded that, as part and parcel of the settlement
– so that he was not involved in additional expense himself,

or obliged to pay for any funeral. Though such a thing was not anticipated, obviously.'

'But you don't know the name of this cautious creditor?'

'I'm afraid I don't – the councillor declined to mention that. The whole thing was clearly embarrassing for him. I wasn't witness to any part of it. He sent for the head of guild to call on him at home – quite a condescension, considering he was dealing with a guild of slaves – and personally made the agreement for all this.'

'So, he didn't come in here?'

A shake of the old head. 'He did not even send a letter, although his steward comes here all the time to pay the household dues. Clearly, he did not want to leave a written record that anyone might find.'

'But you know all about it?' I observed.

'There are only three of us who do – myself and my immediate superior and the head of guild himself, and we were obliged to swear an oath of secrecy.' He seemed to realize that he had said too much. 'Though this can't be relevant to your enquiry. No one would demean a skilled messenger like Celerius by making them a general servant in a tradesman's shop.'

It did seem unlikely. It can take years to train a proper courier – not only must he be able to repeat – verbatim – any message, having heard it only once, but he must also be a rider of some skill. But surely there could not be two separate slaves in Glevum, both at once, on loan from a wealthy councillor in payment of a debt?

'All the same, from everything you say this may be the same man. Would you recognize Celerius if you had sight of him?'

Another shake of the lugubrious head. 'Never seen him, that I know of, citizen. He's never been here either. There was no need of it. His ex-master has always paid his dues – and as I say, he sends his steward with the money every moon.'

'So that steward – or one of the other servants in that house – would recognize a description of the man.'

He pursed his lips. 'I'm very sorry. I really cannot say.

I've helped you all I can. You'll have to make enquiries elsewhere.'

'Difficult to do, if you won't say who the owner is,' I said.

'It isn't that I won't say, citizen. I can't. We had to swear an oath. That's what Thad— That's what that councillor required.' The correction was instant, but I seized on it at once.

'Thaddeus?' I said, without much hope. It was unlikely to be him. I could not imagine him consorting with the guild. And there's more than one councillor whose name begins with 'Th'.

But the man had turned a startled pink again. 'I did not say that, citizen. Please don't misquote my words. I stumbled in mid-sentence, that is all. And now, if you'll excuse me – unless you can identify this corpse you want removed as one of our members, or you're prepared to pay, I'm afraid I cannot help you further, and I've other work to do.' He rose and put away the scrolls, then picked up his lump of chalk as if ready to go back to the chart.

It was as close to a dismissal as he dared to give, given our difference in rank. 'Then I'll bid you good morning – which I assume it is, since I have not heard the midday trumpet sound.' I turned towards the door, but paused at the threshold long enough to say, 'I might call in on Thaddeus's household all the same, and see if the steward there can tell me anything.'

The effect was instantaneous. He put down the chalk at once and hurried to my side. 'Citizen, I beg you, do not say you talked to me. Thaddeus has a lot of influence. He would have me instantly dismissed and punished savagely – and if I survived that, I'd be sure to starve to death. I said too much, because you seemed a kindly man concerned about a slave. But I kept my oath; I did not mention names.' He was so anxious that he started plucking at my toga folds.

'So it was Thaddeus!' I gaped at him, amazed. Thaddeus! He'd visited Vitellius's premises, by his own admission, yesterday. He'd talked to me and Marcus about the missing slave. He'd listened to the neighbour's unflattering account of him. Yet hadn't mentioned once that he knew the man at all.

Of course, that might well be embarrassment about the debt.
But all that discussion at the villa yesterday, pretending to
doubt that there'd even been a slave, and trying to put the
blame on Freckles?

And that story about calling at the workshop earlier – which,
come to think of it, was a strange thing to have done. Most
men in his position would have sent a slave. Even without
the courier, Thaddeus had plenty at his beck and call.

Which raised the question, why pass on Celerius at all,
especially to a task so unsuited to his skills? There must
have been a dozen other slaves he could have sent. Clearly,
I would have to talk to Thaddeus again – or someone would.
Probably not me, on second thoughts. I lacked sufficient rank.
He would just decline to answer, throw me out – or have me
thrown – and make my life a misery for ever more. (If he
didn't trump up some case against me, take me to court,
demand a swingeing fine and ruin me and mine. Such things
are not unknown, if one offends a councillor.)

'Citizen?' The guildsman's voice was piteous.

'Don't be concerned. I will not mention you. I already have
a reason to call in at the house. Thaddeus was with me earlier
today, just before the body of that slave was found. I should
report that discovery to him, anyway, I think.'

'But if the slave was loaned to Vitellius – as I believe you
said – surely it is for him to tell the owner of the loss? There
may be compensation to be paid, on either side, depending
on the circumstances of the death.'

I sighed. 'It would have been better, but it won't be possible.
Vitellius is dead, himself. By the same hand, we think.'

'Murder?' The old man spat upon his hand and rubbed
behind his ear with it to keep bad luck at bay.

I said, 'My turn to rely on your discretion, now. This
must not be mentioned, at least until the aedile has been
informed. But, if the dead slave proves to be Celerius – as I
rather think – his dues will have been paid, and he is entitled
to a guildman's funeral. Perhaps you could send someone
when it is convenient.'

'But if it's not the courier at all?'

'Then I assume Vitellius's heirs will have to pay,' I said. I was improvising wildly. I did not know the law, but it seemed to satisfy my questioner.

'Then we'll arrange to pick the body up as soon as possible. Vitellius's workshop, I believe you said?' He went across and drew a circle on his chart. 'We would have room to put him on the pyre tonight. I presume that, in the circumstances, speed would be required?'

'I will see you get instructions from the aedile,' I said. 'But see they take a cloth to cover up the corpse. It is in several pieces.'

The man turned even whiter, if that were possible. 'Dear Mars,' he muttered. 'I have done this job for many moons, and I have seen the results of dreadful accidents – including that assistant slave who fell into the fire – but I've never had to deal with anyone who had been dismembered quite deliberately.'

'As I said,' I told him as I turned back to the door, 'I rely on your discretion. I will tell Rufus the aedile as much. And now if you will excuse me, I too have work to do. Thank you for your assistance.'

And I went out into the street.

TWELVE

I debated briefly, at the corner of the street, whether I should go straight back to Rufus and report, but decided it could wait. I knew where Thaddeus's town house was. It was not far and it was almost on my way. I wanted to call in on my own workshop, too – poor Tenuis had no notion where I was and might wrongly have supposed that I had stayed at home because of some complication with the birth, which had merely been imminent the last time he had heard. So I could reassure him that everything was well – as I supposed.

I was planning to take my toga off and leave it in the shop – or even send it to the fuller's to be cleaned – since obviously I was going to have to walk back home again. Marcus and gig had long since disappeared, and I had no mule today. A pity, since I had promised I would purchase food and without Arlina's panniers, I would have to carry it – though I would at least have Tenuis to help.

The idea of transport raised another thought. Before I took off my Roman finery, I would call at those other hiring-stables and ask for a description of the slave who had collected the ass on Vitellius's behalf. If the details matched those of Inutilis (or Celerius, as I was now convinced he was called) that at least would prove that he was still alive at noonday yesterday. And if they didn't, we'd have a verbal picture of the murderer.

But first things first. I was back in more salubrious suburbs by this time, and only a step or two from Thaddeus's town house. I found its narrow entry, with a shop on either side, and – greatly daring – rapped upon the gate.

The haughty slave who answered it almost made me quail. He was more resplendent in his azure uniform than I was in my toga, after my long trail through muddy streets. He did not even wait for me to speak, before assuring me, 'If you've come with a petition, I'm afraid there is no point. The master's not at home.'

I tried my most disarming smile. 'Nor the mistress either? Of course, they're probably still staying at the villa, with His Excellence. I should have thought of that. I was at Marcus Septimus's yesterday myself, while they were there, and I heard they were having a new mosaic laid.' Which was strictly true – though not, perhaps, in the way that he supposed.

But the hint that I was somebody of sufficient account to have been a guest of Marcus's had exactly the effect that I had hoped.

'I'm sorry, citizen!' The tone was different. Courteous now, and anxious to assist. 'Is there a message that you wish to leave?'

'I wanted to ask about his courier-slave, that's all. I don't possess a trusty messenger. I don't suppose he'd be available for hire? I didn't think of it when I was talking to Thaddeus last night.' (Also strictly true, I told the listening gods. I don't have a courier. I was fairly certain Celerius was not available for anything. And I had been talking to Thaddeus – even if he wasn't talking much to me.)

The doorkeeper stiffened, and was abrupt again. 'You are mistaken, citizen. Thaddeus does not keep a courier.'

'But surely he had one? Celerius, was he called? Rather tall with long, slim arms and legs, rather pale complexion and . . .' I hesitated, the struggle to rephrase Draco's meaning in more flattering terms momentarily defeating me. 'Large eyes and short yellowish-brown hair.'

The man looked flustered, as if this was pressure he was not ready for. I did the smile again, and eventually he said, 'Celerius is no longer with us.'

I tried to look surprised. 'Really? I understood that he was very skilled. I'm sure that Thaddeus said so.' (That was a reasonable guess. Thaddeus generally claimed that anything he had was better than other people's version of the same.)

It seemed my guess was right, and fortunate. 'Well, if the master discussed him with you, citizen, there's not much point in my denying he was here.' The doorkeeper leaned forward, confidential now. 'He's been sent to another household on temporary loan. So perhaps, if you can find him, there would be hope for you.'

I knew better, so I simply said, 'Does Thaddeus often lend his slaves like that?'

He shook his head. 'I have never known of it before. And I admit I was surprised. Celerius was very much a favourite until very recently – always being called into the master's private rooms, then sent off on "secret errands", which he loftily told us that he could not discuss.'

'There must have been some feeling about that among the other slaves! Of course, a courier has to be discreet, but he does not have to make a show of it,' I said, which wasn't wise. The doorkeeper might have deduced that I had been a slave myself, and refused to talk to me.

But it seemed to have the opposite effect. He became confiding. 'You're quite right, citizen. But Celerius always did. I think he meant to gloat and make us curious. But whatever he was up to, they were profitable trips. More than once he's come in late at night when I was on duty and had to let him in – from somewhere local, clearly, since he didn't take the horse – and every time I saw a bag of money at his belt.'

'Which he meant you to see, presumably, since a purse would be easy to conceal beneath a cloak.'

'I think so, citizen. It wasn't money for his own use, anyway – at least not all of it. He took it straight in to the master every time, then came out with a swagger and refused to say a word to anyone. I imagine he had been given a reward.'

'Really?' This time my surprise was genuine. Slaves are not generally paid for services – though they are sometimes permitted to keep tips from visitors. It suggested he was trusted with some special enterprise – perhaps a risky one. 'But then he fell from favour?'

The gatekeeper tapped his nose. 'I think he must have offended the master in some way. Asked for a bigger tip or something, probably. I know he was saving to buy his freedom – and from the swagger I think he was getting at least something every trip. Perhaps he overstepped the mark, and asked for more. The master is careful with his money – he prefers to spend it on his wife.'

'So, the change was very sudden?'

'Very, citizen. One day he was in the master's confidence, and the next Thaddeus seemed desperate to be rid of him. Called the steward to his room one night and – according to the page who witnessed all of this – started going through the accounts looking to find a creditor who might need a slave. Within a day, Celerius was gone "on temporary loan". My guess is he was offered in payment of the debt, just to be rid of him. Pity you didn't come enquiring earlier; I'm sure Thaddeus would gladly have hired him to you.'

'Obviously it's too late now,' I said, with truth. 'And you don't know where he's gone?'

'No idea. The steward has been sworn to secrecy, on pain of dreadful punishment, he says. And the rest of us are to forget the man was ever here and not to mention him. That page has already been beaten black and blue for reporting what he saw. If asked outright we are to say there is no courier kept – or we shall suffer worse.' He blanched. 'In fact, I've already said too much to you. But since the master told you Celerius was here, what else could I have done?' He tailed off in dismay.

'Don't worry, doorkeeper,' I said. 'You obeyed your orders perfectly, and told me there was no courier here. As I will testify if anyone enquires. I wouldn't wish to cause you trouble with your master. In fact, since Celerius is not available for hire, there's no need to mention that I even called. I won't leave a message – there's no point in doing that – so there's no reason for Thaddeus to know that I was here.' As I spoke, I pressed a coin into his palm.

That earned a grateful smile. 'Thank you, citizen. I think that might be best. I'm only sorry I could not be of help.'

But of course he had been. I was quite certain now that it was Celerius who lay murdered and dismembered in the yard. The only problem was persuading Thaddeus to acknowledge that, so the slave could be buried at the guild's expense. But for now I simply said a quick 'Farewell' and hurried off. I did not want Thaddeus and his litter to arrive, and find me at his gate. Besides, I had another urgent call to make.

It was a little way further to the hiring-stables which had

rented out the ass, but it did not take me long. And questioning the foreman who'd been left in charge – a hefty fellow in a leather apron – was a relatively simple matter, too. My toga, however mud-stained it had recently become, was enough to ensure that I was treated with respect. (Perhaps he, too, had hopes of a substantial tip.) Certainly, he was anxious to assist.

Indeed, he assured me – with a smile that showed a set of yellowed teeth – he recognized Celerius, from my description. 'That was the slave who called and made arrangements for the donkey hire.'

I thought about the implications of that remark. 'But not the one who came in and collected it?'

A shake of the unruly curls. 'That was the other slave. The one who came in afterwards, to request an alteration for the date.' He waved a horny hand towards a heavy piece of slate propped up against the wall – where records for the various animals were chalked.

'An alteration?' That might be significant. 'Changed from when, to when? Can you remember that?' I asked, without much hope. It was clear from the general smudginess that any unneeded record would be rubbed out at once, and quickly overwritten by the next.

And so it proved. 'Might have been able to if you'd asked me the same day, citizen, but I could not tell you now. We have a lot of animals for hire – that's why we keep a written record like we do. We don't even try to keep the details in our heads. The date was brought foward by a day or two, is all I know – though I can tell you at a glance what the new arrangement was.' He went over and consulted the columns on the chart, then came back with a frown. 'In fact, it ought to have been back again by now. He only contracted for it overnight, and now it's overdue.' He made a wry face. 'There'll be extra fees to pay.'

'I am sorry to be the bearer of bad news,' I said. 'But you may find it difficult to get any fees at all. Vitellius is dead.' That was not a secret, I told myself; the news of the undertakers coming to the house would be all over Glevum very soon. 'And of your donkey, I'm afraid, there is no sign at all.' He was about to protest, but I held up a hand. 'It seems the silversmith was robbed and killed. The matter is in the hands of the market aediles and His Excellence Marcus Septimus – in fact it was he who asked me to enquire. Any claims for compensation should be made to them.'

The foreman stared at me in disbelief. 'Then why did no one tell us this before?'

'Because the body was not found until today. But this change in the arrangements-did you not think it was unusual?'

'Not really, citizen. Vitellius had already told the owner of this place, when he met him in the street, that he was not happy with his replacement slave – the one that you described. And the fellow was peculiar when he came in about the ass – so furtive and anxious to be out again that you would think he was reluctant to be here.'

'I understand he'd been demoted suddenly. That might make him sullen,' I observed, thinking about his previous role with Thaddeus.

'Sullen? He seemed as if his mind were somewhere else. So, when the other servant came quite shortly afterwards – a much more lively individual – and said that there had been an error with the starting date, we were not surprised at all. Just assumed the useless slave had simply got it wrong. Which, naturally, cost Vitellius a rearrangement fee. Only a quadrans, but at the time it made us laugh.'

'This lively individual,' I said, ignoring this. 'Could you describe him to me, do you think?'

The man made a dismissive little 'Phhhw!' between loose lips. 'An average sort of person, from what I can recall. Average height, with brownish hair, and neither thin nor fat.'

A description of half the men in Glevum! I pressed a little more. 'Nothing else that you can think of? Could he – for example – have been a Celt, perhaps?'

That was a bit daring, given what I knew. The foreman appeared to think so. He looked doubtful, but I was a citizen. 'I suppose it's possible, since you mention it. But I wasn't paying much attention to the way he looked.' He gave a sudden frown. 'Pardon me for asking, citizen, but what is your interest in him? You think it might be him, and not the useless one, who robbed Vitellius?'

'Something of the kind,' I admitted. 'Though I'd prefer that you kept this information to yourself, at least for now.'

The man looked self-important. 'You can rely on my discretion, citizen.'

I was not sure of that, but I was committed now. 'Then I should tell you that the second man was not Vitellius's slave. The lanky servant is the only one he had – and he is dead as well. So obviously we want to find this other man. Rufus wants him captured and brought in for questioning – on suspicion that he killed both Vitellius and his slave, robbed the shop, and took your donkey too.'

It was the last remark which seemed to prompt the foreman's memory. 'Well, in that case, citizen, I'll try to help, of course. Let me think about the man again. Taller than you, but not as big as me. Darker hair than mine but not as dark as yours. And somewhere between the two of us in age.' He paused and looked at me.

'Go on,' I said. 'You're doing very well. Anything that you can add may help bring back your ass.'

He shrugged his massive shoulders. 'I don't know what more I can tell you, citizen. He was simply unremarkable. Not gangly and goggle-eyed, like the other man, nor strikingly good looking either – just neat and clean and tidily turned out. The kind of servant you might pass in the street without a second glance.'

'What sort of voice?'

'Well spoken, with good Latin – I do remember that – and from the way he came over to the board to watch me change the date, I got the impression he could read. And, like the useless one, he had soft hands – not like my calloused ones.' He spread his own work-hardened fingers out for me to see. 'In my job, you tend to notice things like that.'

'That's helpful,' I remarked. 'So more a steward type than a menial slave – if we're making enquires as to where he might belong? Or a courier even?'

'His face was very tanned, like a man who had spent a lot of time outdoors.' The foreman was clearly flattered by my interest in his views. 'Oh, and he wore an ochre tunic that was rather long for him, and really much too tight. I remember noticing the fact when he pushed aside the cloak to reach his purse. I thought it was because he'd recently been bought, perhaps to take over from the useless one, and was temporarily wearing one of his.'

I said grimly, 'And so he might have been – though, if we are right about him, I doubt that he will be wearing anything like that now. Anyway, foreman, thank you for your help. A description will be issued, through the garrison, to all military units within three days' march of here, to keep a watch on bridges and toll-points and entrances to towns – everywhere the roads are guarded – to look out for him. Let's hope they find him, together with your ass. In the meantime, be careful who you tell. It may be that he's hiding somewhere near the town, and if he hears a rumour that we are seeking him, he may go into hiding until the search is past – and then we'll never find him. You may tell the stable-owner when he comes, but please tell no one else. You know how gossip spreads around the town.'

He nodded, thoughtfully. 'Wise counsel, citizen. And in the meantime, if I think of anything more about the man, I'll send to you with word. If you will tell me where you can be found?'

I hesitated. I could tell him where my workshop was, but then he'd know I was a tradesman like himself, although I had the rank of citizen, and his respect for me would fall. So I said, 'Better to send to the aediles, perhaps. Or you could reach me through Marcus Septimus. I live close to his country residence and he would send me word.'

The parting bow he gave me was so sweeping and so low, I knew I had impressed him – as I'd hoped. A brief visit to the temple to arrange a sacrifice, not merely to purify myself, but in thanksgiving for Cilla's safe delivery and for the fact that the baby was a boy, and then I turned my footsteps to the northern wall.

My workshop lay in the muddy suburb just outside the gate, between a candlemaker's and a tanner's shop. It was a place where few togate citizens ever came on foot – for obvious reasons – and I attracted some attention from strangers as I passed, especially as I was unattended by a slave.

So I was glad to reach the shelter of the shop, and find Tenuis awaiting me.

THIRTEEN

He was eating a midday snack of old bread and a scraping of soft cheese, together with a few leftover salted bean kernels which I had bought hot and toasted (was it only yesterday?) as a tasty treat from a passing street vendor. When he saw me, he scrambled to his feet and instantly offered to share his meagre feast.

'Master, you need to eat,' he said, when I refused.

'All in good time,' I told him, as I shrugged my toga off for him to fold. 'I promised to buy some food to take home anyway, so I can eat some of that if I should feel the need. Meanwhile, I'll have a cup of watered wine. Fetch me one, and then I'll sit and tell you all the news. Quite a lot has happened since I left you here – much of which was at Marcus's behest - and I'll tell you about that as we're walking home. The main thing you'll want to know is that the babe is safely born. A healthy boy. The wisewoman was there, and the mistress has pulled through and is recovering.'

'Thank Minerva.' His face split in a grin. 'I did not dare to ask, but I was worried, when there was no word and you'd been gone so long.' He was already pouring out the wine, which we kept – ready watered, in a jug – in case of customers. (No civilized Roman would drink it undilute, of course.) Not quite a cupful, when he handed it to me.

I looked at him, surprised. 'Is this all we have?'

'There's wine, but not prepared.' His grin was shy but proud. 'I can fetch water and mix some more for you, but a new client called this morning, just before you came, and I gave him most of what we had. He asked to see you, but I explained that you weren't here.'

'Did he say what he wanted?'

The shy grin was even wider, if that were possible. 'A new mosaic in his entrance hall. He enquired about the price, and I quoted the same as you charged for the Cave Canem one.

And, master, he accepted that – and called in a witness to hear the promises exchanged. So, you have the contract. I hope that I did right.'

Not only right, but showing real initiative, I thought. That must be first time in his life that Tenuis had sealed a contract of any kind for anything – a slave can't do so, on his own account, only when acting as his master's agent and for his benefit. And here was timid Tenuis doing that, unasked. New business was especially welcome, too, after my last disaster.

I smiled. 'You did extremely well. I shall have to leave you here more often on your own.' I raised the cup in mock salute and sipped the wine.

He said nothing but he stood a little prouder than before, though unwilling to eat without me doing so.

'Finish your prandium,' I said, gesturing him to come and squat down by my side. 'I'll want you to help me with those errands very soon. You can take that toga to the fuller's, first of all – I've made it filthy round the hems by walking through the mud. Then we'll get those provisions that I mentioned earlier – it might need both of us to carry them. But there's a message which I want to deliver while we're out – I might leave the food with you while I'm doing that. It won't take very long.' I took another sip of watered wine. 'Meantime, tell me more about this contract. Who's the customer? Anybody we already know?' It is not unknown for people to come back a second time, if they are pleased with something we have done. And after the debacle of the lumpy dog, I could do with positive advertisement.

Not this time, it appeared. Tenuis was now eating a scoop of cheese and beans, but he swallowed them quickly. 'Nobody I recognized. A man called Appius Limpnus Corvinus. He came in person – did not send a slave. Clearly a person of some wealth. Or of good family, at least. He's a purple-striper.'

The two were not necessarily the same, I thought, remembering that high-born Thaddeus evidently could not pay his jeweller in cash. I raised an eyebrow. 'Appius Limpnus? I've never heard of him.'

'He's only been in the district for a day or two. He's

staying at the military inn. Retiring from Londinium and the Provincial Court, on grounds of health, he said. He'd heard the air here was salubrious and the soil was good for grapes. So he's bought a villa just outside the town and wants to grow some vines.'

I made a doubtful noise. 'Retiring from the service of Virius Lupus? Much more likely he's been sent here as a spy. Lupus has never forgotten who defeated him in Gaul, and that this whole area supported Clodius.' I sighed. 'What villa has this Appius fellow bought? I hadn't heard of an estate for sale.'

'You know the old Cloelius estate?'

I did! And so did everybody in the town.

Until a year or two ago, it had belonged to one of the wealthier local families, loyal supporters of the previous Governor. But they had been denounced. There were lots of versions of what had occurred, but all agreed on the essential truths. Guards burst into the household late one night, killing several servants who attempted to resist, and seized at sword point every member of the family they could find – including the father who was old and frail. They were all accused of treason, bundled straight into a hold and shipped to Rome for trial before the Emperor – the latter probably at their own request, as it is something any citizen is entitled to demand.

It did them little good. All were condemned and put horribly to death – exactly as Clodius's own family had been – and all their assets declared forfeit to the state. The two or three Cloelii who had escaped arrest (simply because they were not dining there that night), were officially 'proscribed' – declared enemies of state and deprived of 'water and fire' throughout the Empire – making them not only penniless, but perpetual exiles, forbidden to return on pain of death for them and anyone who sheltered them. The handsome villa had stood empty and neglected ever since – so ill-omened, as a place of violent death (most of the slaves were butchered mercilessly) that it was now shunned by all who knew the tale. The newcomer had doubtless bought it very cheap.

I gave a little whistle of surprise. 'He has taken that? And does not fear the curse? Then he's either very brave, or very ill-informed – such a fool he hasn't thought to ask why it's been left to run to ruin. Never mind; his money is as good as anyone's. Perhaps the tiles have lifted in the entrance hall, from damp. What does he want instead? You showed him our designs?' (I keep the samples that my father had, small pattern-pieces backed with linen and displayed on boards precisely so that customers can take their choice from them.)

Tenuis nodded, using his bread to scoop up the last remains of cheese. 'I did, but he wasn't interested in those. He wants to talk to you. Preferably tomorrow, if you will call on him there. He wants a special pattern of his own design – "Vivat Lupus" or something of the kind – and he'd been told that you were able to do such things and make them fit the space. That's why he came to us. One of the councillors recommended you.'

I laughed, a little ruefully. 'I wonder who that was. Not the owner of the Lumpy Dog, I'm sure.'

Tenuis grinned. 'He didn't seem certain of the name himself. A high-born councillor, with certain links to Rome and an expensive younger wife, is all he knows.'

'That's a description of more than half the curia. It might be Marcus – though he hasn't mentioned it. Certainly it can't be Thaddeus!' I said, then realized that – of course – it would be typical. A way of subtly humiliating me, by drawing attention to my supposed ineptitude, while appearing to pay me an outward compliment. (And, incidentally, of disobliging this incomer as well – if I made a mess of this. But I would not do so. Letters were a great deal easier than dogs – even if I did not especially like the text.)

I did not say this to Tenuis, of course. 'Then I must take special care,' I told him with a smile. 'A commendation from a councillor is good for trade – I must make sure that we deserve it. Now, if you have finished eating, you can fetch the money pot, and we'll decide what food we can afford to buy. We'll have to shut the shop this afternoon. Tomorrow is nefas in the morning so we'll be closed then, anyway.' (On semi-nefas days no official business can be done at all, but since the auguries are better after noon, everything else can open once the trumpet sounds.) 'We'll put a notice up to say that we'll be back here in the afternoon – this Appius can't expect me to call on him till then – and you can mind the shop in case some other wealthy customer comes by in search of a new floor.'

I had foolishly failed to bring with me the purse from yesterday, but – thanks to a handsome deposit from our new customer – there was sufficient in the pot to buy what I required. So we put the shutters up and set off into town.

Tenuis hurried with my toga to the fuller's straightaway, while I explored the offerings in the marketplace. I am not skilled at shopping – that is Cilla's realm – but I settled on some leeks and cabbages (our own weren't ready yet), extra turnips, freshly baked bread, a container of soft cheese, and two fine river fish. There was sufficient money left to add a piece of beef (a rare treat recommended by the wisewoman to make a strengthening broth, and a change from our usual ancient chickens, the occasional sheep or goat, and whatever birds and squirrels we could trap). There was a lot to carry, so I purchased two old tunics from the second-hand clothes stall, paid the woman my last quadrans to sew up the hems with twine, and used the armholes to make a pair of bags. Even so, it was an awkward load.

I was wondering if I should have called on Rufus first and told him what I knew, instead of waiting for Tenuis to return and guard my purchases, when to my surprise I saw the aedile himself, striding into the forum marketplace. I struggled over as quickly as I could, with my heavy bags.

'Aedile, I was about to come and look for you.'

He looked at me – for a moment with something resembling alarm – but then his face relaxed. 'Ah, townsman,' he said (carefully not according me my rank). 'I did not recognize you, in your working clothes – especially in the forum. And unattended, too.'

It was a rebuke. Strictly any citizen should be togate in the forum – though it is a rule not much enforced, at least not here in Glevum. For lowlier citizens like me, it is mostly not invoked at all, unless an official wishes to demonstrate his own authority, or vent irritation about something else. That seemed to be a threat. (Revenge for witnessing his weakness when the slave's corpse was found, perhaps?) If I was not careful, I might find myself issued with a fine for conduct unbecoming a Roman citizen.

'I've just sent my only toga to the fuller's, aedile. My slave has gone with it.' I gave him my most sizzling smile. 'But I'm surprised to see you here. I expected to find you at Vitellius's shop.'

The effect of that remark was startling. Now it was Rufus's turn to look rebuked. He glanced around, as if to check that we weren't being overheard, then leaned forward – almost confidentially. 'I left instructions as to where I could be found, and have left them to it. There was nothing further I could usefully achieve. The undertakers are busy with Vitellius as we speak. The other . . .' he let the sentence hang. 'The other matter is a question for the appropriate guild. I thought that you were going to ask them to attend?'

'I did. That was what I wanted to talk to you about. They would not agree to come, unless I promised them that some-body would pay. The question is, who should? Vitellius did not pay the dues. The previous owner was to keep them up – that was part of the agreement for repayment of the debt.'

Rufus looked furtive. 'And they didn't tell you who that owner was?'

I took a deep breath, choosing my words very carefully. 'They couldn't, aedile. They'd heard of the arrangement, but could not say who with. I told the guild they should apply to you for instructions as to what to do. There was no written record, it appears.' That was the truth – although not all of it. I had kept my promise to the guildsman.

Rufus accepted this without demur. 'One could understand why not. Obviously, the former master does not wish to be identified, for fear the news would spread about his debt. So, you don't know who he was and whether he had paid? Well, it looks as if we'll have to tell the fort about the slave and have him put into the common pit.'

With criminals and paupers who died out on the road. When all the time his dues were being paid! I began to feel quite sorry for Celerius. 'Not necessarily, aedile. He must have been a striking man – from what we saw of him, and what the Dacian said. I talked to one or two other slaves around the town who might have seen him come and go, and gave them a description. From their replies I am fairly sure that the man we know as Inutilis was called Celerius before, and . . .' I took a deep breath. 'At one time anyway, he belonged to Thaddeus the decurion.'

'Thaddeus!' Rufus exclaimed, so loudly that a passing woman turned to stare. He looked genuinely startled and – I thought – relieved. 'Well, what do you suggest? That I should send for the councillor at once and get him to go and identify the corpse, so the guild can come and take it to the pyre?'

That was preposterous, given Thaddeus's influence and rank, and it was meant to be. Rufus was throwing the problem back to me. But I was ready. 'That might not be tactful, aedile. If the story's true – which we cannot prove as yet – he will be anxious to conceal the fact that he's in debt, and if it's false, the very suggestion would be an insult to his pride. Besides, that corpse is not a pleasant sight – as you are aware yourself. Hardly a thing to inflict upon a senior magistrate. Better to have a member of his household go and look at it, perhaps? The steward – or any other fellow slave – should be able to confirm if it's Celerius or not.'

Rufus looked at me with something like respect. 'Perhaps the steward, since discretion is required – he might even know about the dues. A good suggestion, citizen. I'll send someone to summon him at once.'

I had been promoted to citizen again, but it was clear whom Rufus was thinking he might send. Fortunately, at that moment I spotted Tenuis. He had come into the forum at the further end, and was standing on a wooden box to get a better view, scanning all the busy stalls in search of me. I put down one makeshift bag and waved a hand at him. He saw me at once, and began to weave his way across the crowd.

'My slave, if you'll excuse me, aedile,' I said. 'I need to hurry home – my wife gave birth last night – a healthy boy – and is wanting these supplies. And, since I have given my report, I have done all that I can usefully do here.' I half-expected a reproof for daring to apply his own words to myself, but he did not seem to notice it.

'Then I won't delay you any longer, citizen. You'll be
wanting to make a sacrifice, no doubt.' He gave me the faintest
of bows and moved away.

I found that I was bristling inwardly. It was insulting to
imply that I'd made no sacrifice as yet – as if I did not care
about the displeasure of the gods. And he'd offered no
congratulations or good wishes on the birth. I said as much
to Tenuis who came hurrying up to me.

'He's only jealous, master, because you have a son,' Tenuis
murmured, with a wicked grin. 'It's common knowledge that
Rufus's own wife has so far only given him three girls, and
he is beginning to contemplate divorce.'

I laughed. 'Of course! I hadn't thought of that!' Aware that
the aedile might be watching, I gave the slave the bags, and
allowed him to carry both – but once we were safely through
the southern gate and out of sight, I took the larger one.

'A reward for that contract you arranged,' I said, when he
protested. 'And it speeds the journey, too. Now I promised to
tell you what's been happening . . .'

I gave him a brief and sanitized account, not dwelling
on the horrors. By tomorrow the details would be all over
town – suitably embellished – but I wanted Tenuis to hear the
news from me. He might be growing fast, but there was no
point in giving him bad dreams.

Even the shortened version – by the time I had explained
about Letigines and the clasp and how I came to be involved
– took most of the journey along the ancient forest track.
It was sticky going, since in places the path is very steep
and often slippery, especially after rain, with both of us
changing hands with our loads from time to time. I was glad
when we emerged on to the narrow lane which led down to
my roundhouse.

'Here we are,' I said. 'I'll be glad to get there, too. I haven't
eaten since this morning and I am peckish now. I've been
promised mushrooms . . . Ah, and here is Brianus, to meet us
in the lane. It's been a dreadful day, but at least it's over now.'

But I had spoken far too soon. As I stepped forward to
greet the older slave, I saw at once from his expression that
there was something wrong.

FOURTEEN

'Brianus, what is it? Not my wife? Is something the matter with the boy?'

He shook his head. 'Both doing well and resting, master,' he replied. 'At least your youngest boy . . .' He tailed off, in distress.

'What do you mean? Don't talk in riddles.' Concern had made me sharp.

'It's Carus – your eldest.' He shook his head again. 'I haven't told the mistress – the wisewoman is still here, and she advised me that it would be dangerous to cause her patient grief and worry in her present state . . .'

'Oh, by all the gods, what's happened?' I was distressed myself. 'He went to gather mushrooms with that Celt – don't tell me he ate something that was poisonous?'

Brianus looked piteously at me. 'Master, I don't know how to tell you this. He did indeed go out to gather mushrooms with the Celt. They left this morning, before you were awake – and they have not come back!'

And I'd thought the day could not possibly get worse! I gazed at Brianus for a moment – deprived of speech and the ability to move, like a man struck by one of Jupiter's thunderbolts.

But my brain was busy with a thousand thoughts – all of them fearful. Something must have happened to prevent them coming home. The rain had long since stopped – the ground round here was dry – so it could not simply be that they were sheltering somewhere.

'You think they've met with wolves? Or bears – or bandits?' I found my tongue at last, but each idea was more dreadful than the last and I could not bear to contemplate any one of them. There were always dangers in the woods. I blamed myself for this. I should not have let the children go there so lightly yesterday. I searched for a more hopeful possibility.

'Though perhaps they have merely lost their way? They must have been heading close to where the wisewoman has her hut – Anlyan found that yesterday all right, and he told us that they'd seen mushrooms on the way – but supposing they ventured off the path? It's very easy to get lost among the trees. Or what if there's been some sort of accident? Suppose that one of them tripped and fell – there are lots of fallen trees and unseen obstacles – or has trodden into one of those vicious hunter's traps! Carus could be lying somewhere with a broken leg – or something worse – unable to return or send word back to us.' I was buzzing with imagined terrors like a tormented bee.

Little Tenuis was tugging at my arm. 'If anyone was hurt, master, surely it would be this Anlyan?' he said, emboldened into uninvited speech by the wish to reassure. 'If Carus was injured, Anlyan would have picked him up and carried him. But just guessing what's happened is not going to help. Should we not go and search?'

'Brianus will have searched already.' I whirled around to him. 'Haven't you?' Anxiety made me very sharp.

'As far as I could do, master.' Brianus was abject with apology. 'But not at first, of course. I did not realize there was any problem for an hour or two. With the mistress so weak there were lots of things to do – and I simply thought that the pair were loitering in the woods. But slowly, I began to be alarmed. I tried to alert the wisewoman, to ask for her advice – she knows that area, if anybody does – but she was only concerned for her patient and the babe, insisting that worry would make the mistress worse. I was hoping you would come – I did not know what to do. I had the other children to take care of too.'

'But you did go and search! As far as you were able, I believe you said?' I was still severe – too worried for my son to spare the feelings of my slave.

'I did, master.' He was so piteous with fear that I almost felt ashamed. 'In the end, I took the toddlers for a "walk" – I told them it was to gather herbs and kindling – and we went along that track, but there was no sign of Carus and the Celt. We even called their names aloud – I pretended they were hiding and it was all a game – but there was no reply, and eventually I was afraid the little ones would guess that there was something wrong. When we reached the hut, I had to bring them back. They were tired and I dared not go too far; I knew the mistress would be needing me again and, besides, I wanted to be here, in case you came. Or – as I was beginning to anticipate – there'd been a message saying Carus had been seized, and demanding money for his safe return.'

'Kidnapped?' This was a horror which had not occurred to me, though perhaps it should have done. There were rumours that the rebels had resorted to this once or twice of late, to fund new weapons, armour and supplies. The stories said that they demanded extortionate amounts, and returned their captives piecemeal if the ransom was not met. I could feel a cold sweat rising on my neck.

'Master.' It was Brianus's turn to try to calm me now. 'There's been no such demand. My fears were probably un-justified, in any case. All the kidnap stories that you ever hear are about the children (or the wives) of very wealthy citizens indeed. And always Roman ones.'

He was right, I told myself. I was not a likely target (though rumours were vague about who the victims were – perhaps because the families concerned were too terrified to talk). I wasn't rich, I live in a humble roundhouse and – despite my toga – people perceive me as half a Celt myself.

All the same, there was one question on my lips. 'Where are the other children now?'

'Asleep in the new sleeping hut, master. I took them to the spring with me first thing when you had gone, to cut new reeds to freshen up the beds – before I realized that anything was wrong. So that second walk tired them and made them hungry, too. I found some nuts and fruit for them, and they were soon asleep.' He nodded at the bags. 'I see you've brought supplies.'

'I have.' I handed him my load, and gestured to Tenuis that he should do the same. 'You take these to the house and get some food prepared to give the children when they wake – and keep a careful watch on them meanwhile. Tenuis and I will go and search the woods. But if we're not back before the sun goes past that west-most oak, you are to tell the mistress where we've gone and why . . .'

He was about to protest, but I held up my hand.

'On my authority – there is no help for it. Then leave your charges in the wisewoman's care and run to Marcus's villa to ask for extra help. They will supply some slaves to help us hunt, I know – ask for the lady Julia if the master is not back.' I was about to turn away, when it occurred to me that Marcus would be expecting a report from town – which it was wise to offer if I was asking him for help. 'If His Excellence is there, you can tell him I have made enquiries and I do have news, but nothing urgent, or significant – except that Inutilis has been found. He's dead, and obviously did not commit the crime. Rufus has been kept informed, and everything possible has been dealt with, for the moment anyway.' It did seem trivial, even as I spoke. Fear for my son had driven the events in Glevum from my mind.

Brianus looked expectant, as if waiting for me to elaborate, but I added nothing and it was not his place to ask. After a moment he simply bowed and said, 'Of course, master. It shall be as you command.' Then, carrying both the heavy bags, he hurried back to the enclosure gate. He seemed surprised to find me following.

This time I did explain. 'I'll call in at the dyehouse and collect the axe.' I said. 'It might be useful in case they've got entangled in some trap.'

This was said for Tenuis's benefit. My intention – obviously – was to arm myself, but he was already clearly nervous at the prospect of what might await us in the woods, and I did not wish to add to his alarm. But I need not have bothered. He was not deceived. He knew it was a weapon and he picked up one himself – a knife I sometimes used for skinning animals.

'Should we go together, master, or walk in different directions?' he enquired as we emerged into the lane again. He was trying to sound resolute, but he was linen-pale.

I thought for a moment – but really, there was no choice to make. Tenuis was bigger and pluckier than he used to be – as he was showing now – but with unknown dangers lurking in the trees he was neither big nor strong enough for me to send him off alone. 'Best to stick together – we don't want more people getting lost,' I answered. 'Two pairs of eyes are of more use than one. And this way I can send you running to fetch extra help, if need be. You're quicker than I am.' Then I added, before he could protest, 'Now, here's the little path we're looking for. Brianus has already searched the forest to the hut, so we will start where he left off, and look near the caves and overhangs a little further on. That's where Anlyan said that they were sheltering yesterday, when they saw the famous fungi. Meanwhile, look out for footprints, or places where the undergrowth is trampled down – as if people might have left the path and gone into the woods.'

We did. The track is very narrow, and very steep in parts, but we searched it thoroughly. And the woods on either side. They seemed unnaturally empty – though full of rustlings. We called and called, and hunted everywhere. The only answer was a startled rook which flew up suddenly and made us jump in fright, and – later – the far off, chilling howling of a wolf.

We left the path – there were too many recent footprints to tell us anything – and began to search the coppices and every shallow cave I knew. And we found nothing – until, just as I was beginning to think of giving up, and mounting a full-scale search party instead, Tenuis's sharp eyes spotted something in the grass. A scattering of Jew's-ear mushrooms, freshly picked, which might have been dropped by someone in a hurry, running by. I looked for the marks of little sandals, in case I saw any which might have been my son's, but there had clearly been riders in this area. There were so many horses' hoofprints in the mud that it was impossible to tell who else had been there recently. Or even which way the horsemen might have gone, except that – apart from where they'd crossed the track – they'd been riding in among the trees and not along the path. You could see the trampling in the undergrowth disappearing into the forest either side.

This was alarming. There must have been about half a dozen horses, judging from the tracks. And bands of forest riders – especially those who kept away from trodden routes –

suggested rebel Celts. What is more, the marks were fairly fresh. Which meant that – though finding the mushrooms made me unwilling to turn back – we needed reinforcements urgently. These horsemen were clearly not very far away, and if they so much as suspected that we were tracking them, we were as good as dead. Even with a knife and axe we were no match for one of their murderous ambushes. Not that I said this to Tenuis!

Instead, reluctantly, I signalled to my slave, who was investigating a clump of bushes near where the mushrooms were. 'We will have to go back and get some help,' I said. 'The sun is already dipping to the west and it will soon be past the marker tree. They'll be concerned for us. Besides, in an hour or so it will be getting dusk. We'll need to organize some torches to go on searching after that.'

Tenuis was looking at me speechlessly. In his hand he held a little woven basket, made of reeds, which I recognized as Cilla's handiwork. He held it out for me to see.

'So Carus has been here? Probably today?'

He was so shaken that he could only nod.

'Hold this.' I handed him the axe. I cupped my hands around my mouth, and shouted, so loudly that it echoed from the trees. 'Carus! Where are you? Do not be afraid. We've come to look for you. It's Tenuis and your father. Carus, answer me!'

Silence.

And then from somewhere, over to our left, I thought I heard a muffled sob, then a faint sound that might have been a wail. 'Pater?' Or had I imagined it?

I looked at Tenuis, but he'd thrown down the basket and the knife and was already hacking at the undergrowth. I picked them up and joined him in the task – choosing a route made easier by the horses' trampling feet. Thorns and nettles and bits of jagged branch snatched at our clothes and legs and arms, but we kept on hacking, working towards the place from which we thought the sound had come.

Every few moments we would pause and shout again, 'Carus!' But if there was an answer it was drowned by the alarm calls of the birds and creatures we'd disturbed. In fact, we'd caused so much rustling and disturbance all around that I was beginning to fear that the riders would be back, and that any moment we'd be set upon.

We'd worked our way into an area where the trees were not so thick – a huge oak had clearly fallen over in a storm, smashing everything beneath it, and letting sunshine in. Its hollow trunk had broken at the base, leaving jagged fingers pointing at the sky, and half of its great leafless branches were crushed against the ground, while the others lay entangled where they fell and formed a kind of twiggy barrier. It blocked our natural progress – though I was sure the sound had come this way – and we paused for a moment to take stock, meanwhile looking round for anything that might lead me to my son. There were faint tracks that might have been a squirrel's trail, but otherwise there was nothing to be seen.

I had been working hard at carving out a path, and was breathing heavily. I was despairing now, and getting more alarmed with every gasp. We would not help Carus by getting killed ourselves. I leaned my back against a friendly elm – half of whose branches had been torn off in its neighbour's fall, and shouted 'Carus!' as loudly as I could – one last final effort, I assured myself.

This time there was an answer. Not just a sob this time, but a despairing cry. 'Pater, I hopeded you would come.' And a small form slithered from the branches overhead and launched itself downwards. I just had time to drop what I was carrying and snatch him with both arms before he hit the ground. 'Carus!' I held him close against my chest. 'What were you doing up in the tree?'

'I hided from the bad men. Anlyan showed me yesterday how I could climb the tree, but when I climbded I couldn't getted down.' His little tunic was torn and smudged with dirt and slime, and his grimy little face was streaked with tears, but I'd never seen anything more lovely in my life.

'Well, we're here now, and I've got you, and we'll take you home,' I said, settling him against my shoulder. I turned to Tenuis, who was grinning with delight, and already trying to carry everything I'd dropped. 'Leave the basket, let me have the knife, and you just take the axe. You can run on ahead and tell them he is found, and we are on our way. I rather think Marcus will have sent his slaves by now.'

Tenuis nodded. 'I was really frightened, master. I thought those riders might have taken him.'

'So did I!' There was no further point in hiding it. My young slave had worked out the dangers for himself. 'But they still may be nearby. The sooner you get home, the safer we shall be. You should be able to get back to the track – just follow where we cut the undergrowth.'

Another nod. 'Master, I'll hurry all the way!' And he was gone.

I followed more slowly, with Carus clinging to my neck. He was still sobbing helplessly, worn out by terror, crying and relief, and I was so concerned with reassuring him – and so relieved at finding him unscathed – that we were almost at the beaten track again before I thought to ask. 'What happened to Anlyan?'

'He stayeded with the bad men, Pater.' Carus's voice was drowsy and I realized that he was already half-asleep.

I said no more, but this news made me doubly vigilant. Anlyan had – mercifully – not hurt my son, but this might be a trap, intended to lure me to the forest, as indeed it had. He and the rebel 'bad men' might be lurking anywhere, ready to seize me too – for some purpose of their own. Though what, I did not know.

Perhaps they hoped His Excellence would ransom us – although, frankly, I was not sure he would. So I was very glad indeed that I still had the knife, and gladder still when I regained the trodden path. There was at least a chance of meeting someone harmless, now: someone collecting kindling, setting traps for birds – going to seek the wisewoman, indeed – or otherwise going about their normal lawful business in the woods.

But when, in fact, I did hear someone coming up ahead, I was alarmed enough to dodge behind a tree, lay the sleeping Carus gently down, and wait – alert and crouching – with my skinning-knife poised ready in my hand.

FIFTEEN

Voices. Several voices – male – and none I recognized. Two of them at least. Calling to each other, as if they were a little way apart. And it was clear, from the scattered phrases I could catch, that they were seeking me.

'If he's left the path and got the boy, he must have left a trail. Once we see that, we've got him.' A young and energetic speaker, by the sound of him.

'Perhaps.' A deeper, resonating tone. 'But keep your ears alert. And don't rush so far ahead. We must coordinate. We don't want him getting past us, out among the trees, because no one happens to be looking that way at the time.' There was no mistaking the vigour and authority in the second voice. And they were getting nearer all the time.

I don't believe I have ever been more frightened in my life. I pressed myself against the tree and tried to hold my breath. Perhaps they would pass by and not find my hiding place. But if they did . . . I clutched the blade more firmly. I would sell my life – and Carus's – as dearly as I could.

My pursuers, meanwhile, were making no attempt to disguise that they were there. I could hear the crackle of twigs and dead leaves underfoot and the swish of something – probably a hefty walking staff at least – sweeping through the foliage at the verge. A murmuring of voices – they were not calling now. A muffled laugh. They must be very close – just beyond the trunk where I was sheltering.

And then the noises stopped. Silence. The searchers had evidently paused. Were they listening for movement, just as I had been? I tried to meld still more into the tree, almost afraid that they would hear the thumping of my heart.

If I was spared, I told myself, I'd count to a thousand before I moved a limb – or would it be safer to jump them from behind and hope to kill them both? Surprise might give me an advantage, and – even if I only managed to stick my knife between one pair of ribs – at least the odds against me would be halved. And it would prevent them doubling back, unseen, and jumping me. Supposing that there really were just the two of them. But I dared not inch my head around the trunk to look.

I was wondering how much longer I could stand statue-still like this, when Carus stirred. Only slightly – he was still asleep where I had left him hidden – but it was enough. I had sensed the movement, and I was not the only one.

'There's something over there – among the undergrowth. Something white. I saw it move.' It was the older voice which spoke. 'It might be just an animal – caught in a snare, perhaps, since it hasn't run away. Or some female creature that will not leave its young. Either way, we should investigate. But be careful. Wait for me. We'll go together. This could be a trap.'

And to my horror I could hear their steps again – now coming directly towards Carus, and my hiding place. There was no longer a decision to be made. My only thought was to protect my son. As they came nearer I edged round the tree – keeping as silent as I could, and praying that the crackle of their own feet through the bracken would disguise the sound of mine. I was trying to make a full circle round the trunk so that I would come out behind them by the time they reached my son.

I had to work around a holly bush and through a stand of nettles on my way – a painful problem which I'd not foreseen and which almost made me curse aloud – but I managed not to draw attention to myself. Just as well! My pursuers were now moving more stealthily themselves – only the faintest crunches underfoot to tell me where they were. And then I saw them. Just the rear half of their sandalled feet, through the lower branches of my shelter tree, but enough to tell me what I needed. Two men, with hairy legs. Their backs were towards me, just as I had hoped – but they had already reached the hiding place where I had put the child. They were bending over it.

'Why, it's a . . .' the younger one began, and I launched myself at him.

Obviously he had been highly trained. He whirled around, and before I could strike him with the blade, he'd caught my wrist and forced my hand uselessly above my head. He was about the age that I was, from the look of him, but hardened, fit and strong. One vicious twist was all it took to make me drop the knife. 'By all the gods! What's this? I'll teach you to . . .' He was already reaching for the cudgel at his belt.

'Don't hurt him!' his companion ordered – surprising me and causing my captor to slacken his grip to less than agony. 'Might be the father. The man we're looking for. I rather think it is.' He had bent over and was picking up the child, who opened one small eye – saw me nearby – and went to sleep again. 'Fits the description we were given, doesn't he?'

I was still trying to wrest myself away, when I realized something that I should have registered before. These men – though every bit as huge and muscular as I'd imagined them – weren't wrapped in Celtic plaid or sporting lime-bleached hair and that distinctive long moustache. They had short Roman haircuts, bore marks of having been shaved by a barber recently, and were dressed in a familiar scarlet uniform. If I'd not been hiding from them, and fighting for my life, I would have seen that earlier.

I stopped my struggling. 'You are His Excellency's men?'

'We are. Magnus and Potens.' He pointed, first to himself and then the younger man. 'Two of his gatekeepers. And you must be the citizen Junio. We're sent to rescue you. Though you don't seem pleased to see us!'

'There have been horsemen hereabouts. Rebel Celts. I think they had my son. I was afraid that you were two of the outlaws coming back.' For the second time this afternoon, I found that I was shaking with relief.

'Never been mistaken for a bandit before in my life,' Magnus replied. (Though it would not have been remarkable – he had the build for it. The very name means 'big' and even now – though he was cradling the child – his brawny arms, huge hands, and massive brow made him look extremely menacing. And it was easy to see why Potens was called 'the powerful', too.)

Potens smiled now, showing a row of rotting broken teeth.

'Fortunate for you, that you were wrong,' he said. 'You would not have lasted long, judging by how easily I overpowered you.' He had picked up my knife, but he did not hand it back.

Magnus looked disapproving at this discourtesy. 'But fortunate that you were armed and brave of you to try. We heard about the rebels. That slave of yours came running to the roundhouse with the news, just as were setting off to look for you. He said you'd found the child. Seemed to think that they had kidnapped him. You'd better have him back.' He put the sleeping Carus into my grateful arms. 'Though how they'd managed to seize him in the first place wasn't clear.'

'I was fool enough to trust a stranger with my son,' I admitted ruefully. 'A Celt who claimed acquaintance with my family, but it appears that he was one of the rebels, or had links with them at least. I don't know what happened – perhaps he changed his mind, or they decided I wasn't rich enough to pay what they required – but it appears he let the child escape.' I hugged Carus to me as I spoke. 'Unharmed, I'm glad to say. I'm rather proud of him – he had the wit to climb a fallen tree and hide, so he was above their eyeline if they came after him.' I gave another squeeze, so hard that he protested with a sleepy groan. 'But he's exhausted. I'd better get him home.'

'And we'll escort you, in case the Celts return,' Potens said. 'Unless you want us to go in search of them? See if we can find the scoundrel who abducted him?'

I shook my head. 'You would never find them. They're on horseback anyway, and rebels know the forest better than most people know the town. They would see those scarlet tunics half a mile away, and you would be lucky if they did not ambush you! As for the traitor, we'll not see him again. Or if we do, I'll have him in the courts. I'd know him anywhere. Besides, the child is safe, and it's possible I may have him to thank.'

'As you wish, citizen.' This was Magnus now. 'His Excellence has already sent a message to the garrison, reporting this abduction to the new commander there. They are on the lookout for the rebels anyway, he says, in connection with some attack in town. And more so after this. Stealing children sets a dangerous precedent. I think His Excellence is worried for his own. He will be waiting for you at your roundhouse, by the way. We were to tell you that.'

I had already started to walk back to the path, but I whirled round, suddenly doubtful. 'Marcus, in my house? I don't believe it. Marcus has never crossed my threshold in his life – I'm sure he would think it below his dignity, though I believe he did call upon my father once when he was ill. But I'm perfectly certain he would not go in today. My wife gave birth there only yesterday and it's not yet been purified. He's very careful about that sort of thing.'

(The Romans hold that newborn children do not yet have souls and may be accompanied into this world by inauspicious spirits from the nether one. So houses where a birth has taken place are almost as inauspicious as a place of death. To be avoided, especially by men – other than the father, whose presence is required to pick up the child and recognize it as legitimate – until a proper period of cleansing is complete. Even young women are sometimes loth to call until the naming day, when appropriate sacrifice can be made and the gods are pacified: though none of this applies to older ones, of course, since – once they begin their monthly courses – females are religiously impure in any case.)

'Besides,' I went on, 'the wisewoman was advising that my wife needed rest. Marcus is too courteous to impose himself on her at such a time.'

That was rather close to being impolite, since that was exactly what I'd just suggested that he had done – and I was speaking to one of Marcus's own men, so my opinion might well reach him. I regretted the words as soon as they were out. But I need not have worried. Potens gave his jagged smile again.

'I'm sorry, citizen. I did not make it clear. I did not mean he would be in the house. I should have said that he'll be waiting in the gig, outside the gate. He had his driver bring him down, so he can sit in comfort there.'

Of course! Marcus would no more walk the thousand paces between his gate and mine – or stand waiting in the lane – than he would launder his own tunic or cook himself a meal.

The privilege of wealth! I should have realized that. 'It was good of him to come at my appeal – and send you to help.'

'Oh, he brought quite a group of us.' Potens seemed anxious to ensure that I could not misunderstand again. 'We were to search the woods. All the bigger land-slaves, and any gate-keepers who weren't on duty at the time. Anyone who might be useful in a fight. But when he heard the child was found, he sent the others home – only sent us to come and be a bodyguard for you. The rest were disappointed. Much more interesting to hunt for people in the woods than go back to digging ditches, herding cows or heaving sacks.' He was talking to me almost as an equal now.

His superior clearly disapproved. 'Potens, enough. This is no time for idle talk. As you say, there are just the two of us. Let's just hope it is enough, and we don't encounter any of the rebels on our way.' He gestured to the drying hoofmarks on the path, which we had just joined again. 'There must have been around a half a dozen beasts through here – and not only riders, but pack animals as well. It would be wise to move – as fast and as silently as possible. We should be outnumbered if we met them coming back. And they would have advantages of speed.'

There was nothing I could usefully reply to that. Magnus was clearly right.

I began to walk as quickly as I could, keeping one armed slave ahead of me and one behind. After that warning I was conscious of every crackle in the woods, and I didn't breathe easily again until we emerged on to the lane. And even there my troubles had not ceased. Even at this distance it was easy to detect that Marcus – sitting in his open gig outside my gate – was beginning to lose patience with the wait.

He was tapping his baton against the outside of the gig and shifting in his seat, while his page (who would have been crouching beside him on the floor when they arrived) was dancing round him, trying to protect him from the wind by rearranging the heavy folds of his cloak. Not to his master's satisfaction, it appeared. We could hear the tetchy grumbling from here. Then Marcus looked up and saw us and his whole demeanour changed.

He signalled impatiently to the page to stop, then gestured with the baton as if to summon us. I thought for a moment he was going to stand up in the vehicle, but that might have been unsteady and undignified. Instead, he leaned over and extended a ringed hand as I approached.

I was still cradling Carus in both arms, but I contrived to shift his weight so I could take the hand and press the seal-ring to my lips. I did not attempt to bow, beyond a solemn nod.

'Citizen Junio! I am relieved to see you safe. And with the boy as well.' To do him justice, he really did sound pleased. 'I cannot imagine how I would have felt if it had been Marcellinus who was seized.' (Marcellinus was his eldest son, now eight or nine years old and very much indulged – so much his father's pride and joy that he was sometimes dressed in military uniform and shown off at dinners, strutting with a sword. I wondered if Thaddeus had been treated to the sight.) 'Though of course my boy is older, and would have put up a fight. Not so easy to have kidnapped him. Though I believe that you were duped into actually admitting the abductor to your house?'

This was a dilemma. What was I to say? Admit that I'd had dealings with a Celt, who could have been a rebel – as it seemed indeed he was? And not only 'admitted him into the house' but accepted him as guard, permitted him to share my children's sleeping space and even, foolishly, to take them to the woods?

I said, very carefully, 'It seems I was deceived. He claimed to have been sent here by an elder of his tribe, who had dealings with my father, and now was hoping for my services. He even produced a document recommending him and written under seal.' That was not strictly accurate, now I came to think of it. I wondered what that famous scroll had actually contained. Producing such a thing promoted confidence, but it was probably no accident that one could not undo the knots.

Marcus was following a different thought. 'Then they'd obviously planned this in advance. They'd never have guessed the boy's rank otherwise. He isn't even wearing a toga, I observe.'

'Not to gather mushrooms in the forest, Excellence,' I said, though he was right, of course. Carus, like any other son of a Roman citizen, has his own little 'boyhood' toga with a wide purple stripe, but (unlike Marcus's own strutting child, who wore his constantly) he rarely dressed in it unless there was a feast, or I was going to take him into town.

'You were not suspicious when this Celt knew so much about you?' Marcus said.

'I thought he knew my reputation,' I replied. 'And he proved extremely helpful yesterday, when hands were needed here and you had sent for me. Took charge of the children and walked them to the well.' I was babbling, but managed to stop short of mentioning that he taken them into the forest on that occasion, too. 'Even helped to finish building the new hut. So when you needed me again today, and he volunteered his help, it did not occur to anyone to question it.' Oh, my foolish tongue! I was so anxious to justify myself, I had almost implied that Marcus was responsible.

If so, he did not notice. 'I see. Bringing gifts and assistance to a house of birth is a Celtic custom, I believe. I remember your own mother doing so when my own babes were born. So perhaps I can understand how you accepted it. Though it seems that you've been fortunate. If he was planning to abduct your child, it is a wonder that he did not do so yesterday, when he had all three of them.'

That was true, and I should have thought of it. 'Perhaps it was today he had arranged to meet his fellow Celts and hand him over,' I suggested, and then doubted it at once. He could not have been certain we would offer him a bed. If Marcus had not called me to the villa straightaway, I would have listened to his message when I first got home and sent him on his way. If Cilla had not been in childbed – which he could not have known – she would have been caring for the little ones herself. And he'd permitted Carus to escape – though he'd preferred, himself, to 'stay with the bad men' according to my son.

That alone, of course, confirmed he was involved with them. No one would even *meet* them voluntarily – given the rebels' grisly treatment of suspected spies – unless there had been an arrangement with them first. But perhaps the kidnapping was his own idea, which had not been approved? Or had he simply realized, having stayed here overnight, that they'd overestimated my ability to pay? In which case he must be a leader of some kind, commanding their respect – they would never have accepted his judgement otherwise.

Anlyan, if that was genuinely his name, seemed more of an enigma the more I thought of him.

But before I could say any of this to His Excellence, he was addressing me. 'Either way, that's not important now. The boy is safe and no ransom has been paid. At least, I assume that is the case?'

I nodded glumly. 'I could hardly have afforded one.' Though I would have done my best, I thought.

'Then no lasting damage has been done. I'm glad of that. It might have set a precedent. I have already sent a message to the garrison, giving a description of this Celt, which I got from your slave. They will seek and seize the villain, and I'll see he pays for this. Though I had better let them know the boy is safe. But he is clearly sleepy. Let him go and rest – give him to your slave, perhaps. I want to talk to you.'

Carus was a little large for Tenuis to lift, but I was ready to obey, when Marcus spoke again. 'On second thoughts, my gig-driver can carry him inside – he can hitch the horse against that tree meanwhile.'

'Then take him into that new sleeping hut,' I said. 'Where the others are asleep. Not to the main house. It might disturb my wife.'

The gig-driver looked startled, but did as he was told, carrying Carus as though he weighed no more than a mobius of wheat. I was about to send Tenuis to accompany him, but Marcus spoke again.

'Your slave can carry these.' He gestured to the interior of the gig. 'Speaking of people who bring presents to a birth, I have some here myself – a few little gifts from my wife to your own. Some strengthening cordial of the kind your mother used to make for her, a little gown and swaddling bands our youngest has outgrown – and, I believe, a jug of cow's milk and piece of boiled sheep. Good for the mother but enough to make a meal for everyone. And she's sent a little brazier for that new sleeping hut – I told her you had built one and she did not wish the children to be cold at night.'

He was passing Tenuis the items as he spoke. The boy was struggling underneath the pile, but the brazier and the jug defeated him.

Marcus smiled. 'My page can help to carry those inside. And I am to tell you, if you require a pig for sacrifice on the naming day, our farm will provide one as a gift to your new babe.'

It was more than generous, and I could only stammer thanks.

His Excellence waved my words aside. 'Thank Julia. I leave these things to her. Which reminds me, page, when you have finished that, don't come back here to me. Run to the villa. Tell them that Letigines is to be released at once. He is to saddle up a horse and take a message to the garrison for me. As fast as possible. He need not wait for me to come – if I'm not still here, I will see him on the road.'

As the servants disappeared, each carrying their burden, he turned to me again. 'I must have learned discretion. Your father would approve. So, quickly, now that the listening ears are gone, tell me about Glevum. I believe that you have something to report?'

SIXTEEN

Glevum! In the immediate fright and fears of what had happened to my son, I had almost forgotten the horrors in the town. And there was so much that Marcus didn't know. I gave him a quick edited account, explaining how the second body had been found, and where.

'It was clearly Inutilis, as we'd heard him called. He was distinctive looking – even in pieces one could see he'd been exactly as Draco had described – and I thought if I asked around the town somebody might recognize the man from a verbal picture. And I was lucky. Several people did, and – since their testimonies agreed – I think we can be certain that he was called Celerius, and was formerly a courier-slave. And quite a useful one, by all accounts.' (I was being deliberately vague about where I'd heard this from. I might need my informants and their good will again – if Marcus kept involving me, as he almost surely would. After his help in hunting Carus, I owed him a formal obligation now.)

Fortunately he did not press me about where I'd heard the news. 'A courier? Passed on to act as a general slave? How very curious. Of course, it was arranged as the settlement of debt – but who could have been so desperate for cash, that he would use a valuable slave as payment, in a role he clearly was not suited for? Or perhaps this Celerius had offended in some way, and this was a kind of punishment. You did not discover who the former master was?'

I thought for a moment, then phrased it carefully. 'Rumour says he may have belonged to Thaddeus at one time.'

Marcus snorted. 'Well, it can hardly have been Thaddeus who gave him to the silversmith. For one thing, surely, he would have mentioned it? In fact, he seemed disinclined to believe that there was a slave at all.'

It was difficult carrying on a discussion in this way, while he was sitting in the gig and I was on the ground, especially

as the horse was getting skittish by this time. Perhaps that's
why I was bold enough to say, 'Or the councillor did not wish
to admit to you that he'd been in debt, perhaps?'

'And that's another thing. I don't believe that Thaddeus
can't pay what he owes – even if his wife does have expensive
tastes. In fact, I'm sure of it. He confided that he'd come into
some money recently. Quite a lot of it.'

'You are sure that's true and not a story to deflect his
creditors?'

'There's every sign of it. He held a birthday banquet for
himself, not half a moon ago, and invited half the curia –
including me, of course. So I can vouch for the fact that he
did not spare expense. Only the best musicians and the finest
food and wine.' The horse was jerking his neck against the
rein, but Marcus seemed completely unperturbed. 'And I know
for a fact that – although he was grumbling about the increases
– he's now paid the taxes on all his properties. And he's
currently having an expensive floor installed – that's why he
angled for my hospitality.'

'Meaning that he spent all his inheritance, perhaps?
Indulged his wife too often, then found he couldn't pay his
jeweller? He hasn't finished paying for the fountain either,
yet, I think?'

'Citizen, you may imply these things to me, but be very
careful what you say elsewhere. Thaddeus may be old and
tedious, but he is a councillor. And he's no fool with money.'
Having rebuked me for my impudence, Marcus showed
that he had thought it through himself. 'A trained courier is
worth twice any general slave. So why would Thaddeus
undervalue his?'

He managed to talk with dignity, even as the gig was being
rocked from side to side by the agitated skittering of the
horse. I had to take the rein and sooth the animal for fear that
it would trample on my feet.

Marcus did not seem to notice. 'He could have sold him at
the slave-market – the trader's sure to know him and would
get him a good price. He could have bought something
cheaper, and more suitable, to pay the debt – and still have
cash in hand.'

I tried to match his calm. 'Or pay Vitellius in coin – which he would surely have preferred. The silversmith did not really want that slave at all. He could have taken an apprentice, who would have paid a fee for serving him.' The horse was still chittering alarmingly and I had to hold him hard against me as I spoke. 'Or at least, have chosen his own slave.'

'Unless the donor was hoping to redeem the courier again, I suppose.' He was still unwilling to admit that Thaddeus was involved. 'Though he clearly won't be able to, if Celerius is dead. At least we know it wasn't him who killed the silversmith. Or stole his stock.' He sighed. 'So I'd better go to Glevum, and tell the garrison. It was Celerius's description I gave them earlier, so they will be seeking the wrong man. Ah – and here is my driver, he can take me to the fort. We will have to be speedy. The day is drawing on. I may have to stay in my town apartment overnight. A nuisance, but it's important that the commander's kept informed. He must be told that the slave's corpse was found.'

'He has been. Rufus has already sent them word,' I said, glad to see the driver coming from my enclosure gate. Wordlessly, I handed him the rein.

'Thank you, citizen, I will take him now. A twitchy animal.' The fellow ran his hand across the horse's nose, whereupon it nuzzled him and stood still instantly.

Even Marcus had the grace to look relieved. 'So, we've finished here. And if the aedile knows that the body has been found, there's no need for me to go to Glevum, after all.' But instead of sitting back and waiting to depart, he leaned across to address his driver slave. 'Is that child asleep?'

'With all the others, master. All of them exhausted with relief. The younger slave is keeping watch on them.'

'And the gifts?'

'The older one is taking them to his mistress, now.'

'Then everything is well.' Marcus smiled down at me. 'In that case, citizen, you are not needed here. You can drive back with me, and we can continue our conversation on the way.' He patted the seat beside him.

This was the last thing that I wanted after a trying day, but

this was Marcus, and I could not refuse. I permitted the driver
to help me to my perch, and watched helpless as he led the
horse around to turn the gig, then expertly vaulted up into
his place. Next moment we were on our way towards the
villa gates.

'Keep a watch out for Letigines,' my host remarked, as
undeterred by bouncing as he'd been by skittering. 'I still want
him to take a message to the fort, and tell them that although
the child is safe, your Celt has not been caught. The guards
can look out for him at the same time as the man who killed
the silversmith.'

'But surely they'll have to call off that search,' I exclaimed,
unguardedly. 'There is no useful description we can give
them, or even any indication of who he might have been.
The only thing we can be certain of is that he left Glevum
with a donkey and a russet birrus cloak. Either of which it
would be possible to sell quite easily – and then there is
nothing by which they could identify the man.' I was clinging
to the gig-seat as we lurched across the bumps.

'Except bags full of silver, gold and jewellery,' Marcus
grumbled. 'Though I suppose you'll say that he will have
hidden them by now.'

'If he hasn't fled the country, which he might easily have
done – there are always trading ships leaving Glevum dock
who would be happy to take paying passengers. Including the
donkey if the price was high enough. It would be possible to
ask. That at least would be remarkable. Otherwise, we can't
even give them a description of his clothes . . .' I let the
sentence hang.

'Because once he took that cloak off, we've no idea what
he was wearing underneath?' Marcus frowned. 'That's true, I
suppose. Though Letigines saw the imposter, didn't he? And
mistook him for a slave. That suggests short tunics and a lack
of sleeves. He might recall the colour of the tunic, too, perhaps.
And here he is, now, coming down the lane. We'll ask him.'
He tapped the driver on the back and ordered him to stop.

Freckle-face was indeed cantering towards us. He was
looking confident and cheerful – quite different from the
nervous lad I'd talked to yesterday – clearly proud to be a

courier again and quite resplendent in his uniform. When he reached the gig, he reined his horse in expertly, slid smoothly to the ground, and led his own mount gently alongside. 'You summoned me, master?' he murmured, with a bow.

'I did. I want you to alert the garrison that the child has been found, but his abductor hasn't. Remind them that he is a Celt, and there's evidence now he has connections to the rebels in the wood. Oh, and you'd better say – for confirmation purposes – that my earlier description of the man who killed and robbed the silversmith was wrong: that person has turned out to be a victim too, and I verify what the aedile has said. You understand the message?'

Letigines, like any courier, could quote it word for word. It was quite impressive.

Marcus heard him out, then turned to me. 'Citizen, you're frowning. Is there something with which you don't agree? Or do you have anything to add?'

'I've been thinking about descriptions of the murderer. It occurs to me that by the time he left the shop, he might have wearing one of Vitellius's Grecian robes. I think he must have been. There were no clean garments in the room upstairs. His own clothes would have been completely soaked in blood. Obviously, he couldn't leave the premises like that – and remember those charred ashes in the fire?'

Marcus nodded. 'It would have been alight, until the silversmith was killed, and very hot as well. So he burnt his garments and probably whatever his victims had been wearing when they died, since they were no doubt gore-soaked, too. And we know he took the cloak, so why not other things? Perhaps that's what he had been searching for so frenziedly upstairs.'

'There were no spare clothes for Celerius either, come to think of it. He might have those as well. It would not have been difficult to walk out wearing both. The robe would hide the tunic, and the cloak would cover that. It's a theory, anyway.'

'Which, unfortunately, is no help at all. Vitellius's robes were always oak-bark brown. The commonest of dyes.' Marcus sighed. 'Which makes him even more difficult to trace. You're right. It's impossible for the army to mount a proper search for him. Luckily they have more details of your Celtic kidnapper. Brianus gave us a good description earlier.' He frowned. 'You don't suppose the two might be connected, in some way? That murder looked like Celtic handiwork.'

'I can't see how Anlyan could have been responsible,' I said, aware of what trouble that would mean for me. But my mind was working like a boiler-slave.

It did seem rather a coincidence – this unknown Celt arriving here, just when all this was happening. And if one thought about it carefully, there would have been time for him to murder Vitellius and his slave, before he came to me. He could have changed his garments somewhere in the woods. Brianus mentioned that he had no baggage with him, though he seemed travel-stained. But no one journeys very far on foot without a bundle of some kind (at least a change of clothes wrapped in a leather sack) because of the near certainty of getting soaked. So if he'd come any distance – as he claimed – presumably he'd had one and had hidden it somewhere. Where better than the forest? There were lots of places there, and he seemed unnaturally familiar with the area.

There might be good motive for the murders, too. We knew that the silversmith had not been paid in cash by at least one of his wealthy customers. Supposing he'd defaulted in a payment to the Celts? They are known to trade illicit silver and they are merciless if they think they've been betrayed. So had Anlyan been sent to Glevum to collect the debt, and punish the defaulter? Perhaps with an accomplice who went to hire the ass? More than possible. Coming to see me might be a clever move – an excuse for being in the area.

It would certainly explain why he was so concerned to keep his distance from Letigines, the night before. Freckle-face would assuredly have recognized the face of the man who'd given him the imitation clasp, and was the source of all his troubles. And now of mine, as well. I sighed. A suspected murderer and rebel that I had actually sheltered underneath my roof. A recipe for serious problems with the law!

Well, there was only one thing I could do. Marcus had invited my comments to his slave. I took a deep breath. 'Letigines,'

I said. 'When you were at my roundhouse yesterday, I think you may have seen a visitor?'

He gave an eager nod. 'Certainly, citizen, a Celtic person by the look of him, although I did not see him close.'

'Did you notice anything about him, in particular? He did not remind you of anyone?'

The young slave shook his head. 'It's funny you should ask. I did think there was something vaguely familiar about the way he walked. It reminded me of someone that I used to know, but I can't place who it was.'

I was not interested in fanciful comparisons. 'He could not, for instance, have been the man who served you in Vitellius's shop and gave you the false clasp? Then, yesterday, refused to take it back? Could he have been the one?'

Freckle-face stared at me as though I'd been struck witless by the moon. 'Not possibly. Your caller was a Celt. The man in Glevum I took to be a slave, because he looked like one. He was dressed exactly like the apprentice that I'd seen there months before. Same yellowy-brown tunic, sandals – everything. Not remotely like your visitor. In fact, the man who served me in the shop had rather Roman looks – as if, perhaps, his mother was a slave and her owner was his sire. That is what I naturally supposed. It's a common enough story.'

As it indeed it was. Very probably it applied to me. But I was chiefly interested in something else. Letigines had mentioned 'Roman looks'. I remembered having thought the same of Anlyan. 'Forget the clothes,' I said. 'They're easy to discard – just think about the man.'

'But, citizen Junio, that is just the point. There's more to Celticness than what you wear. The man in the workshop had dark hair, cropped in a Roman style. Just like a slave in fact.'

'He could have shaved and dyed that later, as part of a disguise,' Marcus said, looking pleased at having thought of that.

'That might take a little time,' I said. 'Lime dye requires longer than an hour or two.'

'Besides, citizen, forgive me,' Letigines put in. 'A man can

cut his hair, but he cannot make it grow. It is not possible to
have no beard at dawn, and have a bushy one by that same
afternoon. Or cultivate a sudden long moustache.' I was
expecting Marcus to declare that these things could be faked,
when Freckle-face went on, 'And certainly one cannot change
one's build and height. The man I saw in Glevum was not
especially large – I thought his tunic seemed rather long for
him. The man I glimpsed with you was clearly taller and
almost twice as broad.'

'So, we can tell the garrison something about the killer
anyway: he's dark-haired, of medium height, and wearing
brownish clothes, which don't fit him very well.'

'That accords with the description of the man who
hired the ass,' I said.

'Though that will hardly help. There must be thousands of
travellers on the road who look like that. But I suppose we
must accept that he was not your visiting kidnapper.' Marcus
sounded disappointed.

'We can hardly describe Anlyan as a kidnapper,' I said,
anxious to extricate myself as far as possible. 'He seems to
have let Carus go, if anything.'

'Perhaps. But that does not alter facts. And I'm much more
hopeful about catching up with him. We know he met his
tribesmen in the woods, today. That gives the garrison an
immediate excuse to hunt for them, and also some indication
as to where they might be found. That will please the
Commandant. Virius Lupus wants them rounded up. So,
Letigines, point out that there is evidence that there are
rebels close to here. Give the description of the dark-haired
man, as well, and say I think he was the murderer. Then
call in at the docks and ask them if they saw anyone of that
description yesterday, who might have had a donkey and was
looking for passage on a ship and – if so – where he went.
You understand?'

Letigines repeated all the messages – flawlessly – including
the one he had been given earlier.

'Good.' Marcus gave him a dismissive nod. 'Then go. Be
quick about it. If it's not too dark, I want you home tonight.
Otherwise, you'll have to stay at my apartment in the town.

The staff there know you, you can share their sleeping space. But make sure you are back here as soon as it is light. There may be a letter I'll be wanting you to take.'

Freckle-face leapt on to his horse and set off at a gallop for the town.

'That letter would be to Thaddeus, I suppose?' I said, daringly.

'To Rufus, if I write one. Thaddeus is still staying at the house, so I can speak to him myself. If I can find out – tactfully – who it was that he sold Celerius to, we'll know who owed the money to the silversmith. Then we may be closer to discovering the truth.'

I wondered what Thaddeus was likely to reply – since I knew full well the debtor was the councillor himself, but I did not say so. I simply made a noncommittal noise and waited till we reached the villa gates, where Marcus graciously permitted me to leave.

But I was uneasy as I walked back down the lane. I could not make sense of the happenings of the day – like the pieces of tessera in the ugly dog, I could not make them fit into a coherent whole.

My mind flicked back to what we had discovered at the murder scene. Had someone killed Vitellius, for some treachery, hacked the body into bits, and then gone calmly down the stairs and acted out the part of serving slave, giving the false fibula to Letigines? It seemed he must have done. Then stayed there overnight to serve him the next day. Was that before or after he killed Celerius? And where were the bodies when the slave was in the shop? Furthermore, if the victims were already dead, why was the showroom not bloodstained until later the next day?

And then it dawned on me. Vitellius was bruised and battered while he lived, but the beheading and dismantling of Celerius might have happened afterwards – quite a long time afterwards. That would make sense of what we found. The blood we saw downstairs probably all belonged to that unhappy slave.

But why would anyone want to mutilate a corpse? Simply to advertise that they were Celts? When it was certain to bring down trouble on the tribes?

And where was Celerius, if he was not killed at once? Had he colluded in his former master's death? Or was he a prisoner somewhere, watching horrified? He must have guessed that he would be the next. So why, when Letigines was there, did he not make a noise – even by banging himself against a wall – to signal his predicament? I sighed. It all seemed inexplicable.

But by now I'd reached my own enclosure gate, and I hurried in – to forget my woes by visiting Cilla and my newborn son. That was very satisfactory, though brief, since I was swiftly hustled out again. So I joined the children in the sleeping hut, to free the slave-boys to be about their tasks.

Keeping the little ones amused – showing them how to wind wool, giving them their food and finding the smallest logs to feed the brazier – kept me fully occupied till it was growing dark. Carus, I was glad to see, seemed none the worse for his appalling fright, and was lying on the trodden floor, engrossed in playing with a little spinning top that I had whittled for him as a gift at Janus-tide.

When the other two were washed and safely in their beds, I tried, very gently, to elicit more from him about what happened in the woods. But he shook his head, more interested in whipping at his toy. Or perhaps it was that he did not want to be reminded of his fears. Better to let him get over it, I thought, and not recall things that might upset his sleep. I would leave my questions until tomorrow – there was nothing to be gained tonight in any case.

I let him play beside the fire until I saw his eyelids droop, then carried him to his mattress where he fell asleep at once. Then, having snatched a hasty meal with the slaves, I blew out the candle and lay down on the bundled reeds between the brazier and the door. After my ill-judged trust of Anlyan yesterday, I had appointed myself watchman to the children overnight.

It was a long time before I allowed myself to sleep.

SEVENTEEN

I t was Carus who woke me, sobbing in the dark. In the faint light of the embers, I groped my way to him. I picked him up and carried him gently to my sleeping place. As his trusting little face looked up into mine, I could see the shine of tears.

'Hush!' I whispered. 'Don't wake the others up.'

'I was frighted, Pater,' he confided, as I held him close to me.

'I know,' I said. 'But it's over now and you are safe with me. I won't let anyone take you to where the bad men are, again.' (Or let strangers take you anywhere, I added privately.) I settled back upon the reeds and perched him on my thighs, letting him sit there while I held both his hands. 'It was bad of Anlyan to take you when he went to meet with them. But you were very brave. You managed to escape, and I am proud of you.'

He brightened at my praise. 'I runned away and hided in a tree.'

'I know. And that was clever. When people are hunting someone they often don't look up. But I didn't know that you could climb so high.'

'I climbded up the fallen down one,' Carus said, his sobs forgotten for a moment in his pride. 'Anlyan showed me how to, yesterday.' He spoke so eagerly that I had to release one hand and put a finger to my lips, to warn him that the smaller ones were still asleep.

'Ssh!'

He dropped to a loud whisper. 'And they didn't look, not either time, they just went riding past.'

'Either time?' With my freed hand I brushed the tears away. 'You mean, they came out twice to look for you? Or once when they went out to search and once when they came back?'

A determined shake of the little head. 'Mmm. Two times. The first one was just after I'd runned away. Two of them came chasing after me, but I climbded up the tree, so I was hiding in the leaves. And they went rushing past. I could hear them shouting in the woods, "where could he have gone to", and they stamped around . . .'

His voice was getting louder, but I touched my lips again and gave him an example by murmuring myself. 'But they didn't find you?'

Another solemn shake. 'They gaved up and went back to the hidey place. When they'd gone, I tried to getted down, but I was stuck. I was afraid to shout in case the bad men heard . . .' The memory had made the tears begin again.

'But then I came with Tenuis,' I said, soothingly.

This time the headshake was a violent one. 'Not then, you didn't. Not for hours and years. I stayed very still and trieded not to cry in case the bad men heard and finded me. Then after a long time someone came and it was you.' He flung himself forward, threw his arms around my neck and buried his sobs against my tunic top.

There were a thousand questions I would have liked to ask, but this was not the time. He was upset enough already, without my making him relive the whole experience. But there were two things I really had to find out if I could. How many rebels were there, and what was their hiding place?

I rubbed his back to comfort him. 'Were there lots and lots of bad men?' I said – although without much hope. (I have begun to teach Carus to read and write his name – instructing him entirely myself, as his mother is not very literate, and Brianus not at all – but I have rather neglected helping him to count.)

He surprised me. 'That many riders,' he said, holding up the fingers of one hand.

Not as large a party of rebels as I'd feared. Though – well-armed, well-horsed and familiar with the woods – even five was a force to be contended with. 'Is that counting Anlyan?' I said.

He pulled away and frowned into my face. 'Not Anlyan, Pater. That's silly. He didn't have a horse.'

'He might have had one hidden in the woods.' I ran my fingers through his curly hair. 'Or borrowed one, or even shared one with a friend.' Carus was still frowning so I added, in an attempt to make him smile, 'It would need to be a big stout horse to carry Anlyan as an extra passenger!'

I had not amused him. I had puzzled him. 'What friend? There was only me.'

'Well, he was friends with the bad men, wasn't he?' I said. 'Or he knew them, anyway.'

'Oh.' Carus let out a long sigh. 'So everything's all right. I thought that they were angry, and that they'd catchded him.' He clearly had been worried about that possibility – more than I'd realized. I could feel the tension ebbing from his little form. 'They were very bad men, Pater, they had swords and everything. But if he was their friend, they won't hurt him after all.'

'Perhaps they were just cross that he had taken you.' I was practically certain that this was the case, but I was still trying to make it sound like a joke. 'Where were you, anyway? A hidey place, you said? Was it in a cave?' I remembered that the mushrooms had been described as 'near the caves'.

'The black one,' he replied, which did not help at all. Then he added, 'With flying monsters in.'

That was even less help. There are lots of little caves and scrapings locally, and there are superstitions about most of them. They are variously rumoured to contain anything from gateways to the other world, to demons, dryads and spirits of the wood – or even (more plausibly) the lairs of bears and wolves. But flying monsters was not a version I had heard. Anlyan must have been spinning scary tales.

'Did Anlyan tell you that?'

A sniff. 'He said it stopted people going there very much.'

I frowned. No wonder the poor child was sobbing in his sleep. 'I don't expect there were really monsters,' I said, soothingly. 'It's just a silly story people tell. You didn't see one, did you?'

'I felt one.' Carus was clearly quite convinced. 'I touched it in the dark and it flyed out at me. That's what made me shout. I didn't keepded quiet like Anlyan told me to. And then the bad men knew that we were there.' He was in tears again.

I tried to comfort him, cursing myself for having upset him a second time. And then I realized what he was telling me. 'Anlyan was hiding from the bad men, too?'

A solemn nod. 'It was supposed to be a secret that he'd come, for now. He didn't want anybody else to know. Excepting us. He said if someone told the soldiers he was here, they'd try to make him tell them where his chieftain was – and if they finded him they'd want to make him dead. So it was a secret, and I had to swear.'

A moment earlier I'd almost been sympathetic to the Celt, but all my irritation came rushing back at that. Leading a small child into an ambush in a cave, and then making him swear secrets – maybe fatal ones! Unforgivable. 'I don't know why he took you to the cave at all,' I said, angrily. 'Those men are worse than flying monsters, from what I know of them.'

'He didn't mean for me to have to stay. He only wented in to get his baggage pack – he tried to get it yesterday, but there was someone there. So we wented back today. But while he was getting it from where he'd hided it, the bad men came . . .'

'And found you?'

'Not at first. He pulleded me inside the hole.'

'The hole?'

'Where he'd gone to get it. He didn't take me first, because you have to wiggle through – but then he heard the bad men and he camed and pulled me in as well. It's long and narrow, specially at the top, and it was low as well. It was difficult for him – but not so bad for me cause I didn't banged my head. But it's hard to walk, because it's slithery and stony. And it's dark. But then you come to another cave behind. It's a long way in, and it's dark in there as well.'

'But that was where he'd put his luggage pack?'

'I don't know. I didn't see it. But it was where the monsters were. And then I shouted, and the bad men heard. They called us to come out. And when we didn't, they started to come in. They had a torch – we saw the light of it.'

'So they must have a flint, which meant they'd come prepared.'

Carus ignored that; his mind was wholly focused on his tale. 'Anlyan whispered me to wait, and when he pusheded me, to run between their legs.'

'And you managed to do that? Though it was dark and slippery.' The bravery of my little lad had touched my heart.

He shook his head again. 'Not zactly, Pater. When I saw them, I gotted too afraid. So I didn't waited any more. Anlyan didn't pushed me, but I did it anyway. I wriggled through their knees into the light, and runned away.'

'You did right,' I told him, and he evidently had. But I was more and more confused about the actions of the Celt. He had evidently done more than just let the boy escape; he had actively facilitated it. And quite cleverly. The rebels would have been coming from the light into the dark, and doubtless holding the torch up high, so it would be hard to see beyond its glow. And since they were not expecting anything so small, Carus was able to dart out between their feet. In that narrow passage, they could not turn round at once – giving him a minute or two to get away. Anlyan must have calculated that. So far, so totally commendable.

'Did they hurt Anlyan?' I said. 'You said they sounded cross.'

'They were. They shouted. But they must have been his friends, Pater, like you said, because I heard him talking to them while I runned away. In some funny language I didn't understand.'

Talking Celtic clearly. So, he was one of them. He had been well aware that outlaws used the cave, and clearly knew the hiding place inside. So was that perhaps a rebel meeting place? A regular hideout where they came from time to time? Or even a safe place to store supplies? The story about monsters might be one they'd helped to spread, in order to keep the inquisitive away. People are unwilling to take unnecessary risks where malevolent spirits are concerned.

Which raised another question, naturally. What was really in that pack of Anlyan's, which made it so important to collect – without his tribesmen knowing he was doing it? Clearly something he should not have had. Could it be illicit silver? The stolen jewellery? If so, how did he come to have it – or was it really Anlyan's pack at all? (Once I had thought of that, it seemed so obvious, I wondered why this had not occurred to me before.)

I thought of asking Carus, but he'd already said that he hadn't seen the baggage pack. Besides, when I looked down I saw that his little eyelids had begun to droop. I was contrite – it wasn't fair to ask him questions in the middle of the night – though it had obviously helped him to talk about his fears. But there was nothing to be gained by keeping him awake. There was nothing I could do until the morning anyway, so I scooped him up and took him back to his cosy sleeping place, where he snuggled down and went to sleep at once.

I only wished that I could do the same. Instead, I lay wakeful, mulling over the happenings of the day, until I heard movement outside the hut. I got up silently, pulled a cloak around myself and went outside – to find that the dawn had already begun to streak the sky, and Tenuis and Brianus were starting their respective morning tasks. Tenuis was feeding poultry and gathering the eggs, while Brianus had picked up the empty water pail, obviously preparing to set off for the spring.

When he saw me, he put it down again. 'You wanted something, master?'

'A word with the wisewoman, when she is astir. I've been talking to Carus about what happened yesterday. It seems that they were hiding in a cave, and it is one where the rebels sometimes meet. Quite a cavern from the sound of it – perhaps a mine or quarry at one time. It's possible the wisewoman could tell us where it is – her hut is in that part of the forest, after all.'

Brianus looked doubtful. 'I believe that there are several in the hills.'

'But not all of them like this. There appears to be some legend about monsters living there. Flying monsters. Have you heard of such a tale?'

Brianus shook his head. 'Never, master.'

'Nor have I – though I have lived near here for years. But perhaps the woman has. She lives in the forest very close to there. If there's any story, the wisewoman will have heard of it.'

'Heard of what?' a familiar voice demanded, at my ear. I turned to find the wisewoman standing next to me, fraying a soft twig into a toothbrush as she spoke.

One could see why some people feared her as a witch. She looked eccentric: short and skinny, in a collection of tunics all of different hues (as dangling hems and sleeves and neck-lines testified) and an apron cloth tied round her waist with rope. With her unruly shock of long grey hair, and brightly coloured amulets on every limb, she was a startling sight.

'Heard what?' she said again. If she looked peculiar, she did not sound it in the least. Her Latin was both fluent and correct. I don't believe that she can either read or write (except perhaps her name), but she can calculate money swiftly in her head, and I've heard my mother say that no one knew more about the properties of herbs, or assisting at a birth. Even the villa used her services – for unguents and potions in particular.

I find her frankly terrifying, I confess, though she stands no higher than my shoulder, but Cilla has a high respect for her, and I am humbly grateful for her skills. So, having asked after her patients – both were doing well – I explained about the cave.

'Rebels, eh?' She glanced up from her task and peered up at me, her blue eyes piercingly intelligent. 'I must say I'm surprised. I've never seen or heard the slightest trace of rebels, in that area. Too close to habitation for them, I would have thought. Even in a cave.'

'But there's some sort of inner opening to another one beyond. Not just an opening but a sort of passageway. Very dark and narrow with an awkward squeeze and tricky underfoot.'

She stopped her whittling. 'So probably the inner system is a natural one. It's not uncommon in the local rock. But I don't know any like that which are close to me.'

'Well, there must be one!' I exclaimed, and earned myself a disapproving glare. I risked another one. 'Carus says there's a story that monsters live in it.'

'Monsters?' She looked at me as if I might be one myself.

'Flying ones, he says. He blundered into one and it flew out at him.'

She frowned for a moment. Then, to my amazement she flung back her head and gave a cackle, startling the hens. 'Then it must be the bat-cave. Well, by Minerva! I knew there was a sort of cleft inside where all the creatures went, but I never guessed that it led anywhere – except the other world, perhaps.'

'You've been in there?' I was genuinely incredulous. I'd heard about there being a bat-cave, naturally – everybody had, but did not know exactly where it was supposed to be. I'd kept away from anything resembling that. Like anyone with any sense at all.

Everyone knows what bats are said to do. They carry departing souls into the afterlife. And when they fly at twilight, silently, on those huge translucent wings, and see the seemingly impossible, then disappear into the dark, I'm not inclined to doubt the truth of that. Certainly no man who fears the gods would venture near their lair, for fear of falling through into the underworld and never coming back.

Even the wisewoman thought so, it appeared. 'I didn't go further than the cave mouth, naturally.' She gave me a sharp glance. 'Bat parts can be useful as ingredients. So I've gone there to catch one, now and then. But I didn't realize the cleft led anywhere. Obviously I don't go blundering very far inside.'

'In case you find yourself transported to the Styx?'

She gave that laugh again. 'More because there may be snakes in there. And – though I'm not sure that it's true about the bats delivering spirits to the ferryman – I'm not anxious to put it to the test by treading on an adder in the dark.'

'Dear gods!' I said, struck by a danger to Carus I hadn't thought about.

She gave me a sly grin. 'But if there's an inner cave, and you weren't afraid of ending up in Dis, I can see how it would make a perfect hiding place.'

'And why there was talk of flying monsters too,' I said, wondering why this explanation had not occurred to me. I'd been envisaging big monsters – gorgons or harpies at the least. I'd not thought of little ones.

'Bats are hardly monsters – though foolish folks are often scared of them.' She was childing me. 'They're quite harmless creatures, unless they get entangled in your hair, in which case they can drive you mad, of course. Generally, though, they're quite benevolent. If one of my ladies sees one when she's great with child, it presages a safe delivery. And the blood is good for snake bites, and their hearts and livers are cures for all sorts of maladies.'

'Precisely because they're supernatural,' I protested. 'You can see that by looking at the things. Everything about them is disquieting.' I meant it, too. I am not fond of bats. 'There's nothing natural about a creature that is half-bird, half-animal – any more than there is about a centaur being partly horse and partly man. I'm surprised that even the rebels use a bat-cave as a base. Who would choose to venture down a passage after bats – just in case it was an entrance to the other world?'

'Clearly it isn't, in this case, citizen.' The woman was amused. 'As your son can testify. Indeed, next time I want ingredients I might go further in myself.' She twirled the brush against her palm to splay the ends.

'But how could the rebels know that it was safe? You would have to go in there to be confident – which I can't imagine anyone would do unless compelled.'

She looked at me wryly. 'You speak like a Roman. We Celts have different attitudes to bats.'

'I'm not so sure of that! I remember stories my adoptive father used to tell, about how they would fly around the Samhain bonfire – hovering – because when the boundary between seasons is crossed, the one between this world and the next is at its thinnest, too. "Shapeshifters", he called them – supernatural creatures taking mortal shape. And – once again – they're said to ferry souls.'

She snorted in disdain. 'Of course,' she said. 'I know all that. I am half-Celt myself. My grandmother used to tell me the same tales when I was small – though she believed it, which I never did. I think the creatures simply come to catch the bugs and moths attracted by the flames. Anyway, Druid practices are illegal now, so nobody lights a Samhain bonfire any more – publicly, at least. Though it's getting near the solstice, so there might be danger of being spirited away – if you were of that persuasion. Which I am not, of course.'

She was so anxious to deny it, that I guessed that it was

true. But I did not press the point. 'So perhaps the rebels did explore the passageway? If they were being chased, I suppose they might have done. And once you knew about the inner cave, it would be a safe place to store things, anyway. Though surely even rebels would not choose to linger there?'

'Either way, I'm sure that is the cave you're looking for. Which is what you asked. So, I've given your answer, citizen.' She said this with a sudden emphasis, suggesting that the talk of Druids had unsettled her. 'And now I must get back to my lady and the child. I've made the brush for her, and I'm waiting for the water that the slave was going to bring. Though I see he has not done so.'

I'd forgotten about Brianus, who'd been waiting close nearby – waiting patiently to be dismissed – and I turned to do so and sent him on his way. But he was already snatching up the pail and rushing off towards the spring.

'When he comes back,' I said, attempting to re-establish some authority, 'I'll send him with a message to His Excellence. Marcus ought to know about the cave, especially if the rebels might be using it. He can tell the fort and they can lay a trap. I know roughly where it is – though I've never ventured there. The best way to reach it is from your hut, I think?'

'So it might be!' she exclaimed, sounding suddenly alarmed. 'But do not send them there. I'll give a different route. I don't want dealings with the authorities. They ask too many questions and make things difficult.'

I wondered for a moment why that should bother her. Afraid of being charged with sorcery? Or with association to the Druids? Or simply that – with her hidden hovel in the woods – she'd escaped the census up to now, and did not want to be called upon for tax. (Every free person in the Empire, living outside Rome, is liable for a levy on anything they earn.)

I did not wish to cause her trouble. We had need of her. 'Well, you can explain to Brianus when he comes back,' I said. 'Or better still – tell Marcus's courier. I've just seen him riding towards us down the road. He must have stayed in Glevum overnight.' I called to Tenuis, who was still collecting eggs and was very close to the enclosure gate. 'Tenuis! Run out and stop Letigines. Tell him that I want to speak to him. I have an urgent message for his master.'

Tenuis put down his egg basket and ran to do as he was told, but the woman turned to me. 'Better you tell His Excellence yourself. If he wants more information you can come to me again, but I've no time to stand here chattering. So listen carefully. Before you reach the clearing with my hut, the path forks left. You'll see a fallen tree.'

'I think I know it,' I said eagerly.

She quelled me with a glance. 'I asked you to listen. That courier's nearly here. Get to the tree and turn so you would face the setting sun . . .'

And that, I'm afraid, is all that I can say, because when the fort commander learned about the cave he insisted on two things. Firstly that, in order to stop outlaws using it again, the inner passage should be filled with heaps of stone (leaving it so that only little flying things could pass – even he was a little worried about offending them). And that all of us who knew of it should be sworn to secrecy – otherwise we would soon find out if it was true about bats and the underworld!

EIGHTEEN

B ut that oath had not been taken yet, of course, so it did
not apply today when I was speaking to Letigines – which
I did now, as the woman went inside, and he pulled up
at the gate. I did not give him directions anyway – following
the wisewoman's advice – just told him to report to Marcus
that there was a cave, which I could lead him to, and it was
probable that rebel bands were using it.

'Tell him that if the army is alerted quickly and set an
ambush there, it's likely that they'll catch several wanted Celts,'
I said. 'Including the one they're looking for, in connection
with the kidnap of my son. That should please the fort
commander, and Virius Lupus too. That's the formal message.
But privately tell Marcus that, from talking to the child, I'm
not sure if Anlyan is with the rebels, or against. He helped
my son escape. It's possible that he may be a rival spy, or
even – as I'm inclined to fear – a renegade who's trying to
cheat them in some way. Probably by stealing a portion of
their spoils.'

'Spoils, citizen? You mean things that they, themselves, had
stolen earlier?'

'Exactly. In this case from Vitellius, I think. I suspect the
rebels killed the silversmith, or one of them at least, and looted
everything – perhaps because they thought he'd cheated them
– and concealed the proceeds in that cave I spoke about. If
so, there is a lot of value for the army to retrieve – and they
will be entitled to a portion as reward. Not just fine jewellery
like your missing clasp, but all sorts of silver goods, unset
gems, and very likely solid ingots, too. Worth a small fortune,
if the rebels could contrive to sell it on. Enough to arm and
feed them for a long, long time.'

'Jupiter!' Freckle-face looked startled. 'Is this certain,
citizen? How much am I to tell His Excellence?'

I realized I had been thinking carelessly aloud and it was

inappropriate. I said, 'The latter part is only speculation, I suppose. Just tell him there were rebels in the cave and things were hidden there. That much I'm sure is true.'

'And you think this Anlyan knew there was treasure there?' the courier asked.

I glanced at him. Properly he should have waited for permission to ask me anything. But he looked so innocent that I answered without offering rebuke. 'I think that he not only knew, but went back to help himself to some of it, when he was sure the others were elsewhere. But they returned and caught him in the act.'

There was a sharp intake of breath, and underneath his freckles the boy had turned quite pale. 'Dear Mercury. They'll kill him. If they haven't already done so. They don't treat traitors kindly. So, if the soldiers *do* find him, it will be without his head, if not his arms and legs, and probably dangling naked from a tree.' He darted me a glance. 'I'm sorry, citizen. He was a friend of yours, I know.'

He was speaking sympathetically, but this was dangerous. I could not afford association with the Celt – especially if my suspicions were correct. It was my fault, of course. I had encouraged Freckle-face, by talking far too freely. 'What do you mean by that?'

'I saw him at your roundhouse. I understand he stayed. And you say he helped your son escape their clutches yesterday.'

I said quickly, in a lofty tone, 'Not a friend. In fact, I was misled into accepting him. He was recommended to me by an elder of his tribe, a one-time client of my father, I believe. So, mistakenly, I trusted him. He may have encouraged Carus to escape, but he led him into danger, quite deliberately it seems. He clearly had knowledge of the rebels' hiding place, which suggests that he'd had dealings with them in the past.'

'Should I tell my master that?'

I sighed. Marcus ought to know what I suspected, but I wanted to distance myself from Anlyan as far as possible. 'It's complex, Letigines,' I said. 'So I have changed my mind. I won't ask you to take the message after all. I'll deliver it myself.' I raised my voice to call to Tenuis, who was collecting goose eggs now. 'Tenuis, leave that and fetch the mule for me.' I turned back to the messenger. 'Wait for a moment and I'll accompany you now. I'll just collect my cloak.' I began to move away.

'Before you do that, citizen . . .' Daringly, he touched my arm – still emboldened by my careless chatter earlier. 'Talking of messages, I have one for you.'

'For me?' I was startled. Nobody sends messages to me, apart from Marcus now and then. Unless it was possibly a customer? 'From whom?'

The answer was even more astonishing. 'From the commander of the fort. I think you know what happened to the jeweller and his slave? The one that they discovered in the yard?' He stopped, darting a look at Tenuis who had obediently put his basket down, and was coming through the gate to do as he was told.

I realized Freckle-face was being professionally discreet. I said, when Tenuis had gone, 'Of course. I was there and helped discover him. So you may speak freely, though I don't understand why the fort should send to me.'

'The message was really for His Excellence,' he said. 'But the aedile insisted you should also be informed.'

'Rufus?' More surprises! 'How did you speak to him?'

'He was with the commandant when I arrived last night, to give my master's messages to the garrison. He was also there reporting news, fresh information about Vitellius and the theft. I gave my message – that your son was found – and when your name was mentioned he pounced on it at once. Said that you'd been tasked with finding out about the murdered slave, by His Excellence himself, and any information sent to Marcus should be passed to you as well.'

'And is there information?'

A bow, indicating that the formal message had begun. 'I am to tell you that the slave you found dismembered in the yard was not the one who served me when I called about the clasp.'

That did not surprise me – I had been sure of it – but the circumstances did. 'You saw him?' I enquired.

'Not willingly.' He gulped. The memory obviously affected him. 'Once the aedile discovered that I'd been into the shop and had spoken to the servant, he wanted to know when. When I told him, he declared that it was just before the crimes and I was probably the last to see the man alive. He insisted that I should be shown the head, at least, before the slave guild took the body off for burial.'

'But it wasn't the same man who served you in the shop?' He shook his head. 'Even in pieces that was very clear. This was a skinny person I had never seen before. Well, you know, you saw him for yourself.'

'That was, in fact, Vitellius's real slave,' I said. 'I told the aedile that, but evidently he did not credit what I said. Doubtless he established it from other witnesses.' I was thinking of Thaddeus's steward, naturally, since someone must have identified the corpse as one whose dues had all been paid, but Rufus had obviously been carefully discreet.

'He did.' Letigines replied. 'Somebody called Draco – another silversmith – and the tradesmen from next door, were all called in, and all declared the same. So, who I spoke to is a mystery. He was new, but I was not surprised at that. I knew that the apprentice, whom I'd met before – on previous errands – once or twice, had been killed in some sort of accident. I just thought this person was the replacement slave. But it appears that he wasn't. This dead one was, although I never heard his name.'

'I can tell you. It's no secret anyway. Anyone could discover by asking round the town, which is how I know myself. He was called Celerius and he was really a courier, like you. But he seems to have offended his master in some way and been passed on as a general slave as punishment.'

'Great Mercury! And in a dangerous workshop – quite unskilled.' Freckle-face looked appalled. 'When I offended Marcus, I would only have been flogged. Though that is bad enough. And the fact that I escaped it is your doing, citizen. For which you have my undying gratitude.'

Explaining why he treated me much like a friend, perhaps? It was quite embarrassing and I was glad to see Tenuis reappear with Arlina. 'Ah,' I said. 'My slave has saddled up the mule. And I already have my cloak. So, let me mount and I will ride to Marcus's with you.'

I did so, and we jogged together at mule-pace down the lane, but there was little chance for conversation on the way. Although Letigines attempted to match his speed to mine, his mount was so much faster that he kept outstripping me and had to pause and linger until I caught him up. But we did contrive to arrive together at the villa gate, which was instantly opened by the gatekeeper.

'The master said to watch for you, since you did not return last night. He's waiting in the house. You are to go straight in,' he said to Freckle-face. He merely nodded an acknowledgement to me, but he let me in before he closed the gates.

A servant was already running out to take the animals, and another to usher us into the house. Straight into the atrium – no quibbling this time – where I stopped at the threshold, utterly aghast.

Marcus was entertaining Thaddeus again! I had completely forgotten that he was still a guest. He was looking splendid, his toga even more dazzling than before – probably a different, newly laundered one. There was Marcus, elegant in a different synthesis – and here was I, in an ancient tunic that I'd been sleeping in, with only a cloak to guard my modesty. But Thaddeus was already rising to his feet, and inclining his head in the tiniest signal of acknowledgement. Clearly yesterday had earned me courtesy. I gave a grateful bow.

'Citizen Junio? I was not expecting you.' Marcus came forward and seized me warmly by both arms, shaking them in greeting, in the Roman way. He was smiling, but all the same, I could detect rebuke.

'Your courier called on me with a message, Excellence. He has one for you, as well – and so do I. But I would like your opinion on what I have to say, so – rather than send it – I decided to deliver it myself.'

It was unconventional, of course, and Marcus frowned. But he signalled to the snowy page to fetch a stool for me, as he and Thaddeus took their seats again. 'It must be urgent then. Not more bad news about your son, I trust?'

'The news comes from him, rather than concerning him,' I said. 'But it's news I think the garrison might be glad to hear. But I can wait. Your courier has a message from the fort.

You should hear him first. It might be relevant.' The stool arrived and Marcus gestured graciously that I should sit on it. I did so, awkwardly aware of my bare knees, which I tried in vain to cover with my cloak.

'Well, then.' Marcus clapped his hands and gestured to Letigines to stand in front of him. 'Let's hear the message, courier.'

Freckle-face bowed deeply, then delivered it – word for word as he'd been given it. It began by reporting that the garrison had alerted every bridge and toll-station along the major road, and all were looking out for stolen goods – and also for my Celt. And then, although more formally expressed, he went to say what he said to me – that the slave found in Vitellius's yard was not the one that he had spoken to.

'Thus confirming what we'd already thought,' Marcus interrupted, with a glance at me. 'Go on, Letigines.'

'I am to tell you that both corpses have been taken from the shop. Celerius – the slave – was cremated yesterday,' he said, smoothly introducing the name that I'd supplied. 'And Vitellius is scheduled for tomorrow night. In view of what had happened to his corpse it was decided that it should not be available for visitors to view, but discreetly disposed of as soon as possible.' He took a breath and seemed about to speak again, but Marcus interrupted him.

'But surely such haste is likely to be objected to? Vitellius was a Roman citizen. Even a tradesman of that rank would expect a day or two on view, so that friends and relations could come and pay respects.'

I could see his point, of course. Anyone entitled to a Roman funeral would want to be washed and perfumed, dressed in his best robe and laid out somewhere near the entrance of his house. (Much status rested on how many people came – and vice versa, naturally.) But obviously, in this case, it would be difficult. The mutilation of the corpse removed all dignity – which was the whole point of visiting at all – and Vitellius had been robbed of all his clothes. Never mind his best ones; he had none at all.

I was wondering if I ought to say as much to Marcus, but Letigines had clearly been prepared for this.

'It appears the jeweller had no living family, Excellence. One or two other members of the guild are detailed to attend the funeral, to demonstrate respect – but most of the mourners will be professional ones. And there won't be a feast. No one can be offended by the lack. The guild themselves are taking care of it. And given the condition of the corpse . . .'

'And what about Inutilis?' Marcus frowned at me. 'Or whatever he was called. I hope that the slave-guild took responsibility? If he was dismembered like his master, as I hear, the undertaker would be justified in quoting extra costs.'

'They may do, Excellence,' I replied. 'But it will all be met. His dues had all been paid, by the owner who passed him to the jeweller, so he was entitled to a proper funeral.' I glanced at Thaddeus to see what he would say – and whether he would admit that it was he himself who'd paid the fees, and thus confess that he had been in debt.

I had forgotten how much the old councillor did not know. 'Dead and hacked to pieces? And the jeweller too?' He might have been prepared to punish his former courier by humiliatingly demoting him to general labourer – and in a dangerous trade – but to give the old man credit, he turned deathly pale at this. The news had evidently shocked him terribly. He was already white around the lips when Marcus turned to me, conspiratorially.

'Did the slave-guild tell you who the former master was?' Clearly he had failed to make his guest confide.

I hesitated. But I saw the tightening of Thaddeus's jaw, and the look of furious panic that flashed across his face. That decided me. The old man would make a powerful enemy – and nothing would humiliate him, in his turn, more than confronting him with evidence of his financial woes in front of Marcus and Letigines. Better to do it privately and later, if at all, and rely on my discretion now to earn me some goodwill.

So I turned to Marcus and responded, truthfully enough. 'I'm afraid they didn't, Excellence. They declined to name the man. It seems it was a promise they had made, a condition for his continuing subscriptions for the slave.' (It was not entirely cowardice, either – or so I told myself. I'd bring wrath down on the guild-clerk, and ensure a flogging for his gatekeeper, if Thaddeus ever guessed at what I'd learned from them.)

He had a question now. 'So how can you be certain of the slave's identity?'

'When I described him in the town, several people suggested the same name. He looked unusual. Besides, not so many slaves are exchanged like that, in settlement of debt. It could not be a mere coincidence. The slave-guild seem to have accepted that this was indeed the man, and that therefore his fees were duly paid.'

'I see,' Thaddeus said, with such evident relief I was surprised that Marcus did not notice it.

But it did not seem so. He was turning to Letigines again. 'And that was all the message?'

The courier gave a bow. 'All of the message from the commandant, Master. But the aedile was present when he was dictating it, and he added something that he thought you ought to know. When the guilds had moved the bodies from the premises, he – Rufus – went back to ensure that all was well and that the cleansing ritual was complete. At the request of the neighbouring silversmiths, apparently. They were afraid that, without official proof that all was purified, potential customers might be deterred from entering the street.'

Marcus nodded. 'That I understand. But there was no problem, surely? The priest would see to that.'

'That's what Rufus thought. But in giving his consent to seal the place, he ordered one of the funeral women to put the shutters up again. And there was something on the wall behind where they had been, smears and streaks of blood. Only in one place, and the board had hidden it – the cleansing ritual had not extended to the walls.'

Marcus was frowning, and Thaddeus was pale. 'So the purge will have to be repeated,' Marcus said. 'As if there were not enough bad omens there, in any case. I presume the aedile will have ordered that – though I'm not sure how the cost is to be met.'

'He hasn't ordered anything,' the courier said. 'That's what he came to see the commandant about. When he examined it – brought in an oil lamp to get a proper look – he realized that it was words. A message – a denunciation, of a kind.'

'Naming the murderer?' His Excellence was sharp. 'I've heard stories of that happening. But that is not possible – his victims had no heads. They could not have written anything.' It was his turn to pale. 'Don't tell me it was a message from the gods!'

'From the murderer himself, apparently. It was smeared and smudged, and it was difficult to read – but Rufus thinks he has deciphered it.'

Thaddeus spoke for all of us. 'And what did it say?'

'It said, "So die all informers" – or Rufus thinks it does,' Letigines explained. 'That is why he thought that you should know. It looks like a motive for the killings, he declared – obviously the man had earned the vengeance of the Celts, by passing information to the authorities.'

Marcus nodded. 'Hence the beheading and dismembering. Mutilation and signs of torture while the victims were alive. Leaving them naked to humiliate them even after death. Such gratuitous violence can only mean one thing – a warning to others not to do the same. Writing messages in blood is part of the same thing.'

These details were clearly new to Thaddeus. He made a sort of strangled noise and staggered to his feet and I thought for a moment he was going to vomit in his cup. But Niveus came quickly forward with a cloth and ushered him outside into the inner court.

Marcus ignored this, like the perfect host. 'But it's very careless of the rebels,' he remarked to me, as if nothing had occurred. 'And most untypical. It virtually tells the commandant who was responsible. If Vitellius was passing information, it would have been to him – the army offers a reward, if information is given about a wanted man. And more if he is caught as a result.'

'So the commandant would know at once which rebels it concerned?'

'Exactly! Though admittedly that may not help us very much. If Vitellius told him where they were – and the rebels found that out – they will have moved by now. They must have dozens of secret hideouts in the forest.'

I was about to say that I had information on that point, but he'd turned to Freckle-face. 'Do we know what information Vitellius had passed?'

'Begging you pardon, Excellence, but that's the mystery. The commander swears he's had no information recently about the rebels, from anyone at all – and certainly none from Vitellius or his slave. The only person to accuse the Celts was you – and that was yesterday. But, given the vengeance they exacted on the jeweller, he felt that you should know – since you had now denounced them too, you might wish to take precautions for your own family. Especially as the perpetrator is still – regrettably – at large.'

Now Marcus had turned pale. 'I ought to see that message on the wall.'

'The commander thought so. The aedile was ready to have it removed and for a priest to re-purify the room, if he could be assured that expenses could be met. But the commander thought that, in the circumstances, it should be left for you, if you wish to see it. You should understand the threat. That is all the message, Excellence.'

NINETEEN

N
ow it was Marcus's turn to look horrified and pale. He was on his feet at once – and, naturally, I had to stand up, too.

'Dear gods,' he said. 'My family! I'll have to buy more guards. Today if possible. I'll go to and speak to the slave-trader this afternoon – see if he's got anything suitable in stock. There's no official trade this morning – the day's nefas until noon – but I don't want to wait for tomorrow's slave-market. I know where he'll be storing what merchandise he has. I'm sure he'll find me something, if he can – I have bought from him many times before, and he will understand the urgency.' He had been talking to himself, but now turned to me. 'Perhaps it was my son they tried to kidnap after all – and that is why your Celtic friend permitted your boy to escape.'

This was nonsensical – clearly – but I did not dare say that. What I did murmur was rather more discreet. 'Excellence, I don't believe you need worry about that. Anlyan was well aware that Carus was my child. Indeed, that's part of what I wished to talk to you about. Something which might be to your advantage, too.'

Marcus put on a patient face. 'Ah, of course. You brought a message. I'd forgotten that.' He folded his hands in front of him. 'So, by all means, speak.'

Unlike a courier, I did not have the words by heart, but I explained about the bat-cave, and what my son had told me about the hidden 'luggage pack'.

'I don't think he meant to kidnap Carus, after all,' I said. 'I'm not sure he wasn't attempting to defraud the other Celts.' I told him what Carus had said about the cave, and how Anlyan had claimed he'd left his baggage there. 'Only I don't think that was a travelling bag that he was looking for, at all – I think it was what the killer stole from Vitellius's shop. It must have been taken somewhere, and not very far away – that theft was discovered much sooner than they planned, and the army was put on watch at once for hallmarked goods. And unmarked silver ingots, come to that.'

Marcus looked thoughtful. 'So if anyone had tried to take it very far, they would have been intercepted, you believe?'

I nodded. 'The military have guards on every bridge or toll-point, on any public road, and those within a long day's ride from here will all have been alerted yesterday. The thieves would realize that. But there was time to get it to the forest, before alarms were raised, and that cave would make a perfect hiding place.' I paused, expecting some encouraging response, but there was none.

Marcus had heard me out in silence. 'I see. Pertinent to the robbery, certainly. But how does that help me? And mine?'

'Because we know for sure that rebels have been using it,' I said. 'If you inform the commandant at once, he can set an ambush at the cave. If he captures them red-handed, you'll earn his gratitude, and that of the Provincial Governor – and possibly a portion of the stolen goods as a reward.' (That is what generally happens, of course, when information leads to an arrest. Not that it would matter to His Excellence, of course, but I admit that I was hoping he might think of me, if he was given something for his pains.)

Marcus, however, was not impressed at all. 'What use is their goodwill, if my family is threatened by the Celts?'

'But, Excellence, if the dissidents are caught – and executed, which they almost certainly would be – the threat against your family would disappear,' I said.

I had thought that was self-evident, but I saw his smile of relief.

I dared to press my point. 'But if the garrison is to act, it must be very soon. The rebels must have other secret places in the forest they can vanish to. Vitellius may not have told the army of their lair – indeed it seems that they prevented that – but they must be worried, now, that Carus might somehow lead the army to the cave. Its otherworldly reputation would not save them then – soldiers fear centurions much more than they fear bats.'

His Excellence was still looking doubtful. 'I suppose you're right. Though I'm not sure it's altogether wise to inform against the Celts. I've already made a formal accusation against them. Look at what happened to the last man who did that! And I've set the army on the trail of one of them – your friend. Thanks to trying to help your family! As doubtless the rebels will very soon find out. They clearly have a sympathizer in the garrison, who is keeping them informed. Otherwise they could not know who was informing about them . . .' He broke off as Thaddeus came back into the room, still escorted by the fair-haired page. Seeing us still talking, he lingered by the door.

Supposing that he was courteously standing back to let us conclude our talk, I continued with my argument. I was alarmed by what Marcus had just said. Not about possible rebel sympathizers at the fort – though I should have thought of it. (Given the recent history of the garrison, it was hardly a surprise if there were people there not wholly sympathetic to the current Emperor.) I was worried by the suggestion that because of Anlyan, Marcus saw me as the cause of a potential threat, not only to himself but also to his family.

That perception could be very dangerous. Especially since I did not think it justified. I had very different notions as to why the jeweller was killed. I was convinced that it was not for passing information about the rebels' whereabouts, or their plans for future raids. It was something to do with their illicit silver trade. And since the Celts had already put their seal on the crimes (not only by the very nature of the deaths, but by that macabre message of revenge), there was more to gain than lose now by saying what I thought. It was time to tell Marcus about my discussion with Draco, earlier.

'Excellence, with your permission, there is something you should know, which – if I'm right – might set your mind at rest. I have a different theory about why Vitellius was murdered . . .' I began.

But Marcus had realized that Thaddeus had come in, and reverted to being the perfect Roman host. Ignoring me, he turned towards his guest. 'You are feeling better, councillor, for a little air? I'm not surprised you felt the need for it. The news has been distressing and it's very hot in here.'

Of course, it was nothing of the kind, but Thaddeus seized
on it. 'Thank you, Excellence, I am much cooler now.' He did
not look it. He was white-faced but sweating heavily. He was
also, I noticed with alarm, looking poisonously at me. Evidently
my achieving a private audience with his superior had offended
his social sensibilities. When he spoke again he was dripping
with disdain. 'I hope that I'm not interrupting anything
of significance? The citizen has another of his speculative
"theories", I think I heard him say?'

Marcus contrived to be courteous to us both. 'A theory, but
quite an interesting one.' He turned back to me and murmured
with a smile, 'He does not believe the jeweller was killed for
informing on the Celts.' (I hadn't thought that he'd been
listening, but he evidently had.) 'That seems unlikely – in the
light of what was scrawled – but I am intrigued to know what
gives him that idea. Go on, citizen Junio.'

Thaddeus gave a ghastly laugh, and said in a voice which
was not quite his own. 'Not executed by the rebels? But of
course he was. And that poor servant, too. Who else would
have murdered them in that gruesome way?'

'Oh, I don't doubt it was the Celts.' I turned towards where
he was still standing at the door. 'But I don't think . . .' I
broke off in dismay. Thaddeus had turned paler than ever. He'd
closed his eyes and for a moment clutched the doorframe for
support.

Marcus, who had turned to me again, evidently did not
notice anything amiss. But he'd seen me glance towards his
guest and misinterpreted my pause. 'You may speak freely in
front of Thaddeus.'

Given what I knew about the murdered slave, and the
thunderous scowl that Thaddeus had just been giving me, I
was not so sure of this. But there was no avoiding it. I took
a long, deep breath.

'Excellence, I was talking about this matter to Draco, at the
scene. We think it's possible the jeweller was trading with
the Celts illegally – buying their unlicensed silver, probably.
If they thought he was "informing" about that, as the message
said, it would not have been to the commandant at all.'

Marcus cocked a brow at me. 'So what are you suggesting?

The market police, perhaps?' He sounded half-convinced. (I carefully hadn't mentioned anyone by name, but he must have thought of Rufus, as I just had myself.)

But Thaddeus, to my intense surprise, joined in – in my support. 'By Jupiter! I do believe you're right.' He sounded brighter, suddenly. 'There were rumours in the curia a moon or two ago, that local tribes still had an active silver seam and weren't declaring it. The fear was that it might be used to forge false currency – you remember there was trouble with a counterfeiter a few years ago? The metal could be sold at an attractive price, to someone who would turn it into arte-facts, and lose it in the general marketplace. Another way of getting funds to arm the dissidents. Though it would be dangerous, if anyone discovered it.'

'For both parties.' Marcus nodded. 'As Vitellius found out, it seems. But it all makes perfect sense. If the rebels thought he was being indiscreet, or deliberately intended to inform on them, they would be merciless in taking their revenge. Even defaulting on a payment – even for a day – would bring certain violent vengeance down on him.'

'It would.' Thaddeus frowned a moment, then said suddenly, 'Trading illegal silver is a capital offence – certainly for the rebels, if it could be proved.'

'And if they could be caught,' I pointed out. 'Though I suppose they might have feared being led into a trap.'

'Self-evidently, citizen!' Thadeus quelled me with a glance. 'But His Excellence is right. They would not want to give the authorities even the faintest suspicion of what was happening. In fact, I wonder if, perhaps, he wasn't informing on anyone at all. That message may have been intended to mislead.'

I did not want to agree with Thaddeus – any more than he'd presumably liked supporting my idea – but, like him, I had to admit that this was possible. Vitellius, as a Roman citizen, would – if convicted – merely face a fine (if one did not count disgrace and the loss of livelihood). For the rebels, it would be certain, painful death. And they could not rely on merely disappearing in the woods, as usual. This Emperor was far more worried about the currency than he was about losing a civilian or two (or even the occasional soldier) who happened to be ambushed in the woods.

Marcus seized on this. 'The mere suspicion of false silver being struck would be enough to have the Governor send down extra troops. With orders to hunt the offenders, night and day, and not to stop till they were seized and brought to court.'

'Or, more likely – to save the bother of a trial – simply executed by their captors on the spot!' I said.

Marcus laughed uneasily, as though this were a jest. 'Certainly the rebels would not want to advertise the possibility that they had been mining unlicensed silver secretly! So that gruesome scrawl might be a cloak to hide the truth – pretending the real grievance was a different one, which no one could be much surprised about.' He turned to Thaddeus. 'Councillor, I think you must be right. We know that Vitellius was not informing – to the garrison, at least. I think we can take the commander's word for that. I wonder who he'd taken his confidences to.'

Thaddeus did not attempt to answer that. 'Or he simply owed them money. The rebels would not be forgiving of a debt – we have seen before how they treat people who defrauded them.'

'And it's more than possible that the silversmith did not have cash at hand, when they demanded it,' Marcus said. 'We know at least one customer paid him with a slave instead.'

That was a dig at Thaddeus, of course, and I looked at the old man again to see how he'd react. But to my amazement he seemed pleased at the remark. 'By Minerva, Excellence, I think you might have hit upon the truth,' he said, ignoring the fact that the whole idea was mine, and he'd supported it. He knew how to flatter and he was doing so. 'And the murdered slave? You think perhaps he was acting as some kind of go-between?'

Marcus said, portentously, 'If he knew his master's contacts, and details of the deals, history suggests the rebels would eliminate them both.'

Thaddeus was actually smiling his thin smile by now, as if a burden had been lifted from his back. As probably it had. If Celerius was butchered in that awful way because of something he'd been doing on Vitellius's account, rather than simply because he happened to be there, then Thaddeus could not altogether blame himself. He turned to me. 'You are in agreement, citizen?'

Condescending as ever, but I did not care. I nodded. 'I think it must be something of the kind.'

'Unless Celerius attempted to blackmail the Celts, and so betrayed his master.' Marcus's suggestion was almost casual. 'In which case he deserves his punishment. I suppose we'll never know. But much more likely that he simply knew too much and they had to silence him. So, citizen.' Marcus, untypically, placed his hand upon my arm. 'Well thought upon. Unlicensed silver! I should have thought of it myself. It explains not just the killings but the robbery as well. Of course, if Vitellius failed to pay, they'd have to punish him themselves – they could not involve the courts. They'd see the goods they seized as settlement.'

'It's what the law would have demanded if they could have called on it.' Thaddeus seemed almost gleeful to agree.

'Worthy of your father, I might almost say.' Marcus gave my arm a friendly squeeze. 'And thank you for your news about the cave as well. I'm sure the garrison will want to act on that. I'll see that they're informed as soon as possible.'

I sensed dismissal and was quite relieved. I gave a little inclination of the head. 'Glad to be of service, Excellence. So now, if you'll excuse me, gentlemen, I will take my leave. I haven't eaten and my family will be wondering where I am.'

Marcus, however, had not released my arm. 'Never fear, citizen. We will send word to them. And Niveus can go and find some sustenance for you.' He nodded to the page, who hurried off at once. 'I think you should accompany me to Glevum, straight away, and explain all this to the commandant yourself. If there's a reward, you should have some part of it.'

'And I should also tell the aedile, perhaps?'

'Rufus?' He frowned, and let me go. 'Why did you not inform him earlier, if you suspected this? Matters of trade should be referred to him.'

'We did not know about the message then,' I said, thinking

fast. 'So there was nothing concrete to report. Vitellius was dead and it looked like Celtic work – the rest was purely speculation on our part. And Draco warned it might be dangerous if we were right and we'd reported our theory to the authorities. Or even if we turned out to be wrong. If the Celts found out that we'd accused them, or even raised the possibility . . .'

'They would silence you, as well? For bringing an enquiry down on them? Astute reasoning, citizen, again.'

'You flatter me, Excellence,' I murmured with a smile. But I did not feel astute. Or very much inclined to smile. Inwardly I was cursing my own stupidity. I'd just reminded Marcus of the danger to himself. He'd want to go to Glevum to buy those slaves and take me with him to the garrison. What had possessed me to call here today myself, instead of simply sending my message with the courier? I'd wanted credit for my news about the cave, but I might have guessed that Marcus would dream up some plan for me. And refusal was – in practice – quite impossible. But there was just one plausible excuse.

'But Excellence, honoured and delighted as I naturally would be to escort you to the fort and assist in any way, I can hardly call on the commander, dressed like this. Not in your company, in a visitor's capacity.'

It was more than special pleading. A citizen is required by law to wear a toga on 'public, civic and festal' occasions at all times – and (though it's not strictly enforced in the forum nowadays) failing to wear one on an official visit to the fort would be insulting to the commandant. And Marcus would have contributed to the offence.

I saw him wavering.

I pressed my point at once. 'I would have no authority to speak to anyone. And I don't have a toga available to wear. Not even in the town. The only one that I possess was sent to the fuller's only yesterday – so it won't be ready yet. And I can hardly borrow Carus's – I am not entitled to the stripe.'

It was a joke – intended to soften my unwillingness. The purple stripe on Carus's little toga is a mark of childhood, supposed to offer protection to the boy. But on an adult such embellishment is a quite a different thing – the sign of a patrician, which I emphatically am not.

Marcus did not laugh. 'I'm afraid I cannot help you in that particular,' he said, as though he'd been considering that he might lend me one, himself. 'All my togas have a stripe as well, of course – and Thaddeus won't have any plain ones here, though he presumably had one when he stood for office last?' He turned towards his guest.

Thaddeus tried to look regretful. 'Hired for the occasion, Excellence. The chalk needs to be freshened every time one is a candidate, and it's better done by those who specialize.' Even those of high patrician birth wear a 'toga candida' at election time. The whiteness is intended to suggest integrity. 'Rufus might oblige you, I suppose?' He had not been present at the discussion earlier, so he could not know the irony of this – but he must have known the aedile and I were not on friendly terms.

'The aedile would hardly welcome lending things to me.' I had no wish to borrow Roman robes from anyone. What I wanted was to go back home, see my children, have some food, and – after all the stress of yesterday – spend the rest of the day pottering quietly around. Though, of course, that was impossible. I would have to go to Glevum later on, in any case, to deal with the new owner of the Cloelius estate. I didn't want Appius Limpnus to take his trade elsewhere.

Travelling with Marcus would save me a long walk – or a long ride on the mule – but all the same, I did not want to go with him and be obliged to pay an embarrassing visit to the fort, dressed disrespectfully. It was likely to be a lengthy call as well – formal ones invariably are – and then I would offend my customer as well! Besides, it would leave me in town without Arlina or a slave and I'd have to walk back unattended in the encroaching dusk. (Tenuis is not the only one to be nervous about forest roads at night.)

Marcus was still insisting. 'Never mind your tunic. Come with me anyway. This is an urgent matter, which I'd like you to explain. You are a citizen and entitled to be heard and the commandant is already hunting a man on your advice. I will take responsibility for your lack of proper dress. And I need to go myself – I still want to buy those guards.'

Thaddeus gave a faint murmur of surprise.

'They may not be strictly necessary, old friend, if your theory is correct,' Marcus went on smoothly, with a nod at him. 'But where my family is concerned I'm not happy to take risks. Ah, citizen, here is Niveus with your meal.' He turned to me again. That's most convenient. He can serve you the tray, then go and tell them to get the gig prepared – and I'll take you into town. Thaddeus, you have your litter – do you wish to come as well?'

Thaddeus gave an awkward little bow. 'Of course I will do so, if you require it, Excellence, but – since this is not a matter in which I am personally concerned, and the curia is not in session for the day, I would be grateful to be spared. You will remember that my wife and I are due to move on tomorrow to another councillor, and I'm sure there are preparations she would like to make.'

Marcus said, 'Of course. And until then please treat the villa as your own. My wife and slaves will entertain you while I've gone. I should be back before you leave – with some new guards, I hope.' He held out his hand to Thaddeus, who kissed the ring and left the room, talking his attendant with him.

My host turned graciously to me. 'Citizen Junio, please enjoy your meal,' he added, indicating the stool where I could sit and eat. 'I'll go and get into something a bit more suitable. Niveus can attend you while I change. Letigines, accompany me please. I'll give you a message you can take to Junio's wife.' And with that he turned, and left me to my tray.

TWENTY

The food was simple, but excellent (of course): soft cheese, fresh fruit and even fresher bread. What's more, I was hungry. I almost forgot my worries as I tucked into it. I was just finishing the final crumbs when Marcus reappeared, looking magisterial in his toga.

'I'm sorry to leave you like that, citizen,' he said. 'But there's some urgency. The gig is waiting – are you ready to depart?'

'Excellence, I have been thinking while I ate,' I told him truthfully. 'You want to buy some guards, which you need to do as soon as practical. This afternoon I need to be in town. I have a customer to contact, and it should be done today. If you wish to summon me from the workshop, later on – as if on impulse – my lack of a toga could not cause the same affront.'

Marcus looked stonily at me. 'And interrupt your dealings with a customer? I hardly thought that you would welcome that. Unless it is somebody of no particular account?'

'You make a good point, Excellence,' I acknowledged ruefully. 'This is a new client and, from what I hear of him, a wealthy one. It would be foolish to offend him, the first time we meet. I've not had the pleasure yet – my slave agreed the terms on my account, and I was hoping to meet the client at the site this afternoon, to finalise the details of the design. It should not take very long. Of course it means I shall not be at the workshop for all the afternoon – but your messenger could find me very easily. I shall be working at the old Cloelius estate, just to the north of town.'

'Really?' Marcus was frostier than grasses in the snow. I'd affronted him, I thought, by making his concerns less pressing than my customer's. I sighed. The stepping stones of social niceties are very slippery.

But I saw a chance to flatter. Marcus as chief magistrate

was certain to have heard of any important new settler in the town. There would be letters of introduction to the curia, presentation of credentials and pleas for patronage – if not for actual hospitality. 'The new owners have arrived. Though no doubt you have heard? One Appius Limpnus Corvinus, who's retiring to Glevum from the Provincial Court?'

A silence, accompanied by a deeper frown. Then Marcus said, 'Appius Limpnus? The name is new to me.' If he was displeased before, he was even less pleased now. 'And retiring from the service of the Governor? How did you come to encounter him?'

I began to wish I'd never mentioned it. 'He sought the workshop out. I believe I may have Thaddeus to thank for recommending me.'

Marcus pursed his lips. 'Then I must speak to Thaddeus, before we leave.' (Still 'we' I noticed, there was no escaping that.) 'This is clearly a man that I should know about.' He gestured to little Niveus who was hovering for my tray. 'Leave that a moment, Niveus. It can wait. Ask the councillor to come here. I want to speak to him.' He turned to me again, more friendly suddenly. 'I'm sorry to delay you, citizen Junio, but I don't like the sound of this. If an ex-official from the Provincial Court has come to settle here, generally I would expect to know of it. But there's been no official word. Which seems to indicate that either he's out of favour with the Governor and has come here in disgrace, or – more likely – that he's sent to spy for him.'

Exactly what I had thought myself! 'He claims that he's coming to plant vines,' I said.

'The two things aren't incompatible,' Marcus almost snapped. 'Lupus is still suspicious of local loyalties. Too many people supported Clodius in his claim, and resent the new Governor for supplanting him. It would not surprise me if Severus has sent a trusted pair of eyes and ears to send him regular reports!' He stopped as there was a rustle at the door and Thaddeus strutted in, accompanied by Niveus and his own attendant page.

'You wished to see me, Excellence?' The old man was obviously flattered to have been called upon.

Marcus did not return the fawning smile. 'Junio has alarmed me by speaking of a newcomer to town, whom I understand that you might know. A man retiring from the service of the Governor. Appius Limpnus Corvinus. You recommended him to Junio's workshop, I believe?'

Thaddeus managed to look both affronted and appalled at the same time. 'Appius Limpnus, Excellence?' he exclaimed. 'I'm afraid I cannot help. I don't believe I've ever met anyone of that name.'

Marcus said sharply, 'You must know. It is unusual enough!'

'Exactly, Excellence. If I'd had the honour of meeting the gentleman concerned, I'm sure I'd not forget. And I assure you I have not. So, I could hardly have recommended your workshop to him, citizen.' He flashed me a leering smile. 'Supposing I were minded to do so anyway!' His tone suggested he would do the opposite. 'In fact, Excellence, as I believe you know, I'm currently having a new corridor pavement installed in my town house – one reason why I sought your hospitality – and have actually engaged a different tradesman for the job. And him I would highly recommend, to anyone.'

It was insulting, and it was meant to be. Especially as I knew the man concerned – there was only one other mosaicist in town, who was slapdash and expensive, in my view. (But was very skilled at flattery and had wealthy patronage.)

Marcus was smiling – rather frostily – at me. 'So, Junio, it appears that you were wrong. You must have some other admirer of your work.' He nodded at his guest. 'Thaddeus, it seems that I was misinformed. I'm sorry to have interrupted you. Niveus, my cloak.'

Snowy hurried off and was already back with it before Thaddeus had finished making his adieus. The page bowed before his master, and prepared to pin the garment on, but as soon as it was placed around his neck Marcus seized the fibula impatiently and dug it himself into the handsome scarlet cloth. And snapped the pin, of course.

'There is a curse on cloak-clasps in this house!' he muttered, clearly furious. 'The wretched things are never strong enough.

Come, Niveus, help me find another one. Citizen Junio, I apologize again. I will meet you at the gig.'

I bowed and he disappeared into the house. I was about to go out to join the vehicle (which would by now be waiting near the gateway at the front) when Thaddeus – from behind me – called my name.

I turned, surprised. I thought that he had gone, but obviously he'd lingered purposely to speak to me.

And in no friendly fashion. He was looking murderous. But there were slaves about. He approached me very closely, before he muttered between gritted teeth, softly enough that only I could hear, 'Citizen, I don't know what you hope to gain by this, but I have advice for you. Leave clever theories to your betters, learn to hold your tongue, and – if you value that little trade of yours – don't get involved in matters which are none of your concern.' He nodded to his attendant, who had been standing against the wall, and raised his voice again. 'Escort me to the peristyle, then tell my wife that I'm waiting for her there.'

I watched him go, and sighed, despairingly. Despite my best attempts, I'd made an enemy – and one who could make my life a misery.

Marcus seemed intent on doing so, as well, when I trailed out to the gig. He was already in it, his striking cloak now fastened with a different fibula. 'Perhaps you could make discreet enquiries of this Limpnus person when you meet,' he said, as Niveus first helped me climb on board, and then crouched down between us on the floor. 'I would be curious to learn who recommended you. Someone obviously knew this man was on his way. And this time it wasn't me.'

It was effectively an order, and one it would be prudent to obey – however much Thaddeus might object to my 'meddling'. Marcus outranked the aged councillor on every count – including the capacity to cause me ill, if crossed. So, 'Excellence, I will do my best,' I said. But I tried to mitigate that promise, all the same. 'Though if this Appius really is spying for the Governor, he may not wish to tell me who his contact was.'

'I suppose that's true enough.' He gave a lofty nod. 'But

try, in any case. I would really like to know. In the meantime, let's be on our way. It's already getting late. At this rate we won't be there till noon.' He tapped the driver's shoulder with his cane. 'Driver, Glevum! As quickly as you can, without bouncing us to death.' The carriage jolted off. He settled back on his seat and turned to me again. 'I'll drop you at the gates. Then I'll take a litter to the slave-trader's storage shed and see what guards I can procure, while you go and prepare to meet your customer.'

However, something had just occurred to me. 'Your pardon, Excellence,' I bleated, between the judderings of the gig. 'To open the workshop I will need the key – which is in my roundhouse. I have just thought of it. My slave was carrying it yesterday. So perhaps it would be better if you let me down and I rode the mule to town – it would be useful to have Arlina to come home later on. Also, it means that I could take a slave with me – who could direct your messenger to find me, if I am not in the workshop when he calls.' And, I thought, I might still have some teeth – which were currently chattering together with every stone and channel on the track.

'The mule. A splendid notion.' Marcus was also clinging to the side panel of the gig, but somehow he contrived to speak with nonchalance. 'I was thinking to offer to bring you home myself, if we finish together at the fort, but of course it is more convenient to have transport of your own. So we will stop and get the key, and you can tell your servant to bring the mule to Glevum later on.' He paused as we went over an especially violent hump, then went on as if nothing had occurred. 'Besides, I may need the gig myself. If I procure these guards, I'll have to send them home – as fast as possible, and under supervision, naturally. The doorkeeper from my Glevum flat could do the job – he's big enough to see they don't attempt to flee – but I can't leave the apartment without a guard itself.'

He looked at me to see that I was following. I was bouncing like a harpastum (the hard-stuffed ball, I mean, not the game they play with it) as we rattled on the ruts, but I assented with a nod.

'So if I succeed in buying something suitable, I'll send this driver home, with orders for them to send a cart to town and a couple of slaves to guard the merchandise. The gig can then either come back for me, or I will hire a litter to take me home tonight – depending on how long it takes to make the purchase, if at all . . .' He had been talking to himself, but he broke off suddenly. 'Oh, I'm talking and we have just gone past your gate! Driver!' He tapped the shoulder with his cane again. 'Stop a moment. Let the citizen dismount.'

The driver reined the horses and shouted a command and the cantering horses came smoothly to a halt (though the same could not be said about the gig, which gave juddering protests as we slowed). It was slickly done – but all the same, we were a hundred paces down the lane beyond my home before we came entirely to a stand.

I prepared to jump down and hurry back towards the house – the lane was too narrow to turn the carriage conveniently around – but Marcus put a restraining hand upon my arm. 'The slave will do it quicker. Let him go for you. You understand what's wanted, Niveus? The master needs the workshop key, he's travelling in with me to see the commandant, but wants his slave and donkey to go to town and meet him there. If the workshop isn't open, they're to wait outside for him.'

Niveus repeated the message to him, faultlessly. Marcus looked at me. I thought of pointing out that Arlina was a mule, but decided it was wiser simply to assent. 'Tell them to leave as soon as possible. If they take the short way – through the forest on the ancient track – we won't get there very much ahead of them.' (That was true, despite our faster speed. In the gig, we had to stay on better roads, though that meant driving several extra miles.)

Snowy prepared to go scampering away, but Marcus bellowed after him, and made him pause. 'And, slave-boy! See if Letigines is there. I sent him with a message to the household earlier and we did not pass him on the road.'

'No doubt he has been offered refreshment, Excellence,' I said, as Niveus bowed and trotted off.

Marcus said, 'Presumably!' in an irritated voice, as though he would not have done the same himself – but he would have done, of course. Especially for a messenger travelling on foot, as Freckles clearly was – there was no sign of any horse tied up outside my gate.

'That Niveus has the makings of a courier himself, one day,' Marcus said, with the pride of complacent ownership. 'If he could learn to ride. That would increase his value in the marketplace. I'll have to see that he is taught. Letigines could do it – ah, and here they are.'

His two slaves were indeed emerging from my gate. But I had seen an opportunity and could not let it pass. 'Speaking of couriers,' I ventured, daringly. 'You know I'm almost certain that Celerius belonged to Thaddeus at one time. But he has not acknowledged that – not even to yourself. Do you not think that is significant?'

Marcus made an impatient clicking with his tongue. 'In relation to what happened to Vitellius, you mean? Citizen, surely you are not returning to that idea again? I tell you Thaddeus could have had no part in the events – he was with me when the murders and robbery occurred. And as for having owned Celerius, I taxed him with the fact.'

'And he denied it?'

'On the contrary. He acknowledged it at once. Explained that he had passed the courier on to someone else, because he caught him stealing – or very nearly so – and did not want to cause a scandal in the house. Especially as the crime could not be proved beyond a doubt. Besides, it would brand the man for ever as a thief – and sentence him to starve if he wasn't flogged to death. Hence the demotion back to general slave was at once a punishment, and a protection for any future purchaser. One cannot have a courier whom one does not trust.'

'So he palmed him off on poor Vitellius?' I said. 'Forced the man to take him, too, from everything we hear. That seems a trifle hard.'

Marcus shook his head emphatically. 'That is not what Thaddeus declares. Agrees he passed him on to someone in financial need, who must then have used him in payment of a debt – though he declines to tell me who it was. A gentleman's agreement, is all that he will say – which suggests that it was somebody of rank – and otherwise he is bound by oath to secrecy. Almost exactly as I thought.'

'But, Excellence . . .' I was ready to tell him what I'd discovered at the guild.

He interrupted me. 'I will hear no more about it. Thaddeus is a patrician and an honourable man and I accept his word. And I should be very careful what you say, to anybody else. He complains to me that you seem to suspect him of complicity, somehow, and he is not a man to anger unnecessarily.' He placed a warning finger on his lips. 'But enough of this, the slaves are almost here.'

They were. Niveus reported that he'd done what he was told, that Tenuis was already saddling the mule, and with a flourish he produced my key and handed it to me. Then he climbed back in the gig and resumed his crouching place.

Marcus, meanwhile, was addressing Freckle-face. 'Go back to the villa and collect the horse, and ride to me in Glevum as soon as possible. You'll find me at my town apartment, or otherwise the fort. I have a feeling I may be delayed in Glevum overnight, but I want to buy some guards. This way I can send a message home with you and keep the gig with me.'

Such was the privilege of wealth, I thought, as Letigines bobbed and scurried off again. If I were ever forced to spend a night in town, my family would have to wait till I got home before they discovered what had become of me. And, not being a man of noble birth, entitled to a stripe, no one would ever take my word for anything, against the evidence.

But there was not time to say anything, even if I wished, because the gig was off again and I was fully occupied with holding on, and trying to protect my bones and teeth from being shaken loose.

TWENTY-ONE

Marcus had his driver set me down, not at the town gates as he said he would, but very close to them, though out of sight of the soldiery on guard. (He would have to dismount at the arch himself, of course, since wheeled transport is not permitted in the colonia by day.) Clearly, he did not wish to be observed arriving in the company of a man dressed in a trademan's tunic – even if that companion was a Roman citizen.

I did not particularly care. It had occurred to me how stupid I had been to allow myself to be swept along to Glevum without intending it. I had not equipped myself with food, nor any money with which to pay for it. And there was nothing at the shop, so it was going to be a long day till I could eat again. Fortunately the 'breakfast' I'd been given was a substantial one. There wasn't even any watered wine awaiting me, and although I could ask Tenuis to mix some when he came, he'd have to go to the fountain and fill the ewer first. Unless I had time to go myself before the trumpet went? If not, I'd have to wait until I'd dealt with Appius. Which I'd have do quite promptly after the noonday signal, if Marcus was going to call me later to the fort.

I had no way of working out what time it was, except that the sun was fairly high by now. But as I passed the sentry at the gate, and went through the arch into the town, I could see that it wasn't yet midday. The streets were almost empty – this morning was 'nefas', so the shops and stalls were closed. Even in the forum there was nobody in evidence, apart from a languid slave sweeping down the entrance to the fishmarket, and a trio of councillors, with purple stripes, talking on the steps of the basilica. (I saw that Rufus, the aedile, was one of them.) I wondered what the conclave was about. It could not be council business – the curia did not meet at all on days that were even partially ill-starred.

Rufus glanced up and I feared he'd notice me, so I slipped around the corner and took a different route, but I had not reached the northern walls before the noonday trumpet blew. Trade was permitted in the afternoon, and this was the signal that it could begin. People began emerging from shops and premises, taking down shutters and piling goods on view: builders appeared with buckets, ropes and hoists, clattering up ladders and swearing at their slaves, and the streets were quickly filled with people, handcarts and animals. I found myself elbowing my way towards the gate.

I was glad to reach the relative quiet of the muddy little suburb outside the walls, where the workshop lay – though there was hubbub even there. Already the businesses on either side were hard at work again: the tanner on the right adding his daily stenches to the smell of rendering fat coming from the candlemaker's on the left. At my door I took out the key and let myself inside. Was it really only yesterday that I was last here?

I hung my cloak up on the nail behind the door and looked around. The fire was out, of course, and it took a little while with tinder-cloth and flint and kindling to get it going again. Without its heat the shop was very cold, and also I might want hot water later to ensure the stones I wanted to turn to tesserae were clean enough to use.

Then I collected up the tools that I was going to need: a strip of leather marked at intervals, for measuring; a slate and chalk for sketching a design, and for calculating how many tesserae I'd need; and a plumbline on a frame for gauging levelness. Mindful of the reputation of the house where I was going, I found my protective amulet and slipped it on my arm. Foolish, but I felt a little better for the charm. When Tenuis arrived I'd leave him in the shop and go over to the site and see what was required.

I did not have long to wait. I was just selecting a variety of sample stones, to illustrate what colours I was able to provide, when I heard his footsteps at the door.

'Master?' He came in, carrying a bag. It looked very heavy. He put it on the floor.

I frowned at him. 'What is it you have there?'

He grinned. 'Some of it is food, and there's a clean tunic too. The mistress insisted I should bring a clean one in. You couldn't go to visit an important customer, especially a new one, dressed in the one that you were sleeping in, she said. She is amazed you went to Marcus's like that.'

I found that I was smiling. 'She is recovered, then?'

'Much more herself, this morning,' Tenuis replied. 'Wanting to get up and make the stew herself, and put some nut bread in the baking pot. But the wisewoman says that she should just instruct the slaves today, and do things herself tomorrow – if she is strong enough. I'm to tell you that the babe is out of danger now – there's always a risk for the first day or two, but he is sucking strongly and it's likely that he'll thrive. So you can start to choose a name for him – I presume he'll have a bulla day, as Carus did?'

'Marcus has already promised us a pig,' I said. 'But if I'm to call on Appius, I had better go at once. It's quite a long walk to the Cloelius estate – the Limpnus Corvinus estate I suppose I should say now.'

'Well, you can take Arlina,' Tenuis said. 'I thought you might need her. I've tied her up in the alleyway outside. But don't you want to eat before you go, and look at what is in the parcel that I brought? The mistress has sent you cold meat and everything. And there's . . .'

I raised a hand to stop the flow. 'All in good time. Food can wait till I come back. I ate at Marcus's. He has a plan to summon me a little later on, but I want to do this first, or I might lose the contract. I'll have the tunic, though.'

He took it out. It had been freshly laundered – by Cilla, in the stream, so it smelled much fresher than anything the fuller cleans. I pulled it on, on top of what I wore. Instantly I felt a great deal more respectable. I left Tenuis to fetch water and then mind the shop for me.

'Put some water in the pan above the fire to heat, and mix the rest into the wine. Then you can sort and wash that pile of stones and sweep the floors. I should be back within an hour or two at most. And if Marcus sends a slave for me, meanwhile, you know where I will be.' I went out, found Arlina, and set off to my task.

It did not take long to reach the villa on the mule. The Cloelius estate is not far from the town, though it was not a place I'd ever been before. I knew that it had fallen into ruin – its dreadful ill-omened history had seen to that – and I expected to find collapsing walls and a gate that had fallen off its hinge. But Appius Limpnus had wasted little time. There were builders already busily at work, and a burly slave in orange uniform was on duty at the entrance gate. He was armed with a cudgel and he looked at me suspiciously.

I explained my business and his manner changed. He stood back to let me pass. 'You'll find the master in the atrium,' he said. 'If you can call it that. Don't wait to be escorted. He's only bought a dozen slaves, as yet – including me – and most of them are clearing dust and debris from the rooms, or cleaning out the underground amphorae by the kitchen block, so he can safely store his oil and grain.' He looked at Arlina. 'You'd better leave that here. I'll keep an eye on it.'

It was friendly. I attempted to respond. 'I've never met this Appius Limpnus,' I confided with a smile. 'What kind of man is he?'

A step too far. The smile was not returned. 'You'll find out, tradesman.' He seemed to realize that he'd taken me aback, and he hastened to atone. 'He only bought me yesterday, so I don't know myself. But much what you'd expect from a man who served at the Provincial Court – from what I see of him. Thinks himself an eagle, too important catch flies.'

I was actually grinning as I walked across the court – or what might have been a court and garden if it had been cleared. At the moment it was a wilderness of bracken, scrub and weeds – though one could see bits of statue hidden in the leaves, and a stone circle which had clearly held a fountain once. This must have been a splendid villa in its time.

I picked my way across the broken paving stones and reached the portico. As I had been warned, there was no slave on duty and a tentative tapping did not bring one out.

The door was open. Very daringly, I ventured in. The house was beautiful – or had been – and in a better state than I'd imagined it. Appius Limpnus was fortunate, if he did not mind a curse. Even the painted murals in the passageway – though streaked with mould and grime – would clean, and the loops of leaves and flowers would come to life again. Unlike the previous inhabitants, I thought! It was chilling to think of what had happened here. I touched the lucky bracelet round my arm and took the last few steps towards the atrium.

Appius Limpnus was standing in the middle of the room, talking to a slave in Grecian robes who was furiously scribbling on a wax tablet as his master spoke.

If Appius thought himself an eagle (as the gatekeeper had said) it was certain that he resembled one. The hooked nose was prominent enough to be a beak, the hair was thin and grey and fluffy on the top – reminding me of down – while the cold grey eyes were set unusually high, so that they made him look like some human bird of prey. No toga, naturally, since he was at home. Instead he was dressed in a tunic of white wool – a long one, with decorative bands at the neck and hem and also round the sleeves, which reached almost to his wrists. It was fastened at the waist with a multicoloured plaited fabric belt. (Obviously fashionable in Londinium – much shorter hems and sleeves were customary here, and that fancy girdle would be thought effeminate.)

But he had seen me, and had turned in my direction now – leaving the servant poring over whatever he had written in the wax. 'Who are you?' The voice was sharp as ice. 'What are you doing here? How did you pass the gate? This is a private residence.'

I scraped a bow, and introduced myself. 'I understand you wanted a pavement, citizen? I was asked to call on you.' It occurred to me that it was not obvious where this mosaic should be put. The floors were dirty, and had lifted here and there, but generally they seemed in reasonable repair, and the patterns were attractive, as far as I could see. The one in this room depicted hunting scenes.

Appius saw me looking. 'Not here. It's wanted in the passage to the summer dining wing. My steward here will show you. It must be changed and soon. Sylvanus, take him there.'

Sylvanus put his writing-block away and escorted me towards an inner door. 'This way, tradesman, if you'd like to follow me?' And he led the way into the interior.

There clearly had been some attempt to clean the place – dust had been swept into piles here and there, and we passed a slave-girl scurrying with a pail. I noticed votive offerings at the household shrine – someone was attempting to appease the gods – and there was a sharp smell of incense in the air. All the same there was an eerie atmosphere. Once I thought I saw old bloodstains on the wall and I was glad of the comforting presence of my charm.

What I was not prepared for was the 'passageway'. I had envisaged some narrow corridor, but this was a proper little anteroom. (Perhaps I should not have been surprised – the whole notion of a separate 'summer dining wing' is an advertisement of wealth.)

It was a striking floor, in very good repair, but I could see why Appius wanted it removed.

A simple pavement, paved in black and white with a stylish key pattern around the edge, featuring some kind of creature like a snake with legs and teeth, and underneath, in Roman script, the words 'Vivat Albinus' picked out in vivid red. Of course the Cloelii, and no doubt their dinner guests, were supporters of that unhappy governor. That, indeed, had been the reason for their fall. No wonder that Appius required something different. And why he'd chosen 'Vivat Lupus' as a substitute.

Of course, it would depend on how much he wanted changed, but the job need not be difficult (beyond the inevitable task of taking up existing tiles). I got out my plumbline frame and set it on the floor. The string that held the dangling weight hung straight across the mark, indicating that the present pavement was still lying flat. It would be possible, I thought, to lift just the centre of the right-hand side, and substitute the word. With care I might be able to reuse some stones. The last two letters might even stay intact.

I got out my leather tape and measured up the area. Spacing the words would be the hardest thing. The new design was shorter, but the result must still look balanced in the end. If I placed each downstroke just a little more apart . . . I seized my slate and started sketching frantically.

'Ah, there you are, Sylvanus.' It was Appius approaching

from the rear. I had forgotten that the steward was still there. 'And the pavement-maker too. Making drawings, I observe. Is this a contract you can easily fulfil?'

It was my father's precept that, with any customer, if you found a way to save him money you should tell him so. It would redound to your advantage later on. So I explained my plan. 'If that would be satisfactory?' I enquired.

To my surprise he shook his head. 'I want that crocodilius removed,' he said, pointing at what I'd thought to be a snake. 'It was a symbol for the traitorous governor – they have the creatures in the part of Africa where he was born apparently, and he favoured the design. Replace it with something more appropriate.'

I resisted the temptation to suggest a bird of prey. 'A wolf, perhaps,' I said – since, after all, that is what Lupus means. 'Or a big dog at least.'

He gave me a look that suggested that he had heard about my last attempt at that. 'Perhaps a harvest scene. Or food, like apples, bread and meat. Whatever's easiest. And if you've finished here, I would like my steward back. He has other tasks to do. When can I expect you to begin the task? Tomorrow?'

'Not tomorrow,' I said quickly. 'I am required elsewhere. But perhaps the next day, if it isn't an ill-omened one.' I was sure it wasn't but I wanted to look keen. 'I'll check the market calendar. It will take a little time to take up unwanted tiles – that pavement has been laid with quality. That is the first thing to be done., and I'll certainly send my slave to get to work on that. Meantime, I can make a start on the design. The lettering is quite simple, if I can keep it square – and a plate of fruit and bread would not be difficult.' I sketched out something quickly on my slate, and held it out for him. 'A bit like this perhaps? I can draw that on to a piece of cloth and stick the tiles to it, and bring it here in one piece on a cart. Then I can lay it upside down in new cement and soak the fabric off. It should not take me many days – though it is skilled, of course.' I added that quickly. I didn't want him quibbling about the price.

Too late. Appius was uninterested in technicalities. 'Very

well. And when you've finished to my satisfaction, I will see that you are paid. I take it that, in the light of what you say, you will not expect the full amount? Shall we say a discount of ten per cent? In the meantime, here is the advance that I agreed.' He handed me a meagre five denarii.

That was entirely my own fault, of course, but I was glad to have the coins. And really, I would have quoted even less for the whole job, if I had seen it and costed it myself. Tenuis had done very well for me. So I thanked Appius (who clearly thought he had a bargain now), then allowed the steward to show me to the gate, where Arlina was waiting patiently.

I took her from the burly gatekeeper and rode her to the shop.

TWENTY-TWO

Tenuis was waiting with a cup of watered wine, which he thrust into my hands as soon as I arrived. 'Should I take Arlina to the hiring-stables?' he enquired. (I have an arrangement, dating from my father's time, to leave her in their care when I am working in the shop, rather than simply tethering her outside for many hours.)

But I shook my head. 'Marcus will be sending for me very soon, so I can ride her to the fort, and we'll take her home from there. Which means that you had better come as well, and hold her while I'm talking to the commandant.' I looked around. 'You've done a good job sorting out the stones, and I see you've washed them too, so we have finished here. Except for copying my sketch on to a cloth and making sure the measurements are right.'

I showed him the quick drawing that I'd done.

'Bread and apples and an amphora?' he hazarded.

'I'm glad that you can tell. I've made it as simple a design as possible. It's got to fit in where a crocodilius was. We'll have to lift that first, and several of the letters on the existing floor – but I've told him we can't do that for a day or two. We can make a start on marking out the linen backing today – but even that can wait, if Marcus's summons comes. In the meantime, what about that food you promised me? I'm beginning to feel like something – it's a long time since I ate.'

Tenuis grinned and fetched the sack from where he'd hidden it. 'A piece of meat, a piece of bread and a twist of roasted beans,' he said, producing each of them in turn. 'And Brianus said I was to bring you this. I don't know what it is. He had to change all the youngsters' bedding-reeds today – you know what children are: he had to remove them and throw them all away, instead of simply putting fresh ones on the top. He

found this hidden underneath them, by the wall.' He handed
me a stained and tattered linen bag.

For a moment I stared stupidly at it. Then I realized what
it was. 'This belonged to Anlyan,' I said. Tenuis, of course,
had never seen it up till now. 'He didn't take it with him, when
he went?'

'It doesn't seem so, master. Brianus was surprised. He has
not told the mistress, I don't think – she may be stronger, but
he did not want to remind her of her fright of yesterday.
But he thought that you should see it.'

I had already taken out the scroll and was picking ineffectu-
ally at the knots again. 'It's a letter recommending him. I don't
know what use it can be now – except it might tell us more
about the Celt I suppose.' In retrospect, it frightened me how
little I had known, and how easily I'd been persuaded to let
him in my house. I frowned at Tenuis. 'Why did you not tell
me about this before?'

'I did try, master,' he replied. 'But you were in a hurry to
be gone. Besides, I didn't think it was important now. It was
clearly Anlyan's. Whoever he was, he obviously isn't coming
back. Though I rather wish I'd met him, from what I hear of
him. He might have taught me how to make a roundhouse, so
I could be more use to you.'

I looked at the little slave-boy in surprise. It had not occurred
to me that he might have ambitions of that kind. 'I'll have to
show you,' I said. 'Though it may not be of use – the mistress
has ambitions to have a stone house soon.' He looked disappointed and I tried a little jest. 'But you'll have to ask
Carus, when it comes to climbing trees. And someone ought
to teach me how to undo knots!' I was still plucking at them
uselessly. 'Though why should I be careful? The Celt has
clearly gone. He won't be needing to use the scroll again. Pass
me that knife and I will cut the strings.'

Tenuis did as I requested, pausing only to whet the blade
against my sharpening stone. It was strange to be cutting the
restraining ties – years of being careful of some things
are hard to overcome – but I put the knife against each knot
and cut the ribbon free. A scroll of parchment cascaded through

my hands – the squid ink blurred and blotted with old age, and everywhere crossed with writing going the other way. I found the beginning – which had rolled down to the floor – and I began to read it.

'*To Junio best beloved. From Arthekgour, elder of the Dumnonoii and owner of the ox.*'

I frowned. The name meant nothing to me. As for the tribe, I had scarcely heard of them. But the ox . . .?

'Master, what is it?' Tenuis was alarmed. 'You have turned quite pale.'

'It's a letter from . . .' I was about to say 'my father' when I realized that I should not. The writer – whom I had last seen driving southwards in an oxcart – was carefully avoiding identifying himself that way in the text. That was to protect the messenger, of course. If he'd been intercepted and the letter read, Anlyan – who was not a citizen – might have been subjected to the torturers. They'd force him to tell them where the exile was, and – more fatally – confess the crime of having helped him to escape arrest and trial. And the same thing might be dangerous for me. I had brought father the oxcart, after all, when Marcus thought he was escaping on a northbound ship.

Fortunately, I had been reading silently. And though it was written in standard script and all the ink had run, I realized that this was indeed a dear familiar hand. I found that there was moisture in my eyes. I looked up to find Tenuis staring anxiously at me.

'From somebody I know,' I finished, when I could speak again. 'At least it claims to be. Let me see what else he has to say.'

'*By the time this reaches you,*' the manuscript went on, '*I will almost certainly be dead.*' I gulped. I was seriously in danger of most un-Roman tears, but mindful of Tenuis's anxious scrutiny, I persevered. '*I am old and failing and when the seasons change and the veil between this world and the next is at its flimsiest, I shall slip through it and go meet my wife. But do not grieve for me. Like the autumn leaves I have had my golden years, and like them I will flutter to my allotted close. Until then, be assured, I am among my people, accepted and revered. If you are reading this, it means that my messenger*'

*has managed to travel safely and find you alive and well. (I
have warned him to say nothing – to anyone but you – at least
till I am dead, and I counsel you to do the same. By autumn
there will be no danger connected with my name.) You can
tell Anlyan that was I right about the dog – and he will tell
you everything. Incidentally, do you like the name? I gave it
to him when I freed him last Samhain. It means 'the smallest
one' although that scarcely describes him any more . . .'*

I put down the scroll again. 'Freed him?' I exclaimed aloud.

So Anlyan had told the truth – throughout. He *had* brought
a letter from an elder of his tribe (who certainly had known
the workshop years ago) and he himself had been in servitude!
So my instinct to trust him had been justified. And then it
dawned on me. Dear gods! 'The smallest one.' In Latin,
Minimus! My father's loyal slave – one of the two who'd fled
the Empire with him. That hunking, bearded Celt? It wasn't
possible!

But it was, of course. He was always a redhead and had
been growing fast. He would have matured to manhood in the
last few years, and of course the beard and long moustache
disguised his face. Not surprising – since he had been living
with the Celts, he would obviously have adopted Celtic ways
and dress. But like his new name, they were also a disguise
– a protection against possible recognition and arrest for
'consorting with a proscribed person and offering succour to
the same', which was itself a capital offence. One which I had
been guilty of myself!

But no wonder Anlyan had known his way up to the spring
– and where to find the mushrooms, and the wisewoman.
And probably the cave! He had lived in the area longer than
I had done myself. Before my father ever built his roundhouse there, or even owned the land, Minimus had been a
slave of Marcus's – one of a fashionable matching pair that
ceased to match. I had never actually shared a house with
him – he hadn't joined my father's household till I'd moved
from it – but I'd known him well, of course. Yet I had not
recognized him in the least, neither his appearance nor his
voice – which had broken to a baritone since I saw him last.
Though I'd registered something oddly familiar about him,

which I'd completely failed to place. If I'd made a hundred guesses I would not have got it right.

I wondered if Tenuis might have known him instantly – they had been slaves together and shared a sleeping-hut. Perhaps he would have done – but, of course, he hadn't seen the 'Celt'. He'd stayed in the workshop the day Anlyan arrived, and when he went home yesterday with me, our visitor had gone into the forest with my son. Where he'd tried to retrieve his luggage (which I now totally believed) and ran into some rebels in that cave. Dear Jupiter! He was not in league with them at all! He was in mortal danger – if he was not already dead and hanging from a tree – and I was doing nothing to assist.

I found that I was already on my feet. 'Never mind Marcus and his messenger,' I said. 'We have to go at once. Anlyan is not an enemy. This letter proves the fact. He's a messenger from someone I respect and love – and he's fallen into rebel hands by accident. They'll think he is a spy.'

'And kill him? Chop his head off?' Tenuis was shocked. He would have been a thousand times more horrified, if he'd realized who it was.

'At the very least.' I was already flinging on my cloak.

My slave was beside me, instantly, attempting to assist. 'I'm very sorry, master. That must grieve you very much. Someone you respected?' He was too well trained to question any more, and I did not explain.

'We'll have to try and find him, whatever they have done. If it's no more than his body, we can give it burial.'

'Are you going to send for help?' He had turned whiter than the wood ash on the hearth. 'I will come with you, of course. But suppose we meet the rebels? There are only two of us – and we know from the hoof-tracks that there were lots of them. If we surprise them, we'll be killed as well.'

He was right – in all respects. Right about the danger, and almost certainly right in thinking Anlyan was dead. (I'd have to remember to call him by that name – using his old one could be very dangerous. At least, until the leaves began to fall.) My eyes were treacherously wet again.

'Perhaps it would be wise to call into the fort. I know that

His Excellence is likely to be there, and the commander could be talked into sending soldiers out – they are already searching for Anlyan, in any case, mistakenly thinking he was a kidnapper. But there simply isn't time. Anlyan is in mortal danger, if he's not already dead. Though it's just possible they might have spared a fellow Celt – if only to ask questions, and find out what he knew. They wouldn't be asking politely, if I am any judge, so even in that case, I might well be too late. But while there is the slightest chance that he's alive, I owe it to my . . .' I hesitated. 'My family honour to try to rescue him.' I was collecting items as I spoke: money, food (with some foolish notion that the rebels might be bribed) and a hammer, knife and sharpened chisel from my bag of tools, which was all I could muster as makeshift weaponry. (Inwardly I knew that the hope was quite forlorn: five denarii and half my prandium was hardly an inducement to negotiate – even if I had a chance to offer it, and the outlaws were desperate for supplies!) At least, I told myself, if I was going to die, I wouldn't do it without putting up a fight.

I looked around for a bag to put them in, but there was nothing visible except the sack which Tenuis had brought. He guessed at once what I was going to need, and before I asked he'd brought it to my side. He held it open, while I stuffed my things inside, and wordlessly handed me a piece of string to tie around the neck. I was about to do so, when I thought about the scroll. If anything should happen and I did not return – which was not impossible – I did not want it falling into hostile hands. (Rufus, for instance, was not a stupid man, and – if he demanded entrance to the shop, as he was entitled to – I could envisage trouble for my family, if and when he worked out who the writer was.) I picked it up and stuffed it – and its bag – into the sack, and tied the whole thing tight.

The thought of my family had given me a jolt. What would become of them if I was killed? Tenuis was right. I needed help – and soon.

I picked up the workshop key and turned to him. 'I am going to take Arlina and ride straight to the cave. Don't protest. If Anlyan is dead they will have left the place by now, and if he isn't, there is no time to spare. In the meantime I want you to go back to the fort, as fast as you can run, give them a message and tell them where I've gone. Say that I need reinforcements urgently. A small detachment, fully armed, if possible. If Marcus is already there, I'm quite sure he'll give you his support – especially if you say there is a possibility of catching the rebels in the act, and recovering the stolen jewels and silver from Vitellius's shop.'

Tenuis was already tying on his cloak. 'And if His Excellence is not there?'

'You'll have to do your best. But he won't be long in coming, anyway. I had expected to get a message from him before now. If he sends Letigines to me, you may see him on the street, in which case you can tell him to let his master know.'

'And come to find you?' I could hear the terror in his voice.

'Better to wait for the soldiers if you can. No point in putting both of us in danger,' I replied. 'But it's more likely that if a courier comes here, it will be someone from the garrison. Marcus was planning to send Freckle-face back home, to send a cart to fetch his guard-slaves in.'

Tenuis nodded. 'Marcus could send those guards to rescue you,' he said. 'Should I ask him to divert them, if it is not too late?'

It was a sensible suggestion and I was surprised. That possibility had not occurred to me. 'Someone on horseback could catch up with them, perhaps,' I said. 'And obviously that would be excellent for me. But I would need the soldiers anyway.'

Tenuis nodded, and before I'd locked the door he was already running towards the city gate. I unhitched Arlina, swung my bag on to her back, climbed up after it and urged her to a trot.

TWENTY-THREE

I took the long route round Glevum, outside the city walls. Longer, and stonier, and boggier in bits, but probably quicker because there were no crowds, no gates and sentries to be passed, and very few other vehicles to clog the track. People do not often choose to come that way. But Arlina is sure-footed – though she is sometimes slow (and occasionally stubborn when you try to urge her on). Today though, she seemed to sense the urgency, and she kept up a pace which I could not have matched on foot. All that impeded me were branches in my face, in places where the track was overgrown, and people wanting to sell me watercress when I had to cross a stream.

I was headed for the cave, of course, and when I reached the south gate and joined the southern road, the going was easier – though not long afterwards I had to turn off on to the ancient forest track. But Arlina was so familiar with the route that she hardly slowed below a walk, though after a time I was beginning to rather wish she would. What was I doing, coming here alone? Supposing that I met the rebels in the cave? My family were likely to discover me, naked and head-less – and armless too, perhaps – upside-down and dangling from a tree!

I was almost tempted to go directly home, and try to pretend that I'd discovered nothing new about the 'Celt'. Merely a stranger who had offered me his services, foisted himself upon my hospitality and disappeared again. I wouldn't be expected to risk myself for him. No one had ever read that scroll but me.

But Tenuis knew what I had – rashly – planned to do, and he would tell the fort. That was both a comfort and a curse. A comfort, because the troops would surely come (I tried not to think that it might not be in time), but a curse because my intention was now known. And as a Roman citizen, my repu-tation – which meant my future trade and patronage – depended on behaving in a manly way. Not running away, like a coward, in the face of threat.

I reached the junction with the path that led up to the cave, and brought Arlina to a stop. Was it worth the ignominy to preserve my wretched skin? After all, I had my family to think about. But this was Minimus – Anlyan – who had saved Carus from the Celts. Honour required that I should repay the debt. If it was not too late! They would probably have killed him, thinking him a spy.

In which case, they would certainly have left – for fear that their secret lair was compromised – and there was therefore nothing for me to fear myself. If not, they might still have him captive in the cave. Doing dreadful things to him to make him talk?

There was really no decision to be made. Whatever else, I told myself, the rebels weren't expecting me – which gave me the advantage of surprise – and if I was careful, I might choose a moment when most of them weren't there. (From what Carus had told me, they clearly came and went.) With my hammer and a knife, I might overcome a single guard – even an armed one – if I could simply take him unawares.

Well, there was only one way to find out. And the time had come for that. I was so seized with terror that I was almost numb, but – like a mechanical ballista when the twisted skein is fully wound – I seemed to be beyond the reach of human thought. Like the Emperor Augustus's famed automaton, acting of itself, I turned Arlina up the track, and felt the perspiration prick my brow.

My heart was thumping like a woman's laundry stone. Just as it had the last time I was here. The mule was trotting nimbly up the track and we quickly reached the clearing where the wisewoman had her hut, and – almost too soon afterwards – I saw the fallen tree.

I had not been in special danger up to now, I realized, stupidly. This was a public pathway through the woods, and travellers and foragers often passed this way. There was nothing to suggest that I wasn't one of them. But as I slid down from the mule and tied her to a tree, my senses were so stretched I felt that they might snap. The bag seemed heavy and awkward as I hefted it, slinging the string round my neck to keep both arms free. The weight pulled it down against my side, and I wished I'd taken more trouble with the knot. It would take me moments to untie it. But that was for later. First I had to reach Carus's former hiding place – and then locate the cave. By this time, I could almost taste the fear.

The forest was quite silent – unnervingly so. I took a hesitant step forward, off the path, the trampled grass showing where I had been the day before. A startled bird flew up from just beside my feet, squawking loudly with alarm. I all but did the same – biting my tongue as I bit back the sound – and had to lean against a tree to collect myself. As if the squawk had been a signal, other birds replied and there was a rustle in the bushes, from what proved to be a fox. Nothing else – except a snort from Arlina. No human sound at all. Nor – I realized with relief – the noise or shuffling from any horse ahead.

A prickle of sweat and hope ran down my spine. Another step. Still nothing. And another yet. Only the whisper of the leaves. Another dozen paces. There was the fallen tree. But then I stopped and drew back behind a bush. Hoofprints – fresh ones, by the look of it – criss-crossed the ground again, and there were signs where the horsemen had ridden through the trees.

I paused for what seemed minutes, listening to the thudding of my heart, but there was nothing else. Cautiously, I moved forward to get a closer look, and contrived to tread sharply on a stick. It sounded like whip-crack, and I held my breath. But there was still no sound or reaction up ahead.

I turned my attention to the tracks again. It had not been raining since I came this way before, but here and there it was still damp enough for them to be quite clear. They seemed to lead in two directions – towards the cave ahead, and back through the woods behind me to my right. I had not crossed their path till now, and they were clearly going nowhere near the track at any point. Yet they had found a route which let their horses pass. Clearly riders who knew the forest well.

I only wished that I did – especially when a snake uncoiled itself suddenly from somewhere near my feet and slithered off into the undergrowth, reminding me of what the wisewoman had said about the cave. I did not dare to take a stick and thump the ground, as one is supposed to do, for fear of warning more than snakes of my approach. But I kept a sharp lookout as I edged along between the trees and came to where the rocky slope became a cliff.

Even then, I might have missed the place, if it were not for the evidence of trampling that I found. I was in a little clearing by a stand of furze, with a heap of stones beside the hill as if there'd been a slip. Nothing else that I could see. The hoof-prints went no further, but there were lots of them – and other evidence that there had been several horses here. Especially at the foot of a pair of largish trees that were growing further down the slope.

I went down and looked between them but the thick undergrowth beyond was undisturbed. No one had ridden that way and I backed out again. Very cautiously I tiptoed over to the slip.

And then I realized. It was not a slip at all – someone had been excavating the hill here in the past. On the far side, almost hidden by the furze, there was clear proof of it – part of the cliff-face had been hacked away, to leave an overhang. And at one end, a sort of cleft, an opening in the rock. The entrance to the cave.

If my mouth was dry before, it was like tinder now.

Tinder! I could have kicked my stupid self. Why had I not packed some kindling and a flint when I filled the bag? I was going into a cave and I'd brought no means of light. I cast around to see what I could find. There were unlikely to be flintstones lying handily about. I had my knife, so I could cut some wood – so I could make a bow and rub a point against a log . . . but that was little use. It would take far too long to make a useful glow. The Celts weren't here, that much was evident, but at any moment they might come riding back.

I was about to take a deep breath and plunge into the dark when I glimpsed the sheen of something shiny by the entranceway. I crept over, silently – all was black inside, but there might be a trap – and picked it up. Fool's gold was spark-ling at me from a broken piece of rock. Either the gods were on my side, or the rebel gang themselves had left it there. Now with my knife blade I could strike a spark – all that I needed was dry grass to act as kindling and then, with care, I could set a soft-wood branch alight and make a torch. And under the overhang, the foliage was dry. There was even a dead elder tree whose brittle spindly branches would burn quite readily.

It took me far too many strikes to do it, even then. It was not easy to get the angle right and make the spark land where I wanted it, nor to blow the smouldering stems into a flame. Especially when most of my attention was elsewhere, listening for voices and approaching hooves! But at last I managed it, and – with one piece of elder acting as a flare, and another to light from it before it failed – I made my way into the cave. My knife, at the ready, was in my other hand, the sack slung round my neck.

Even with my light, it was difficult to see – and there was nothing much to look at anyway, even when my eyes had adjusted to the gloom. The outer cave was empty, except for a pile of broken wood, which might once have been a crate. A damaged pannier-bag. A discarded cloak and what looked like the ashes of a fire suggested that the Celts had been here recently. I even found a silver coin that had rolled under a ledge in the back wall of the cave. I used my knife to flick it out, and put it in my bag. I was confident by now that no one else was here.

Using my flame I felt my way along the rear, and found the entry to the natural passageway. Daringly, I called out: 'Anlyan!' And for good measure: 'Minimus?' Then I flattened myself against the cave-wall with my knife prepared. But there was no reply. Good – there was no guard waiting to leap out at me – but at the same time bad, because if Anlyan was not here, it was unlikely he was anywhere alive. The rebels don't take prisoners, as a rule – they leave dreadful warnings to others not to interfere.

On the other hand, I had not found anything hanging in the trees, either here or on the path – though it did not mean that there wasn't something further up the track, past the point where I had branched away. I would have to go and check. A sickening thought. If I found him, I'd have to make sure the children did not see the gruesome corpse – but at least I could secure him a decent burial.

In the meantime, there was work to do. If there was no one here, I could brave the bats and look inside the inner cave – in case the Celts had left anything behind. I was almost praying that they had. Preferably some of Vitellius's goods, but almost anything would do. I was going to look very foolish otherwise, when the garrison sent a party of armed troops at my request. Which they would be doing very soon if Marcus had anything to do with it. And they would be furious if a humble tradesman like myself had dragged them over here for just a folded cloak and one denarius. And none of the promised Celts at all.

I lit my second flare and stamped the other out. I could come back to it, with luck, but elder burns quickly and I did not fancy being in the bat-cave in the dark. Then, ready as I could be, I edged into the little aperture.

Carus was right – it was quite low in there, and narrow at the top. I had to hold the flame aloft and stoop, dodging my head to prevent it rapping against protruding stone. I thought of clever Carus, ducking out of here – seizing his chance to scramble out between the knees, while their owners were preoccupied. I wondered again at his agility – and bravery. It was borne in me how great a risk it was. Thank all the gods they had not captured him. I could not bear to think about it, even now. Though he was right again: there was no room here for a pursuer to turn round quickly and chase after him. And presumably – thinking they were safe – none of the party had been left outside on guard. Though Carus – and Anlyan – could not have known that, at the time.

I found that I was sweating, still more heavily. (I had already been perspiring with fear.) Bats or not, I was glad to reach the inner cave and be able to stand upright again.

This would have to be quick, as my torch would soon burn down, and I would not relish groping back along that passage in the dark. I held the flame aloft and looked around. There were things strewn around the rocky floor – lumpy shadows in the gloom. Elder makes a soft glow, not a searching one, and I'd have to approach things to see clearly what they were.

I was reluctant. I am not keen on bats – especially their association with the underworld. They hadn't borne Carus's soul away into the afterlife, but would they spare my own? I could see them hanging – upside-down, like one of the rebels' victims – on the rock ceiling to the rear. What's more, I was disturbing them: I could hear the rustling as they stirred.

Heart in mouth, I approached the nearest lump of something on the floor. It proved to be a bulging bag – most of a goatskin, by the look of it – and fastened with a strap. I was excited, for a moment, hoping it held booty from the jeweller's shop. But a prod with my left foot persuaded me that it was soft. Disappointment flooded over me – until I realized that this might be Anlyan's baggage-roll. If so, I could see why he had left it here. It was clearly too bulky to carry unnecessarily. If I had not been at the roundhouse – which he could not know for sure – perhaps he would have decided to bed down in this cave. It was warm and dry, if you didn't mind the bats.

Either way, trying to retrieve it had cost him very dear. I decided I would take it with me when I left.

Another goatskin, soft and floppy, with one leg formed to make a spout. I put my knife between my teeth and pulled the stopper out. I don't know what I was expecting – victims' blood perhaps? But it was only watered wine. Mostly water, and not much of that. I let it fall again.

The next lump proved more promising. It was heavier and solid, and it proved to be a sacking bag which held a wooden chest. Locked. And no key visible, of course. But I did have my chisel. I looked around for somewhere I could support the light, securely and high enough to see the task. But there was nowhere obvious. Then as I took another step, two things occurred at once. Something black and horrible flew past and brushed my face. And another. And another.

I ducked away, and they swooped after me. They seemed to be attracted by my torch – or perhaps the little cave moths that were flapping round the flame. But as I bent over, I got my second fright. Worse horrors still. One of the bags, was moving – by itself.

I thought about that snake and poked it sharply with the handle of my flare. It writhed, and made a sort of muffled grunt. Only a faint one, but discernible. No snake then. Perhaps it was a pig, or some other animal. Rebels have to eat – indeed are known to raid and rob for their supplies – and might well keep something trussed up alive, since they can't go to market like anybody else.

I prodded it again, and got the same result. It wasn't lively, whatever it might be – perhaps they had stunned it and thought that it was dead. But it was clearly still living – evidently roped or it would have broken free.

Now this was difficult. Cornered pigs can be very dangerous, especially wounded ones, and this was large enough to last a gang for several meals. And like the bats, which were swarming round me still – but which I'd half-forgotten in this greater fright – I had disturbed it now. It was twitching violently. Perhaps it would be prudent to leave at once and let the garrison take care of it.

'Oh, dear gods!' I said the words aloud, and as I did so the creature moved again. An enormous heave which turned it on its side – and I realized what anyone, not scared out of their wits, would undoubtedly have recognized at once.

There was a human tied up in that sack. A burly human, with a bag around its head. And I thought I knew which human. I let out a cry.

'Anlyan?'

Another muffled sound. I wasted no more time. My knife was in my hand. I wedged my makeshift torch between my knees and used both hands to cut the cord. That freed the bag from round the head. I pulled it free.

Anlyan. With a gag tied round his mouth. I did not try to wrestle with the knot, I simply cut the cloth away beside his ear. Not easy, because the gag was very tight, and I was afraid of nicking him – I did, a little, but he did not seem to care.

'Water!' he managed. I dropped the knife, grabbed the goatskin-carrier, pulled the stopper out and held it to his mouth. He drank it greedily, the liquid dribbling down his chin, till I could squeeze no more from it.

'Master Junio,' he gasped, when he could speak again. 'Thank Jupiter you've come. I thought they were going to leave me here to die.'

I had already thrown the goatskin to the ground, and was sawing through a second rope that held the sack in place. It had been too small to cover all of him – hence the separate bag around the head – and it had been pulled up around his neck so tight that his bound legs were forced to bend. When I released it, he let out a sigh, and straightened them. I pulled him from the bag.

He was still secured at his arms, legs, hands and feet, and I still had to saw through all his bonds. But my torch was running low, and holding it this way was impeding me – though at least the bats had been deterred. Now they were merely flapping overhead.

He saw my dilemma. 'Arms first,' he said. 'Then you can rest the flare between my hands – and if you free my legs and feet I think that I could walk. Then leave me if you have to, I'll find my own way out.'

'I'll light another torch and come back for you,' I said. 'But there should be soldiers coming very shortly, anyway. If you can't walk, they'll help me carry you. And they will have brought tapers and a pitch-torch – or the means of making one.' Unlike my stupid self, I thought, remorsefully.

'Master Junio, no one could be carried through that passageway.' I had contrived to free his arms by now, and he flexed them gratefully. I accepted his suggestion for the torch, but it was burning low and I feared that he'd be burnt. So I did not free his feet, but went on sawing frantically at the rope that held his hands. It parted and I just caught the elm branch as it fell.

'I'll get another torch,' I said. 'You wait here, Minimus.'

He actually smiled. 'I do not have much choice. And call me Anlyan. It is my name these days. But I am glad you recognized me in the end. I did not dare to tell you openly . . .'

'I know,' I said. I handed him the knife. 'I worked it out at last – and there's so much I want to hear. But now I'm going to set fire to that sack, while I still have a spark. It will be smoky but it will give you light while I am gone – though it will burn out fast.' I pulled the bag towards the centre of the cave and held the guttering branch to it. It smouldered for a moment, then burst into sullen flame.

It was smoky. It made me cough at once, and I was prepared to stamp it out but Anlyan signalled that I should leave it as it was and go. He was moving his stiff fingers so that he could use the knife, so I turned away towards the passage and the open air.

But even as I did so, I heard noises from outside.

'The soldiers!' I was so relieved I squeaked. 'Though they'll be disappointed that they didn't catch the rebel Celts.'

'Celts?' I could not see his face, but I could tell he was perplexed.

'The men who captured you.' I was puzzled now. 'Carus said that they were talking Celtic – or something that he did not understand. I supposed that they were rebels.'

'So did I at first,' the captive said. 'That's why I used Celtic when I called out to them. I thought that it might save my life, and I believe it did. One of the servants spoke it, and he answered me – I had to learn it, living with the tribe, but it isn't perfect and I make mistakes. But all dialects differ, so he put it down to that if he did not always understand me, or me him. All of the rest spoke Latin all the time. Educated, too. Fortunately, they didn't think I understood – and I pretended not to, beyond a word or two . . .'

'Then who . . .?' I said, and then – unlike the lumpy dog – the pieces of mosaic fell perfectly in place. Dear heaven, what would I tell the soldiers now? Well, I'd have to think of something. They were in the outer cave.

'In here!' I shouted. 'And bring a light with you.' I trod out the embers of the sacking as I spoke. A moment later, I had to drop the flare as well – the remaining handle was too short and hot to hold. But it no longer mattered. There was a light approaching down the passage. I could already see the glow.

And then a figure with a proper pitch-torch in his hand. Followed by a second and third. The sudden light was so intense that I was forced to blink. But not before I'd seen what was confronting me.

These were not soldiers. They were not even Celts. Three men in merchant's tunics, with cudgels at their belts. So similar, they looked like a father and two sons. And behind them, another individual in a brown slave's uniform. Of average height, with brownish hair, and neither thin nor fat – unremarkable in every way, except that he had a steely look about the eyes and a drawn sword in his hand.

TWENTY-FOUR

I don't know what possessed me – perhaps the bats had brought some hero's spirit to my side – but I did not hesitate. 'Members of the Cloelius family, I believe?'

The oldest man, whose long grey whiskers could not entirely disguise his Roman nose and chin, looked at me rather sadly. 'We'll have to kill him, too. But do it cleanly, Interfector. This man was not involved in what happened to my clan.'

Interfector? A hired assassin then. This was not looking good. I said, 'I'd not advise it. The fort is sending soldiers. They know where I am and they'll be here at any time.'

The Cloelii – for it was clearly them – exchanged a worried glance. 'Then this must be quick,' the youngest one exclaimed. 'They must not find us here.' He turned towards the interfector, but I intervened.

'Don't make it worse,' I blurted, just in time. 'You have already murdered the wrong man.'

The paterfamilias looked wholly shocked. 'What do you mean?'

'It was not the jeweller who betrayed your family. What made you think it was? Discovered which courier had brought the message to the fort – then followed him the next time that you saw him in the town to see where he led you and who his owner was? Well, that was your mistake. The person who denounced you found out there was a threat – I don't know what happened, perhaps he got a glimpse of you somehow . . .?'

'My fault.' The father had turned deathly pale by now. 'I sent a sealed message – by that same messenger – to his owner, we didn't know the name, anonymously warning that we knew what he had done. I wanted him to sweat.'

'He did that all right,' I told him, thinking of how Thaddeus had squirmed and paled.

'So you know who he is?' the older son demanded. He looked fanatical.

'I know he is a senior councillor,' I hedged. I did not care for Thaddeus, but I would not wish a death like that on anyone. 'I learned that from the slave-guild when I went to arrange the courier's funeral. They would not give his name. But you clearly frightened him, because he suddenly passed on the slave in payment of a debt. It wasn't much welcomed, I discovered that, but since he was a wealthy, influential man the poor recipient had very little choice. It was a death sentence, of course, as the donor must have known. Vitellius was entirely innocent . . .'

'So that's why it took Interfector so long to find the courier again?' the younger one exclaimed. 'We thought our betrayer had simply stopped sending his wicked denunciations to the fort. We thought we'd frightened him.'

'The fort where you have fellow sympathizers, I suppose? Otherwise, how could you have learned of it?' Marcus's deduction, but it had an instantaneous effect.

The young man stepped forward as if to silence me himself, but his father pulled him back and turned to me. 'One soldier loyal to his former Governor, that is all it takes. He found himself responsible for doling out rewards – including those for naming so-called "traitors to the state". The army is meticulous in keeping records of accounts, and it was not hard to match the date when my family was denounced – though the recipient was only noted by a code. Precisely for fear of reprisals if it was ever found, I suppose. All that was needed was to match that code to the courier again. Or so we mistakenly supposed.'

'And the courier was conspicuous enough in looks to later pick him out around the town?'

'Exactly. Interfector even followed him to the hiring-stables one day and discovered that the owner was going to leave the town. So we planned to do the deed when he would not be missed for days – giving us time to leave the district and make a getaway.'

'And the mutilation of the bodies?'

'Did you not hear what happened to Albinus Clodius?'

I had, of course. Not just beheaded, but Severus had him stripped and laid down on the ground so that he could get his horse to trample him until his limbs came off – with the pieces thrown into the river afterwards. I nodded silently.

'His wife and children were treated the same way – were you aware of that? Despite the fact they were offered amnesty. Except that the soldiers did the mutilation rather than the horse. And it's happened to several of Clodius's supporters since.'

'Your family included?' This was making sense.

His turn to nod. 'All fifteen of them who were taken off to Rome – women, children, my old grandfather. Better that they'd been killed with the servants on the night of the arrest. There would have been more honour – and more chance of an escape.'

Another little tessera slid into its place. 'But one of the little slave-boys managed it, I hear?' I said. 'Nervous little fellow with striking snowy hair. But loyal to his former masters, all the same. I rather think you've been in touch with him – and he has been supplying you with food. I ought to warn you that His Excellence has noticed it was gone.'

Interfector moved towards me with his sword. 'Enough of this. The soldiers will arrive – and they know that we are here. Let me kill him – and the Celt as well. You should have let me despatch him earlier. Then give me my reward and let me go – before I turn my sword on you as well.'

'Then go at once,' a voice behind me said. Anlyan had freed himself, and worked the circulation back into his legs. He was a big man and he was carrying the knife. 'Anyone who hurts this citizen will have to deal with me. But you still have a chance. The garrison is coming and they know what you have done – but they think that you are rebel Celts. They won't be looking for honest merchants on the lane.'

'Provided that you are not carrying Vitellius's goods. They're looking out for them, and they carry a hallmark, so they can be identified,' I joined in at once. 'Or illicit ingot silver – but I don't suppose you are. That was a mistaken notion that I had.' Marcus had been right. Vitellius was too honest to deal with rebels and illegal goods, and he had a licence for sufficient anyway.

But I was talking to myself. Interfector darted past me and picked up the bag which held the little chest. 'You do what you like. Stay and be arrested. I'm taking this,' he said. He snatched a torch from the father and made off down the passageway. He banged his head in passing and we could hear him swear. 'And I'll have the horses too,' he shouted – and was gone.

The old man looked at me uncertainly. And at Anlyan and the knife. 'I don't want to kill you.'

'Then don't,' I said. It was unlikely that they could, but we were still outnumbered and they had weapons, too. 'My father is an exile, so I have some sympathy. And this man – who does speak perfect Latin, as you see – used to be his servant and was a fugitive, like you, although he's now been freed. I will have to tell the army what I know – but I don't have to tell them yet. The explanation can occur to me – preferably when another councillor is there to hear. The story will be round the curia next day and your betrayer will spend his whole life afterwards perspiring with fear. A living death. Surely that's revenge?'

Cloelius senior looked thoughtfully at me. 'You would let us go? Even after our treatment of your friend?'

'You didn't kill him, or my son,' I said. 'Although you could have done. Which shows that you're not by nature murderers. You wanted vengeance – and I am not surprised. In any other circumstance the law would grant it to you – and the goods you seized as recompense for what you'd lost. But this time the state – and therefore the law – was itself your enemy. So, I would let you go. I doubt that your assassin will have seized that hired ass – so you will look like traders, though more humble ones. But there are conditions.'

He looked at me. 'I feared there might be. You want money, I suppose.'

'Enough to pay the stables for their animal,' I said. 'You have no quarrel with them, but they are traders too. I have already told them that Vitellius is dead. They will assume the donkey is, as well, and won't start sending people out to search for it.'

The old man nodded. 'That can be arranged.' He fumbled

at his belt and tossed me a small purse. It was more than adequate.

I stuffed it in my bag. 'Stolen?'

He shook his head. 'That was all hidden not very far from here – the house of another loyal family. We did not dare to stay there, or go near the town ourselves – too many people know our faces there. We had to hire someone – and Interfector was recommended by a friend. We do not know his proper name. We suspect that he's an exile too, but he wasn't known in Glevum, so he could move freely in the town.'

'And even pretend to take over at the shop! And that's the other thing. Though you'll have to tell me quickly, or the soldiers will be here. What happened to make Interfector stay there overnight and pretend to be a servant – even after the jeweller had been killed? That seems strange, and it proved unfortunate – without it the deaths might not have been discovered even yet.'

He sighed. 'He killed the jeweller, as arranged – I am sorry about that – and I believe he beat him, too, before he died, trying to make him admit to what he'd done. Which he hadn't done at all, I am forced to realize.'

'But Interfector chopped him up – the way your family were.'

'Only after he was dead. And that was partly to terrify the slave – because, although he had confessed to taking messages to the fort and receiving money in return – thereby confirming his master's guilt, we thought – he stolidly refused to say any more than that. He wouldn't tell Interfector where to find the safe, or keys, even when threatened with similar himself. He was kept alive – trussed up, rather like your friend – and questioned quite repeatedly. He held out for many hours before he talked at all – and even then he never mentioned he'd been someone else's slave.'

'Poor Celerius,' I said. I had misjudged him terribly. He must have feared that this would happen, when the swap was made. No wonder he had scarcely left the workshop after that, and kept away from people in the street. 'He protected his master to his dying breath? So he was still alive when Marcus's courier came?'

The old man sighed. 'Unfortunately so. We had instructed Interfector to bring us what he could to recompense for what our family had lost – and that's what he tried to do, though everything in the shop would not account for half of it. So he did not want to leave until he'd found the safe, and keys. Before he left, he couldn't strip the shelves and close the shop. The neighbours would have realized there was something wrong. He did not go seeking out customers, of course, and he evaded most that came into the shop by saying that his master was away and recommending they returned another day. But then that little slave arrived, wanting a piece of mended jewellery. He almost panicked then. But he found something from a drawer which seemed to meet the description of the clasp, so he gave it to the slave, and thought he'd dealt with it. But it alarmed him, and he put more pressure on his prisoner that night, and the man broke down and agreed to show him where he could find the safe and keys.'

'And Interfector rewarded him by killing him?' I said.

The old man seemed shamed by this description of events. 'Brought him in to show him where it was, then put him out of his misery,' he said. 'Dealt with the corpse as he'd done the other one, which made a lot of blood – but this was not the real betrayer. This was just a slave, so he dragged the body out and put the pieces back in the storage box, where he'd held him up till then.'

'Just as well he'd gone there earlier and killed the dog,' I said. 'It would have barked and howled and sniffed around till people came. And bitten him, no doubt.'

'That's what Interfector said himself – although I don't know how you knew. When he found out where the servant lived, and learned there was a dog, he threw poisoned meat across the wall to it. As it was the mongrel next door barked at him and threatened to arouse the neighbourhood. Did it again when he took out the corpse.'

'That was the morning the slave-boy came again?' I prompted. 'Shortly after he had left the premises, I presume.'

'You knew that, too? He almost caught Interfector in the act this time. He'd just extorted the information about where the keys were kept–' he was about to kill his prisoner and clear the shop then did what he had to with his prisoner. Got rid of him as quickly as he could, and went and got the donkey and piled things on to it – it came with panniers, and the silversmith had several bags and chests and crates. He'd intended to leave earlier, as the jeweller would have done – shortly after dawn, when there was nobody about. Wrapped in his victim's rather handsome cloak, at a casual glance he would have passed for him – but the arrival of the slave put paid to that. And the boy was threatening to bring his master to the premises. So Interfector grabbed everything he could, scribbled a message on the door in chalk to say the place was closed, and left – trying to look as casual as possible, though it was noon by then. Fortunately it was raining, and nobody approached. He went around the corner and took off the cloak, and after that he melded in with other people driving loaded donkeys in the street. Nobody paid attention, even at the gate, and he brought the ass and came to meet us here.'

'A man who's unremarkable in any crowd,' I said. 'A valuable skill. And he had the wit to move the head downstairs and make the murders look like rebel work. The stolen cloak, I suppose, is the one I saw outside. But the warning scrawled in blood? That was your idea, again?'

'I fear so.'

'Well, it will have hit its mark by now,' I said. 'The rumour will be all around the town. News travels swiftly – and I suggest that you do, too. The troops must surely be almost here by now. I'll stay and wait for them. But I'll have that torch, with your permission. It's dark in here, and I do not care for bats.' Though they seemed to have been discouraged by the smoke from swooping round my head.

'I rather like them,' Cloelius said, to my surprise. 'Bats are a symbol of my family. I have one on my seal. They're supposed to bring us luck. Perhaps they do, considering what has happened here. Though I'm not sure I can trust you.' He glanced at Anlyan. 'Or your Celtic friend.'

'We have a knife and you have none,' I pointed out. 'Someone would be wounded if you tried to kill us now – and we're not attacking you. And every moment matters, so what have you to lose?'

'He's right. Come Father, quickly.' The younger man had

sprung to life again. He seized his father's torch and thrust it in my hand.

The old man was being propelled towards the exit by the other son. He said, across his shoulder, 'If we escape from this, we won't forget. We'll make a sacrifice for you to all the gods – though we will have to flee the Empire.'

'Then take a boat from Glevum,' Anlyan called, to his retreating back. 'That's what my master did, when he escaped. The authorities will be looking for horses – and for Celts. For the moment anyhow. They won't be expecting anyone like you.'

The old man paused and seemed about to answer this, but his son was still pulling at his arm. 'Father, come, or we will go without you.' Indeed, his brother had already gone. The flickering torchlight was receding from our sight. And then they followed it, towards the outer cave.

I wondered if the donkey would still be there, and what would become of those three fugitives. And their Celtic-speaking servant – I had forgotten him. (He was discovered later, hanging from a tree – Interfector was efficient at his trade and clearly the poor slave had witnessed far too much. Perhaps he'd tried to protect the horses, too.)

For now though, I was unaware of this. I turned to Anlyan and – with the hand that didn't hold the torch – enfolded my old friend in an embrace. My wretched eyes were getting damp again. I tore myself away. 'You have much to tell me, I believe.'

'Indeed I do,' he answered. 'Let's go out into the light.'

He was still telling me when the troops arrived.

TWENTY-FIVE

The soldiers were not pleased to find there were no rebels in the cave. Especially the commander, who had ridden out himself, to take credit for the ambush (and was, no doubt, the cause of their delay in getting there).

In fact, I had difficulty in dissuading them from arresting Anlyan on the spot. 'If you had not arranged to meet the rebels, what were you doing in the cave?' The commandant was still sitting on his horse. The height – and the flowing cloak he wore over his burnished uniform – only added to his authority. 'Seize him, guards.'

Two burly soldiers were prodded forward by a stout centurion, and pinioned Anlyan, one on either side, at the same time clamping a hand across his mouth. The army were never going to listen to a Celt. Something must be done.

'Commandant, your indulgence. I am the citizen whose son had disappeared. I believe His Excellence, Marcus Septimus Aurelius, reported it to you?'

The commander still looked scornful, but the name of Marcus worked its magic charm – and perhaps the fact I was a citizen, myself. He stopped to listen. 'And?'

'This is the man that you are looking for. It was supposed that he was a kidnapper. But all he'd done was take my child to gather mushrooms in the wood. They happened on the cave, explored inside and then got trapped in it. He actually helped my son escape.'

A glance towards the stout centurion, who snapped a straight arm in salute. 'Sir, that would accord with what we have been told. I brought you the message that the boy was safe.'

The commander turned flinty eyes on me. 'And the Celt?'

'Was taken prisoner and tied up inside. I have just freed him.' Inspiration struck. 'If you examine him you'll see the rope marks round his arms and legs – and the severed bonds are still inside the cave. He was the prisoner, not the friend, of the outlaws using it.'

The centurion marched over, freed one of Anlyan's arms, and looked it, then held it out for inspection by his superior. 'Worthiness, that seems to be the case.'

A deep sigh. 'Very well, release him. But be warned. Any trouble and I'll know where to come. Now leave us. I want to search the cave – to see if the rebels have left anything behind that may lead us to them, since it seems they got away.' And, as Anlyan stretched his shoulders, which had been forced cruelly back, he added, 'Celt, you're lucky to survive. We've already found their lastest victim hanging in the lane.'

Obviously the body of that slave-interpreter, I thought! It was clear that saying they'd not been Celts at all was not going to be believed, so I didn't say it. And nor did Anlyan. It was evident they did not trust him, even now. They searched his baggage pack down to the stitching on the base before we were permitted to depart with it.

(Marcus's slave-guards joined them later, he told me afterwards, but simply had to watch while the army did their work. They hunted through the cave with torches for several hours, he said, and did recover one tiny bag of jewels – something that Interfector had been due, no doubt. The haul did not include that clasp of Julia's, but they found a pair of toe-rings, of no especial worth.)

For now, though, there was no one else in sight. I led the way back to the path, glad to find Arlina still tied up by her tree – I'd feared the Cloelii might have taken her. Poor Anlyan was still shaky from what he had endured, so I helped him on to her, together with his bag, and led them gently home. As we walked, I noticed the first gold among the leaves. Autumn was on its way. The veil between this world and the next was already getting thin. Of course, Anlyan must have taken moons to get to us.

My slaves came out to greet us at the gate. Tenuis – delighted to have got home ahead of me – took charge of Arlina, while Brianus helped her passenger dismount. I wondered what they'd say when I told them who he was. Meanwhile, it was heartwarming to see the children running out to hug him round the knees.

'Later!' I said, as they did the same to me. 'First we need to eat. Anlyan has had nothing since yesterday at dawn, except the remnants of my lunch.' I had given them to him, while we waited at the cave, and now I was hungry too.

Brianus was soon fussing round us with a welcome stew, and Anlyan ate hungrily at first, but suddenly ran out of appetite. 'I have not slept,' he said, apologetically. 'I need to rest.' We were sitting in the sleeping-hut of course, and the soft reeds looked inviting, even to myself.

'Then I'll leave you to it,' I said graciously. 'The children will join you in a little while. I'll try to see that you are not disturbed.'

I had some notion of going to see my wife, but before I reached the roundhouse door the wisewoman appeared. She had her cloak and basket, and seemed ready to depart.

'There you are!' she chided. 'I don't know where you've been – and I don't want to know. Important business, I've no doubt you'll say, though I can't see what's more important than your wife and child. But she's out of danger now. Been up all the morning, overseeing chores, and I've put her back to bed again. And if you see she does that every day until the Kalends she should do very well. Meanwhile, you don't need me any more, and other people will.'

I'd left my bag, and the purse that the Cloelii had given me, in the hut where Anlyan was fast asleep, but I found the cash-pot in the dyehouse and paid her what I owed – and even added a little more for luck.

She eyed me – with malicious glee, I thought. 'Now I'm gone, you can sleep in there tonight. Though you're not to touch her till the bleeding stops. I hope that's understood. Though probably you wouldn't anyway, till she's been purified.'

I muttered promises, and she took her leave, stomping off towards the forest like a storm on legs. The slaves had taken the children to the spring by now, 'to tire them out' as Cilla always said, and I found myself alone. Surrounded by sleeping people, and with no task to do. I went to the dyehouse and picked up my cloak, from where I'd hung it on a nail. Time to visit Marcus and tell him what I knew.

I'd timed it perfectly – by accident. I found him in company with Thaddeus, who was fussily preparing to depart. His Excellence came towards me, when I was announced, his hand outstretched for me to kiss. He did not look thrilled to see me.

Nor did the councillor. 'To what do we owe this constant pleasure, citizen?' he said, as soon as the proper courtesies had been exchanged.

It was insulting, and it was meant to be. I had the greatest pleasure in saying to my host, 'Excellence, I think I have an explanation for the murders and the thefts. You heard that I had rescued Anlyan from the cave?'

'Naturally, the commander sent me a report back with my guards.' Marcus did not sound especially friendly, either. 'Said you insisted that the man was freed.' Of course, it must have been embarrassing for Marcus, too. The troops had been summoned to catch Celts, at his behest.

And on my behalf. Time for an explanation, if only half of one. 'He proved to be a messenger from outside the Empire, Excellence. Not a member of the local tribes at all. My father is dying and he came to tell me so.'

'Ah!' Marcus had been very fond of his old protégé. One could see it in the softening of his expression now.

Not so Thaddeus. 'That fugitive?' he said, dismissively.

Marcus ignored him. 'That's what you came to say?'

'I came to tell you that Anlyan saw his captors before they tied him up,' I said. I didn't mention that I'd seen them for myself. 'And they were not Celts at all – he spoke to them in Celtic and they did not understand, but their Latin was impeccable. Educated citizens, he is quite convinced – although not dressed as such. You'd take them for humble merchants, from their general attire.'

'Educated citizens? But what in Jove's name would such men be doing in a cave?'

'Excellence, that is exactly what I thought at first. But an idea occurred to me. I have a contract – I think I mentioned it – to lay a passage pavement at the old Cloelius house. And I realized there might be a connection with the deaths. It's known that some members of the family escaped. It's generally assumed that they had fled abroad. But suppose that they came back, and thought they knew who had denounced them to the fort?'

'Not Vitellius, surely!' Marcus was appalled. 'The jeweller was an honourable man.'

I was trying not to look at Thaddeus all this time, but I could sense that he was growing ever more alarmed, and the imputation of that last remark had struck him like a knife.

'Not Vitellius,' I answered. 'That was a mistake – and from what Anlyan contrived to overhear, they are aware of it. I do not think they did the crimes themselves – there was someone with them, demanding to be paid. They called him Interfector – you see the force of that.'

'Assassin,' Marcus murmured. 'The executioner.'

'Precisely, Excellence. And a man who didn't know the town. So he could come and go and not be recognized. And the nature of the killings might suggest it was revenge. You must have heard what happened to Albinus Clodius – and to his family and his followers afterwards.'

Marcus nodded grimly. 'I have indeed. And I concede that mutilation of that kind is reminiscent of what the rebels do. But why Vitellius?'

'Because Interfector did not know the man. Or anyone in town. The family had simply identified the slave who had carried the denunciation to the fort. The killer picked him out and followed him for days – planning with the family how best to bring about the deed. But they made a bad mistake – they sent a message by the courier, warning his owner that he would meet his fate and why. So the master found a way to pass him on to someone else. This was all said in Anlyan's hearing in the cave. And we know that Celerius was suddenly on loan – I was told that by the funeral guild – though they were careful not to give his former owner's name.'

I added that quickly. Marcus knew of my suspicions about that, and I did not want them aired to Thaddeus.

But the bald old man was already panicking. 'This is pure nonsense, Excellence,' he muttered, although it lacked conviction. He waved his hands about.

Marcus raised his own to silence him. 'On the contrary. This starts to interest me. Citizen, you don't know who the owner was?'

'All they would tell me is it was a member of the curia.' I turned to Thaddeus. 'I don't suppose that you know, councillor?' And before he had a chance to expostulate again, I added sweetly, 'If you do, it might be kind to warn him, don't you think? The Cloelii are unavenged and are aware of their mistake. He might wish to do what you did, and find excuses not to be at home.'

It shook him – even more than I could hope. 'There's nothing unlawful about what I did!' he said, abandoning pretence. 'In fact, denouncing traitors is a patriotic act. Do you not think so, Excellence?'

That was a trick question – failure to agree was treason against the Emperor – but Marcus parried it. 'And no doubt a most rewarding one. Useful when it comes for paying extra tax, and providing pretty trinkets for one's wife.' There was no mistaking the contempt. 'If you want some extra guard-slaves, I have some to spare – I shan't be needing them. Though at a price, of course.'

Thaddeus muttered something about preferring to leave town – hinting that he wished to go as soon as possible. So I made my own excuses and bowed myself away, leaving him to make his own farewells.

You never saw anyone leave a house more rapidly. Before I was fairly halfway down the lane his litter-boys ran by with his double litter. The curtains were all closed, but I could hear him and his lady quarrelling inside. I wondered if he'd choose to leave the town by boat – and whom he might encounter if he did. But I would never know.

And around me the leaves were still turning gold.

EPILOGUE

When I returned home I found my bag, and finally read the remainder of my father's scroll. Anlyan had told me much of it by then, in any case, and Cilla had recovered sufficiently for me to tell her too, that night, after the children were safely in their beds. Brianus was guarding them in the sleeping room, and Tenuis was tucked up in the slave-hut next to it.

My wife was feeding the newborn by the fire, and she looked up from her task. 'Well, of course it's Minimus,' she said, with the certainty of someone who had not had to guess. 'I could have told you that. I am surprised that Brianus did not know him at a glance.'

'I was afraid he would. That's why I kept away from him as much as possible.' Anlyan – who still looked nothing like his former self to me – was squatting in the shadows, drinking heated mead, exactly as my father used to do. 'But when we concluded it was safe to tell the servants my identity, he was reassuringly surprised. Tenuis didn't recognize me either, till I laughed. Master Junio has sworn them both to secrecy, of course. We don't want all Glevum knowing who I am. And there's no need to tell the children – not for now, at least. They would ask too many questions, and it would not be safe.'

Cilla moved the baby to the other breast. Anlyan had been my father's household slave – there was no call for modesty in front of him. 'Have you told Marcus?' she enquired of me. 'I know you went to see him, earlier today.'

'I didn't tell him everything. Only that this was a member of a tribe outside the Empire, where my father had found refuge,' I replied. I outlined what I'd said.

My wife was quite contemptuous of my restraint. 'And that was all? You didn't tell him the exciting parts? How your father had gone back to his tribe: his cleverness in buying all those pots and pans at once, so he got a big discount from the

stallholder for taking all the stock, then selling it from the
oxcart as he travelled south. And getting through all the Roman
checkpoints on the way, because he looked like any trader on
the road?' She was clearly better – or very nearly so.

'Hardly the moment. Thaddeus was there,' I told her, peace-
ably. I'd already told the story of how the councillor had fled
– and why.

'Well, it might have given him some lessons in good business sense!' she said, softening the retort with her old cheeky
smile. 'Then he might not have needed to cravenly denounce
his colleagues on the curia, simply for reward. I'm still amazed
at how your father managed his affairs. Selling his pots and
pans for cash to buy supplies, and even allowing him to stop
at inns – to say nothing of restocking when his load of goods
ran out! Though he had gold to start with, I suppose. He'd
just been paid and he took a load of money when he went.
But I'm sure that Marcus would have been impressed.'

'Marcus still thinks that he escaped by ship, and imagines
he's in Caledonia, beyond the northern wall. It's not up to me
to tell him otherwise – he'd only think I'd been deceiving him
for years. Though he'd enjoy the vision of my father as a
bard!'

One of Anlyan's stories had involved the way that, as he
neared his home, my father had employed a different strategy.
'You would not believe it,' Anlyan had said. 'There is a sort
of tradition among Celts (the tribes down there, in any case)
that they welcome "berdh" – wandering poets and people
who tell heroic tales. They take them in and give them hospitality, in return for entertainment for the night. Your old father
was very good at it. There were some sagas he already knew
by heart – learned them when he was very young, he said,
and had not forgotten them, though they were long and he
occasionally had to improvise. I didn't really understand the
words, although I might do now. I do know that they were
generally about the High Kings of the Celts, and the fabled
battles and history of the tribe. Dumnonnii and Cornovii – he
seemed to know them both.'

'He loved to tell a story.' I could imagine that.

'And when he'd finished with the old ones, they would often

ask for more, and then he'd tell them tales – he almost made them poems – about Glevum and the things that happened here. Life there is very different, and they relished every word.'

'In what ways different? They're not Roman, I'm aware, but surely they live in roundhouses very much like this?' Cilla rearranged her tunic folds. 'And keep animals and farm, as people do round here?'

'Up to a point. Not really. They do not live in towns. And their roundhouses are mostly made of stone. It is very windy and they don't have many trees. Not big ones, anyway, with nice straight boughs for making frames and walls. Theirs tend to be scrubby and bent over in the gale.'

'But lots of stone?' It was expensive here – as I was always saying to my wife.

'Enormous quantities. You cannot put a spade into the ground, without digging granite up. So it makes sense to drag the pieces out and use them when you can. And they do. They have walls instead of fences – even for the cows. And granite makes snug houses in the cold and wet – even platforms you can sleep on, lifted off the floor. With straw on top you have a cosy bed – no draughts, despite the winds! Amazing how quickly you can get used to that!'

I laughed. 'He used to say that Celts had cleverer things than Romans in some ways – though don't tell Marcus that! Soap instead of oils and strigilling – he swore it made you clean, and that educated people would adopt it in the end. Though I see no sign of that! And those outlandish trousers – he said the same of them, though I never saw him wearing any and I can't envisage it.'

'He does, though, all the time. Not at first of course – he only had a robe, a sort of long-sleeved tunic, and a cloak. One of the reasons that he chose to be a bard, perhaps. They all dress like that, apparently – rather like a druid – though he never pretended to have a bough with bells, which is the sign of formal training in the art. But when he found his family he went back to the trews. Made of the tribal plaid – exactly the same pattern as your mother used to weave. The one I'm wearing now. I thought that you might recognize the pattern – if not me.'

'I thought it was familiar,' I mumbled sheepishly. 'But I was not expecting you. Any more than his people were expecting him. But they accepted him?'

Anlyan made a little face. 'Well, in the end, they did. It wasn't easy though. They'd thought that he was dead. When he first arrived they welcomed him and let him tell his tales, but when he told them who he was, they tried to drive him off with stones and sticks. I thought he wrote about it in that scroll?'

He had. It had not made for comfortable reading. He'd found the place – that had not been too hard – but most of the family that he'd known were dead, and the only people still alive were very old: two aged ladies, one of whom was blind, and the cousin who (by general consent) had succeeded him as chieftain of the tribe. And also his wife – although he'd not been married when my father was first seized, captured by pirates and sold to slavery. But now there were children – nine of them, in fact. My father was amused.

'*At least,*' he wrote, '*succession is assured. You are my son, and a beloved one, but it was not a job for you. This was my father's bloodline, and I know that it goes on. And they were right to doubt that I was who I am. They saw me captured. My cousin's wife, Skental, saw me dragged away – and went and told the others in the tribe. They had all hidden in the fogou when the ships came into sight, and had sent to warn me, but I'd missed the call somehow. And Gwellia was with me, so she was seized as well. They mourned us for a week – the Celtic way, with songs and feasts and praise – convinced that we were lost for ever, and would soon be dead – even if we did not perish on the way, crammed in those stuffy holds.*'

I said all this to Cilla, and then turned to Anlyan. 'Whatever is a "fogou", anyway?' I asked.

He laughed. 'It's a sort of a building underground, where crops and animals and even people can be put for safety in times of danger to the tribe. Human or otherwise. I've known them use it in a thunderstorm.'

'Made of more stone, no doubt!' I said, and made him laugh again. I tried to imagine my father cowering in a place like that, and failed.

'You think he really missed the warning? Or decided not to follow it, and tried to brave it out?'

'I am sure he didn't get it – everyone who was present at the time swears that they remember the message being sent. It didn't get to him. It seems that the messenger was captured too. But I am convinced my master thinks that was no accident.'

I frowned at him. 'What do you mean by that.'

'He never said as much, but that is my belief. He did say that his beloved dog had disappeared.'

Ah, the dog! I thought, remembering the letter. Aloud I said, 'Is that significant?'

'He seemed to think so. It was a large and faithful one, and could be very fierce – although Libertus swears that it was as gentle as a lamb.'

'He was obviously very fond of it indeed.'

'More than that.' Anlyan took another sip of mead. 'It was the dog that made the tribe accept him in the end. One of the old women – the one who lost her sight – set him a question that she thought would be a trap. If he was who he claimed, she told the tribe, he could describe his pet, and say what it was called.'

'Which he could do, of course.'

'Of course, although his cousin's wife was rather sceptical. Said that anyone could guess that it would be a dog, and what it would look like from others in the tribe. They were all related, like the people. And that "Brengi" – "noble hound" – was a common name for them, which he might have learned from listening to talk. But then he told a story about how he'd chosen it, from a litter that the sightless woman had, though she wasn't sightless then – how he'd almost selected another brindled pup, but finally picked that one because it licked his hand. The woman got up and flung her arms around his neck – nobody had witnessed that event but her, and only he could possibly have known. And that convinced them all, and after that they tried to make it up to him. The chief especially.'

'So my father owed a great deal to the dog.'

'And might have owed a great deal more, had it been there that day. It would bark and growl at strangers – so everybody says – and once attacked an angry bull because it thought its master might be under threat. It never left his side, apparently, but the day the pirates came it simply wasn't there. He whistled for it, and called its name repeatedly, but it did not come. He worried that it might have got caught up in a snare. In fact, he was looking for it when the pirates came. That is how they took him unawares. The dog would have barked to warn him, he declares, and probably bitten at least one of them, giving him a chance to run away. But it was not there. I'm sure he thinks that someone poisoned it. On purpose, on that day. Someone who knew the ships were coming, at the very least.'

'Dear Mercury!' I said. 'Someone betrayed him to the slave-traders? That's what he believes?' Such things were not unknown – and a sturdy young male would fetch a healthy price, and earn the traitor a sizeable reward. 'Whom does he suspect? Anyone still living? His cousin, I suppose? He would be the only one to benefit.'

Anlyan gave a shrug. 'He hasn't mentioned anything to me. I told you that. And his cousin seemed more pleased than anyone at his return – once Libertus had convinced them who he was. But I'm quite sure I'm right that he thinks he was betrayed. In public he is cheerful and polite – to everyone – but alone with us at night it is clear that he's upset. We used to find him sitting, thinking—'

'We?' I interrupted. 'And you said "us" before. There was someone else with you?'

'Well, Kurso was with still us, at that time, naturally. It was only last spring he asked for permission to be wed. Your father granted it, of course, and set him free at once – which isn't difficult according to their laws. Though they seem to let their slaves have wives in any case, and they don't have dozens of them like the Romans do.'

I could hardly credit this. Kurso, my mother's little kitchen slave – so accustomed to mistreatment that when he first arrived he could move faster backwards than ahead. And so shy that he could hardly speak, even to my father! 'I can't imagine Kurso marrying!'

Anlyan permitted himself a little grin. 'She chose him,